PAGE ONE: VANISHED

A Robin Hamilton Mystery

Nancy Barr

A

Arbutus Press
Traverse City, Michigan

Page One: Vanished
A Robin Hamilton Mystery

ISBN 978-1-933926-16-2

Arbutus Press
Traverse City, Michigan
www.Arbutuspress.com

Printed in the United States of America

Library of Congress Cataloging-in-Publication Data

Barr, Nancy, 1972-
Page one. Vanished: a Robin Hamilton mystery / Nancy Barr
p.c,m
ISBN 978-1-933926-16-2
1. Reporters and reporting—Fiction.
2. Copper Harbor (Mich.)—Fiction.
3. Missing persons—Fiction.
I. Title. II Title: Vanished.

PS3602.A777435P34 2007
813'.6—dc22

2007007469

Other books by Nancy Barr
Page One: Hit and Run

To Jeanne Vizanko Asplund Olsen

for showing a kid with nothing that anything was possible

if she just dared to dream big enough.

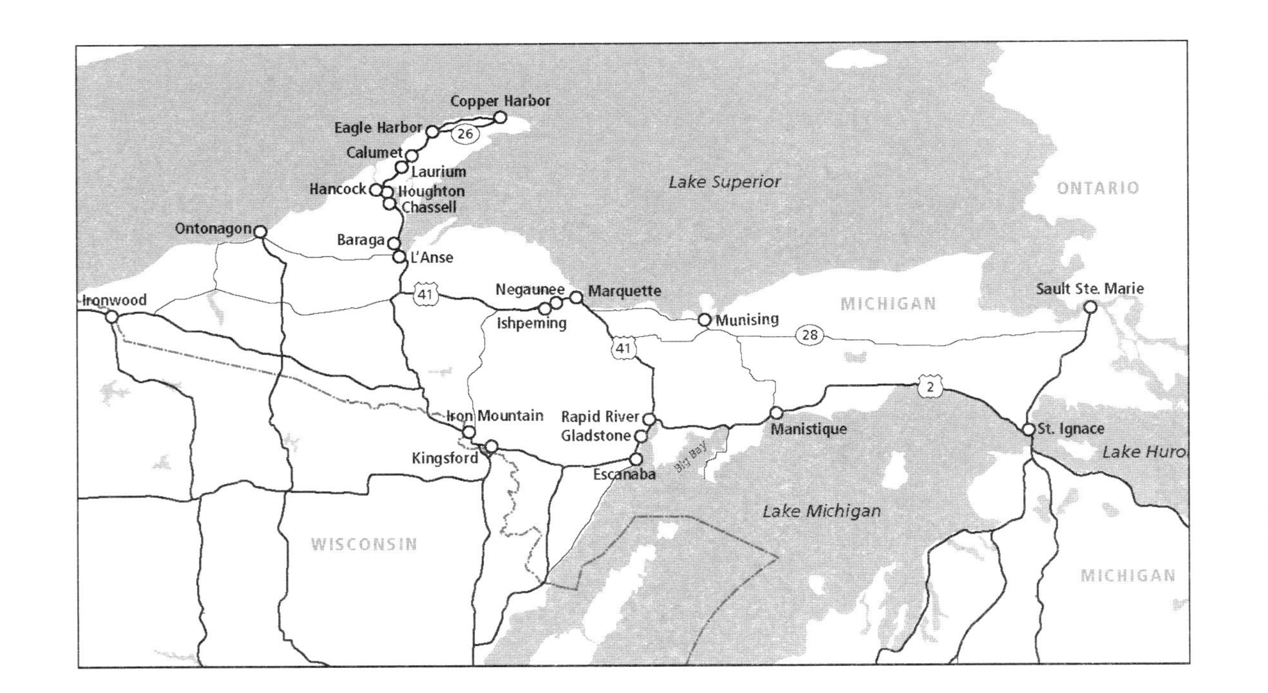

Michigan's Upper Peninsula contains 16,452 square miles. The maximum east-west distance in the Upper Peninsula is about 320 miles and the maximum north-south distance is about 125 miles. It is bounded on the north by Lake Superior, on the east by St. Mary's River, on the south by Lake Michigan and Lake Huron, and on the west by Wisconsin. It has about 1,700 miles of continuous shoreline with the Great Lakes.

Author's Note

When an author chooses to set a fictional story in real places, inevitably some characteristics about those places must be tweaked in the interest of privacy and plot development. In the case of this novel, the street names of all the towns mentioned will be recognizable to those familiar with these delightful hamlets; however, the people and home descriptions are entirely fictional and are based on no one and nothing in particular.

Also, the Great Lakes Summer Institute is a figment of my imagination, but a very good idea, (hint to all those billionaires out there looking to make a lasting contribution to society).

This book could not have been completed without help from the following people and organizations who aided me in research: Dr. Dawn Nulf, Houghton County Medical Examiner; Jim Lowell, executive director of the Calumet Theatre (one of the Midwest's finest examples of history that lives and breathes with the spirit of every performer who has ever graced its magnificent stage); Erik Nordberg and his staff at the Michigan Technological University Archives; Mark Dennis of the O'Neill-Dennis Funeral Home in Hancock, Dr. Kimberly Dovin of the Medical Arts Health Care Center in Houghton and JoJean Miller at the law firm Butch, Quinn, Rosemurgy, Jardis, Burkhart, Lewandowski and Miller in Escanaba. As always, any errors in fact are mine and mine alone.

Again, thanks go to Arbutus Press publisher Susan Bays, for making the dream a reality, and to my family, friends and colleagues for their support throughout my career (with a special nod to Carolyn "Candy" Peterson for help with proofreading this manuscript). Finally, a special heartfelt thank you to the readers, who have made the "Page One" series such a success.

Prologue

June 7, 1974

She had never felt so grown up as she did holding the glass of golden liquid that fizzed and tickled her nose when she tasted it. She knew it would be like this when he had asked her to join him after school. He saw her as a young woman, not a child. He talked to her like a woman, about things that mattered — art, music, politics, where the world was heading.

Dad would not be happy that she was drinking alcohol, but then again, how would he find out? She could never tell her parents about him, how he made her feel. They wouldn't understand.

"Mary Jo, don't be in such a hurry to grow up. You'll be an adult soon enough."

Her mother's voice rang in her ears. Come to think of it, every sound in the room seemed to be ringing in her ears. The buzz came from within and the room, with its plush furniture and dark-colored walls, began to spin. She felt herself falling, fading, and then she was gone.

Chapter One

Saturday, September 23, 2006

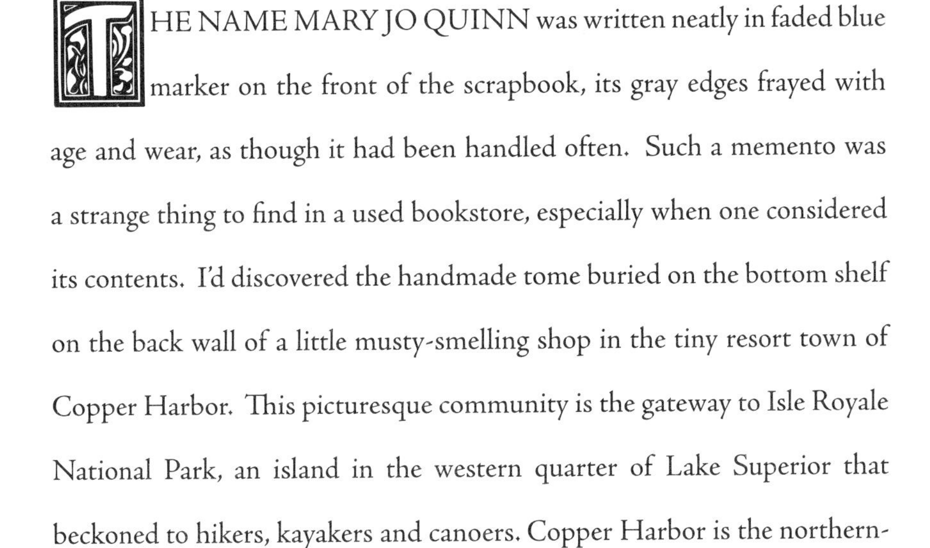

THE NAME MARY JO QUINN was written neatly in faded blue marker on the front of the scrapbook, its gray edges frayed with age and wear, as though it had been handled often. Such a memento was a strange thing to find in a used bookstore, especially when one considered its contents. I'd discovered the handmade tome buried on the bottom shelf on the back wall of a little musty-smelling shop in the tiny resort town of Copper Harbor. This picturesque community is the gateway to Isle Royale National Park, an island in the western quarter of Lake Superior that beckoned to hikers, kayakers and canoers. Copper Harbor is the northern-most bastion of civilization in Michigan on a crooked finger of land called the Keweenaw Peninsula. Its remote, pristine shoreline provided an excellent respite from a hellacious year for my best friend from high school and me on a late September weekend.

Michaela O'Bryan (or Mick, as everyone except her mother called her) and I had spent the morning touring the old army outpost at Fort Wilkins State Park and snapping photos of the Copper Harbor Lighthouse, accessible only by boat, and were now hitting the gift and specialty shops that lined the streets. The bookstore had been my idea, tucked away at the end of a dead-end street and filled with antiques and musty, ancient volumes on every topic imaginable, most missing their dust jackets but still treasures to the person who loved to read.

I opened my odd discovery, which crackled dangerously in my fingers, as though it would disintegrate at any moment if the handler were not careful with its contents. I was confronted by a pair of golden brown eyes peering at me from the faded color photo of a young girl on the verge of womanhood. Her blonde hair fell in wheat-colored waves to her waist. Her smile was tentative, shy, perhaps self-conscious about the braces on her teeth. Underneath the photo, probably taken at school from the look of the plain gray background, her birth and death dates, 1960-1974, were written in that same blue marker. So young, yet those eyes were so full of life, soulful eyes that seemed to watch me.

"Find anything interesting?"

I jumped and gasped.

"Mick, jeez, don't sneak up on me like that," I said, and tapped her sandaled foot, planted next to me on the floor.

"Jumpy, aren't we? I'm not the boogeyman. What are you looking at anyway?"

"It's some sort of scrapbook about a dead girl."

"Eww! Robin, that's gross. Why would anyone make such a horrifying thing?"

"That's exactly what makes it so interesting, doesn't it?" I said and stood up, or at least tried, but stumbled forward, nearly dropping my discovery in the process.

"Careful, you don't want to end up in another cast," Mick said and reached for my arm.

"I'm fine, but this damn ankle just isn't cooperating." I flexed my left foot and cringed. My ankle had broken when its panicked owner jumped from the second story window of a burning building two and a half months before. The cast had come off on Wednesday; it was now Saturday—too soon to be putting much stress on it, but I was tired of being treated like an invalid.

I limped to the counter and put down the scrapbook along with a few hardcover Lord Peter Wimsey mysteries by Dorothy L. Sayers, from the 1920s.

"You're not actually buying that thing, are you?" Mick whispered as she dumped a bunch of Jackie Collins paperbacks next to my pile.

"Why not? I'm curious. There must be a good reason someone went through the trouble of making this and then got rid of it," I said, then looked around the otherwise empty store. "What happened to the clerk?"

"I'm here," called a voice from the back room.

A petite woman in her mid-fifties with long curly graying hair tied back with a light blue satin ribbon trotted to the counter.

"I see you found some things," she said with a bright smile and a quick look at our selections. Then the smile slowly faded. "Oh, the scrapbook. I'd forgotten all about that."

"What's the story behind it? I didn't really look through it, but it piqued my interest," I said, lightly tracing the name on the cover.

Mick was eyeing a ghastly abstract painting of what I guessed to be Lake Superior during a summer storm. She glanced at the proprietress with curiosity and then shifted her gaze back to the painting hanging behind the counter.

"Well, I remember it was in a box of books and papers I picked up at an estate sale in Houghton this spring. Now, what was her name?" The woman squeezed her eyes shut and pinched her lower lip. "Oh yeah, I remember. Astrid Heikkinen. She was 86 when she fell down the stairs with a basket of laundry. Beautiful old house, too. She was a retired school teacher, never married."

"Was the girl one of her students?" I asked, tracing the name on the cover again with my finger.

"Could be. That's filled with news clippings about the girl's disappearance. I didn't read them all, but she apparently vanished while walking home on the last day of school. They never found her body either, poor thing," she said and shivered, as if imagining what horrible fate could befall a pretty young girl who didn't come right home from school. "I wasn't going to sell it, but then I figured someone would come along who would be interested. You'd be amazed at some of the things people buy. That'll be nine dollars and fifty-four cents, please."

I fished a ten-dollar bill from my pocket, not sure why I even wanted the tattered old thing. Maybe it was something in the girl's eyes, some unfinished business, but I felt she had a story to tell me. Mick stared at me pointedly, then at the books and shook her head. Turning to the woman behind the counter, she pointed up at the painting and asked if it was for sale.

"Of course, everything in here is for sale, even me if the right offer comes along." She erupted in deep throaty laughter and then added soberly, "Hundred bucks and it's yours."

"Sold."

When we stepped into the bright morning sunshine, me carrying two plastic bags of books and Mick balancing the hideous canvas, I said, "I don't even know if that god-awful thing's going to fit in the back seat. What is it anyway?"

I opened the passenger side door of my aging white Jeep Wrangler and frowned.

"Robin, you obviously don't know anything about art, or books for that matter," she said in exasperation and huffed a little as she shifted the weight of the painting from her hip and slipped it behind the front bucket seats so it leaned back, painted side up. The frame was chipped and too ornate for the unusual style expressed.

"I know the difference between a Claude Monet and a Norman Rockwell, and I know that thing is ugly. What was that crack about the books? Dorothy L. Sayers was one of the pre-eminent mystery writers of her day."

"Exactly. You don't realize that you practically stole those books. I can tell from the bindings they're early editions, probably worth a lot more than the three bucks apiece you paid."

I started to tell her that just proved what a good shopper I was when a Ford Explorer pulled into the parking space next to me and deposited a family of five, all talking at once.

"This place is soooo boring. There are no cute guys, no malls, nothing," whined a tall, lanky blonde with a pouty face covered with too much make-up for someone barely out of middle school.

"Shut up, why don't ya? Dad, can we take the boat to Isle Royale? I want see a moose," said a pre-teen boy wearing a Detroit Red Wings t-shirt.

Their harried-looking father said, "We don't have time," and herded the pair into the store behind their mother and little sister.

Rolling my eyes at Mick, I got in the Jeep and started it. "I missed out on all that," I said as I buckled my seat belt.

"What, bratty little brothers? Please, I had two of them. You don't know how lucky you are to be an only child," she said, then cringed. "Oh God, I forgot about Evan. I'm so sorry."

"Don't worry about it. I barely remember him. It's almost like being an only child. I was only three when he died. Now, what's the deal with this monstrosity?" I jerked my thumb at the painting.

"That's by a guy named Karl Maki. His paintings caught the eye of a gallery owner in New York about four or five years ago and may be worth something someday. His work is very moving, full of emotion." She swept a strand of ketchup-colored hair from her pale forehead and turned up her nose.

"Uh-huh, whatever," I said with a snort and drove us back to the log cabin situated about halfway between the summer tourist havens of Eagle Harbor and Copper Harbor on a rocky Lake Superior shoreline. As we headed west on the state highway, I hummed along as Stevie Nicks belted out a live version of "Edge of Seventeen" and Mick watched the lake bathe the giant boulders of basalt lava rock along the shore.

The cabin had been Mick's idea. We hadn't seen much of each other since she'd gotten promoted to an acquisitions editor position at Random House two years ago. The New York publishing scene suited her well, but it was hard on our friendship. She had been in England working with a particularly recalcitrant author the week I buried my fiancé during an elaborate police funeral complete with a multitude of solemn-faced uniformed cops and a flag-draped coffin carried on the shoulders of six fellow officers near Chicago in April. Mick had tried to draw me out over a series of phone calls, but I wasn't comfortable talking about the intimate details of my tragedies when all I had to look at and hold was a cold plastic receiver. For me, conversation was as much about seeing a person's expression as listening to his or her words. She finally gave up and suggested that when my cast came off we should spend a weekend catching up on each other's lives. Since we sought peace and quiet, it made sense for her to come back to Michigan's remote but breathtakingly beautiful Upper Peninsula than for me to board a plane to New York. With my basset hound, Belle, still in the care of my much put-upon father, I had picked Mick up at the Delta County Airport in our hometown of Escanaba and driven three hours north to the Keweenaw Peninsula the previous afternoon.

"You've been pretty quiet so far this weekend. Usually you're the one regaling me with tales of life among the privileged set in New York. What's up?" I asked as I turned onto the hard-packed gravel parking lot in front of the cozy log cabin.

"I'd forgotten how beautiful it was up here in the fall. I never really appreciated the U.P. when I lived here." She opened the door and slowly slid from her seat, chewing her bottom lip. She took a deep breath, exhaled and turned toward the water, which was crashing in massive milky waves on the rocks. After adjusting her retro-style horn-rimmed eyeglasses on her straight little nose (courtesy of a highly-skilled plastic surgeon), she faced me.

"I have something to tell you. I haven't told anyone about this yet. I don't know how everyone will react."

I studied her slumping shoulders and wide blue eyes.

"Mick, whatever it is, you know I'll be okay with it," I said and meant it, although my mind was playing over the possibilities — gay, pregnant, both. She was known for dropping bombshells, like the time between her freshman and sophomore years in college when she announced she was going to become a nun, even went to a convent in Wisconsin, but lasted a whole six days before calling me in tears at two o'clock in the morning, begging me to come get her, which I had done.

"I got married three weeks ago."

"You mean when you were in Mexico? I thought it was a business trip and that you went alone."

"I did. I met Miguel on the plane trip down there. He teaches Latin American Culture at NYU. He's wonderful, Robin."

"I see." I massaged the steering wheel. "Um, what's so wonderful about him that made you get married in the space of a week and not tell a soul?"

"It just happened so fast. We started talking before the plane was off the ground in New York. Miguel is the smartest, most cultured man I've ever met, and he's so romantic."

"Of course he's romantic. All men are romantic the first few months of a relationship. What do you really know about him?"

"I know he's the one I will spend the rest of my life with, and that's enough."

I knew from the firm set of her jaw that she wouldn't hear any protests. Besides, it was too late now. I got out of the Jeep and began unloading our recent purchases.

"So when do I get to meet this guy? Are there going to be little Michaelas and Miguels running around this time next year? Or are you going to do the honorable thing and name your firstborn after me? Robin can be a boy or girl's name, you know."

She laughed and came around the side of the Jeep. Tears were streaming down her face as she wrapped her arms around my thin shoulders.

"Stop it; you're getting my shirt wet. Look, are you going to take this thing or are you going to make me lug it inside?"

"You're the best, you know that?" she said and hauled her ugly painting into the cabin.

Around noon we packed a lunch and drove up a winding road to Brockway Mountain, one of the highest points on the peninsula, with spectacular views of Lake Superior and the northern tip of the Keweenaw Peninsula. Below us was a carpet of brilliant orange, gold and red leaves from birch, aspen and maple with shades of evergreen mixed in for contrast. The sky was a crisp blue only seen in regions far from factories and heavy traffic. We could see the southeastern shore of Isle Royale about 50 miles to the northwest. Much closer were the peaks of Mount Lookout, Mount Houghton, Mount Bohemia and Mount Horace Greeley, steep protrusions from the rocky earth mined by Native Americans a thousand years before and then by settlers from the Northeastern United States and Europe in the nineteenth century.

We spread our picnic out on one of several stone slabs that served as a boundary along the south side of the road overlooking the peninsula. The sun was high in the late September sky, but a brisk wind off the lake required visitors to the mountain to don lightweight jackets to ward off the chill. After finishing the sandwiches and fruit we'd packed, Mick trotted off to the gift shop that occupied the center of the mountain top while I pulled the scrapbook from my pack. I read through each newspaper article, starting with Mary Jo Quinn's disappearance and ending with an update of sorts on the twentieth anniversary. Either nothing else had been written since June 6, 1994, or the scrapbook's creator had stopped collecting articles. Each of the roughly twenty stories was neatly affixed to its own page with the newspaper's flag and date of publication pasted at the top. Most of the articles were from the *Daily Mining Gazette* in Houghton, but a few were from the *Detroit Free Press*. Every once in a while, the big Detroit daily would pick up a story in the Upper Peninsula.

Car doors slammed and people milled around the mountain top "oohing" and "ahhing" at the view, snapping photos and sharing tidbits of information they'd picked up about the area. I was oblivious to their conversations, though, engrossed as I was in the story of an ordinary fourteen-year-old girl, probably excited at the prospect of going to high school the next fall, but who never made it home from school on a late spring day thirty-two years ago. According to the police, not a single person recalled seeing Mary Jo Quinn after she left school that day. Although well-liked, she often walked alone to the house she shared with her parents, a preschool-age brother and her grandmother.

Hundreds of residents and students from nearby Michigan Technological University had fanned out across the neighborhood, the town and the surrounding woods for days afterward but to no avail. "Gone without a trace" was the headline on the twentieth anniversary article, which provided an in-depth look at the investigation, including an interview with her parents, Joe and Coleen Quinn. They had been shattered by their only daughter's disappearance. Both coming from large families, they had hoped to have a houseful of children, but Coleen had miscarried many times between Mary Jo's and Joe Junior's births. At the time the article ran, the son was in medical school, following in his father's footsteps.

The police speculated the girl may have simply run away from home, although no one would admit she had a reason to do so. "People don't just disappear into thin air, not around here. This isn't Chicago or Detroit," the chief of police was quoted as saying in an article written a year after she had vanished. Typical small town attitude, I thought. Nothing bad can happen here. I snorted and shook my head.

"You look like a bull getting ready to charge."

I looked up to find Mick holding a couple of plastic bags of merchandise.

"More stuff? You're not going to be able to fit all that in your suitcase," I said, snapping the scrapbook shut and stuffing it back in the pack.

"I wanted to pick up a few things for Miguel. Besides, they have some lovely copper earrings in there." She surveyed the landscape and inhaled deeply. "God, what a beautiful place. I can't believe there aren't more people up here all the time. This is amazing. Look at all the color, especially the deep blue of the water. I could stay up here forever."

I must have been giving her a strange look because she added, "Oh, don't get me wrong. I love New York and can't imagine ever moving back to the U.P., not with my career and Miguel's. But it is a great place to raise a family. It's so peaceful."

"Yeah, I know what you mean. Too bad I don't feel any peace," I mumbled and picked up the pack. "Ready?"

"Yeah. Are you okay?"

"Fine. Let's get going. We've still got a lot of sightseeing to do."

On the way back down the mountain, we stopped at a plateau that overlooked Copper Harbor and nearby Lake Fanny Hooe and Fort Wilkins State Park. A small group of Girl Scouts from the Fort's campground enjoyed the view while listening to a lecture from the troop leader. They looked to be about middle school age and I wondered if Mary Jo Quinn had ever gone camping.

Chapter Two

"OKAY, I'VE TOLD YOU MY big secret, now tell me what the hell is going on with you," Mick said. We had just returned from dinner at an expensive Copper Harbor restaurant that featured waitresses dressed in German folk costumes and views of the water and were now enjoying a nightcap on the back porch of the cabin.

I took another sip of red wine and continued staring at the lake as it undulated over the rocks and then retreated.

"What do you mean?"

"Robin, you downed a bottle of wine last night and you've practically finished this one. You never used to drink. You were always the one who stayed away from camp parties in high school and the drunken bashes in college," she said, snatching the nearly-empty bottle of Merlot off the table. "And what's with that music you're listening to now? Stevie Nicks, folk music, Enya? You used to blast AC/DC and Ozzy Osborne so loud your dad would wear earplugs around the house."

I smiled, remembering Hank Hamilton telling me a hundred times that I was going to be deaf before I hit twenty if I didn't turn the stereo down. But that was a long time ago.

"You ever really listen to the words of some of that stuff? It's all about death, darkness, depression. I need to hear about life, light and love." I stared out at the lake, watching the sun sink lower and lower, about to be swallowed by the dark blue water.

"I don't understand," Mick said and dumped the bottle next to her chair. The liquid made a red stain on the wooden decking, spreading until it slipped between the boards.

"There is no peace in me, there's never any quiet, even when I'm alone. I always hear a noise in my head, like a thousand voices all talking at once. I don't sleep well, haven't in months."

"And that helps?" Mick pointed at my glass.

"No, not really. It helps me sleep sometimes, but it doesn't quiet the voices."

"So am I going to hear on CNN that you went to the roof of Harbor Tower with a rifle and picked off a dozen people?" she asked, referring to Escanaba's tallest building, an eighteen-story apartment complex for senior citizens.

I laughed bitterly.

"No, I'm not crazy, not yet anyway. I don't want to hurt myself or anyone else. Well, maybe the bastard who killed Mitch, but I think that's normal." I swirled the remaining wine in the glass and then drained it. The buzz in my head seemed louder.

"I'm sorry I wasn't there for you when he died. He really loved you. I knew that as soon I saw the two of you together, but —" she paused and grasped my hand, "is this how he would want you to live?"

I looked at her with eyes wide and leaned forward.

"I don't know. We never discussed the possibility of someone blowing the back of his head off." I jumped up and clamored over the rocks until the waves lapped at my sneaker-clad feet.

"Robin!" Mick followed me, stepping carefully in her sandals.

"Look, I know what you mean. I just need to handle this my way. I'll be fine," I yelled over my shoulder and gazed longingly at the water, now a warm gold, set afire by the setting sun, wishing I could float away from all my memories.

"Okay. It's getting cold," Mick said. "I'm going in to build a fire and call my mom and tell her about Miguel."

I turned and gave her a weak smile.

"Good luck. I'll be inside in a bit." I sat down on a rock and listened to Lake Superior. It amazed me how much noise it made even though only a light breeze shifted the water, but it was enough to send waves over the rocks in a mesmerizing rhythm.

I had come down there intending to think about Mitch and have yet another personal pity party. Instead, I found my thoughts drifting to Mary Jo Quinn again. More than three decades had passed since she was last seen alive. Did she run away? Was she living somewhere far from Houghton, a middle-aged woman, maybe with a husband and family? The whole idea of her fate intrigued me and provided a welcome distraction from my own misery.

"Good evening" called a voice behind me. Alex and Karen Breyers, the owners of the cottage and neighboring house, were making their way over the rocks toward me.

I waved, stood, brushed off my jeans and said, "Hello. You have a beautiful place. We're really enjoying ourselves; we've both needed a break."

"Oh, don't get up. We're just out for our evening stroll," Alex said and held out a steadying hand to his wife.

"Are we interrupting? You looked deep in thought," Karen asked rhetorically.

It wasn't my nature to be rude so I waved off her concern and invited them to pull up a rock and sit a while.

"Listen, I know we're intruding, but I couldn't wait to talk to you. Alex said you're in the publishing business," she said, nearly breathless. "I've written a novel and, well, I'm clueless as to how to get it published. I've tried everything short of shelling out the money to do it myself."

I laughed and held out my hand.

"Congratulations. Writing a novel is no small feat. Unfortunately, you're talking to the wrong person."

"Oh." She dropped my hand and looked crestfallen.

"I'm a reporter and copy editor for the *Daily Press* in Escanaba. My friend Michaela is the book editor. She's with Random House and specializes in celebrity acquisitions, biographies, Washington insider tell-alls, that kind of thing, but she might be able to help. What's your book about?"

"It's a romance, kind of a coming-of-age tale about a woman in the Peace Corps in the mid-Eighties. It's sort of our story, only more exciting," Karen said and giggled, then gave her husband a shy smile.

"Real life is sometimes more exciting than anything an author could imagine," I said and zipped my fleece jacket against the advancing fall chill, but it didn't do much to block the raw wind off the big lake. "Mick's on the phone with her mother right now, but I'll tell her to talk to you before we leave tomorrow. She loves finding new talent."

Karen beamed as bright as the setting sun. "Oh, that would be wonderful. I'd be so grateful."

"No problem. Hey, are you from around here?" I asked, still thinking about the mysterious scrapbook.

"I am," Alex answered. "She's a New Englander, Vermont actually. I'm from Houghton. I graduated from Michigan Tech in Houghton with a master's degree in industrial archeology. Now I'm working as a research assistant at the university and completing my doctorate."

"And what exactly does an industrial archeologist do?" I asked.

Laughing, he said, "We study the history of industry in an area. Take this area for instance. It's an archeologist's dream with all the old copper mining sites scattered across the Keweenaw Peninsula and into Ontonagon County. It's my job to study how they built and operated the mines, more specifically, the smelting plants where they processed the copper."

"Sounds interesting, but how does that translate into a Peace Corps job?"

"Well, a lot of those Third World countries are working with technology that's centuries old, but, to be honest, I just needed a break from my work and spent two years helping people in an African village develop their economy by teaching them how to capitalize on their talent for turning the wood from surrounding trees and shrubs into beautiful—and highly sought-after—jewelry. I met Karen there while she was teaching the children to read and write their language and English. That was sixteen years ago."

I guessed he was in his mid to late forties, with Karen maybe seven or eight years younger. That would have made him about Mary Jo's age. I filled them in on my find at the store in Copper Harbor and watched Alex's expression go dark in the waning light.

"Oh God, yes, I remember her. We sat next to each other in several classes over the years. In fact, I remember sitting behind her in sixth grade and my best friend sat next to her. We both had huge crushes on her, but she was more interested in Karl than me. She had the most beautiful hair. You wouldn't believe the way it glistened in the sunlight. It entranced me." He rubbed his temples and then gazed at nothing on the horizon. Karen reached for his hand.

"I didn't know any of this," she said, then turned to me. "We just moved here two years ago. I teach English at the high school in Calumet. We had been living in Massachusetts where he'd been working on a project to study the textile mills of the eighteenth and nineteenth centuries."

Alex broke his silence, but kept staring out at the lake. "I was one of the searchers, with my dad and two older brothers. Day after day, dawn to dusk. Never found a damn thing." He ran a hand through his thick graying hair and adjusted himself on the rock.

"The thing is, I know she didn't run away. That's just a smokescreen put up by the cops who couldn't handle anything more complicated than a bar fight or bustin' some college kids for smoking weed. She was a happy kid. Her parents were awesome. Her old man worked a lot, but they always seemed to get along. Christ, she was fourteen. Where the hell was a fourteen-year-old going to run to?"

"What do you think happened?" Karen asked with genuine concern as she tucked a stray strand of brown hair behind her ear and studied her husband.

"I don't know. I always felt like she knew the person who got her. She was trusting, but not stupid." His blue eyes were shrouded in a film of tears as the last light of the day faded to midnight blue. "I lost more than her friendship when she disappeared. Karl and I were never the same. *He was never the same.* His personality seemed to darken and he took to painting these brooding scenes. He still lives in Houghton running the family business. He's done well for himself with his art, too. Those paintings speak to people, but they creep me out."

"Mick just bought one," I said and cringed internally. "It's different, I'll say that." I didn't really find it creepy, just a bit disconcerting, like it had a hidden message, and not a pleasant one either. "What was Mary Jo like? Any hobbies? Any enemies?"

"You sound like a cop, but that's okay. It's good that someone still cares after all these years," Alex said, turning to me, his face barely visible. "I remember she was very creative. She was really into fashion, even made some of her own clothes and not because she had to, either. I mean, her old man was a doctor, you know."

He looked at his wife and smiled. "You remind me of her in a way. She was really nice, always the first one to welcome a new kid in class. She even talked about becoming a teacher."

It was dark and I was freezing. I wanted to hear more but I was too cold and sore from sitting on a million-year-old hunk of conglomerate rock for the last hour. I stood and stretched.

"I'm sorry for dredging up bad memories for you, Alex. It's just that I have a natural curiosity about the strange or unusual." Turning to his wife, I added, "See what I mean about real life being more exciting than books sometimes?"

"Jeez, no kidding," Karen said, holding her husband's hand as we walked back toward the cottage, hopping from rock to rock. When we reached the fork in the path leading to their house a few hundred feet from the cottage, I stopped and considered how to word my last question of the evening.

"Why would Astrid Heikkinen keep a scrapbook of Mary Jo's disappearance?"

A porch light near the cabin's back door cast an eerie glow on our faces and made Alex's smirk seem foul.

"Miss Heikkinen was our English teacher that year. She was pretty cool, if a bit weird. She wasn't your stereotypical spinster school teacher.

Actually, she was a bit of a radical, sort of a Mrs. Robinson-type, if you get my drift. She was in her early fifties but looked about forty in those miniskirts she wore." The recollection made him laugh. "She even drove a lime green Volkswagen Beetle with a peace sign bumper sticker. Her problem was that she was born about thirty years too soon."

His face turned serious as he continued. "She was in the woods right along with us. I remember her crying when the cops called off the search. I guess she just really cared. Miss Heikkinen took a shine to Mary Jo. We all did."

The couple, arms wrapped around each other's waist, said good night and walked back to their own log home, which appeared warm and inviting with soft light emanating from the downstairs windows. They looked content. I turned on my heel and went into the cabin.

Mick built a roaring blaze in the large stone fireplace in the living room, then curled up in an overstuffed chair drawn close to the heat to read a typed manuscript. She looked up when I approached the fire to warm my wind-chilled hands.

"You seem happy. Were your mom and dad okay with the wedding news?" I asked, settling into a chair across from her.

"I swear my mother is the most unpredictable person in the world. You know what she said? 'Oh, how wonderful. When can we meet him?' I'm like, 'Mom, I thought you'd be pissed.' She said my happiness was all that mattered and that she understood these things sometimes happen. Her mom and dad knew each other two weeks before they got married. Then two days later my grandfather was on a boat headed for the Philippines in World War II."

Mick put the manuscript down and stared into the fire for a few seconds, then said, "I guess I should have known. Years ago, when my dad was bugging me about marrying Gary, Mom pulled me aside and told me to make up my own mind based on what I felt, not what the rest of the world thought. It was good advice, since he turned out to be a jerk. I'm really lucky to have her, you know."

I wondered what my mother would think of my life. She had died of cancer when I was ten. My father had done his best to fill the void over the years, but a kid needed both parents. Would she approve of the choices I'd made, the path I had taken? Then I thought of Mary Jo again. What would having a child vanish into thin air do to a mother?

I quickly told Mick about Karen's literary aspirations and then went to bed, but it was a long time before I fell into a fitful sleep, dreaming of a golden-haired girl running through the woods.

I pulled a slip of paper from my pocket and checked the address I had scribbled on it. Mick swallowed a forkful of syrup-drenched pancakes and mumbled, "Whazat?"

"It's impolite to talk with your mouth full," I said and stuffed the paper in my pocket. "It's the address where that Quinn girl lived."

Mick rolled her eyes. We had stopped at Slim's Café, a family-style restaurant in a little old mining town called Mohawk that lined both sides of U.S. Highway 41 for about half a mile. The crowded tables suggested that Slim had created a popular gathering place for locals and tourists alike.

"You're not seriously going to try to find a kid who disappeared more than thirty years ago, are you?" Her eyes were wide with disbelief.

I squirmed in my seat and focused on downing a tall glass of orange juice.

"No, not really. I don't know. I'm just curious."

"Uh-huh. Remember what happened the last time you played detective? Are you trying to break the other ankle?" she asked, wiping her plate clean with the last bite of pancake.

"Spare me the lecture. I get enough of that from my dad."

I began figuring out who owed what from the check the waitress had just slapped down between us. Mary Jo Quinn had taken up residence in the dark spaces of my mind and refused to leave. When we were back on the highway heading south toward the Houghton-Hancock area, the business and residential center of the region known as the Copper Country, I told Mick what Alex Breyers had shared the night before.

"So why didn't the cops look for someone locally if Alex thinks she was murdered?" she asked. "Don't those things usually turn out to be perpetrated by family members or acquaintances?"

"He probably never told the police he suspected murder. Who cares what a 14-year-old boy thinks, especially one with a crush on the girl? Maybe they would have accused him."

"Maybe he did kill her. Maybe he was jealous of her relationship with his best friend. Fourteen's old enough to develop a pretty serious attachment," Mick said, as she turned her face to the half-open passenger window and let the wind whip her hair around her flushed face.

"A crime of passion? Hmm, I hadn't thought of that."

"There, case solved. Now let's not talk about dead girls anymore. It's too depressing." Mick went back to reading the thick manuscript of a biography of some French courtesan she had started the night before while I drove the next fifteen miles in silence, paying no attention to the riotous mix of autumnal brilliance along the road, instead thinking of nothing except Mary Jo and Alex and his friend Karl and all the possibilities. We passed through several more little towns along the way with names like Ahmeek, Allouez, Centennial, and Calumet, some with visible evidence of past mining operations. Finally we reached the fifty-year-old lift bridge that spanned the Portage Lake shipping canal and joined Hancock and Houghton geographically, if not communally. The two communities were well known as friendly rivals in everything from business to high school hockey.

"So where is this girl's house? I assume that's our next stop," Mick asked and sighed.

"I have no idea. It's on Edwards Street, wherever that is." I pulled into a gas station just south of the bridge on the Houghton side of the canal. While Mick filled the gas tank, I grilled the clerk for directions to the Quinn house and the junior high school. Then it occurred to me the school might be long gone, a distinct possibility considering the age of the town, another relic of the 19th century copper mining boom. On the Hancock side of the canal, atop a sweeping hill, stood an imposing silver shaft house from the Quincy Mine, a sentinel watching over the descendants of miners from a hundred years before as they built new families and new industries.

"Yeah, the middle school is fairly new. It's part of the high school," the twenty-something clerk said, scrunching her forehead as she tried to remember her local history lesson. "I'd say it was built in the last ten, fifteen years , but the old one was just a few blocks away on Houghton Avenue. I think that was both the junior high and high school, but they tore it down a few years ago. Now the site is just an empty lot." She tugged at the front of her blue and white Finlandia University sweatshirt as she thought.

"What is that, something to do with Finland?" I pointed at her shirt.

"Yeah, it's a Lutheran school. My last name is Ahola. Where else would I go to college?" she said with a shrug and a smile.

"Well, good luck," I said as Mick paid the bill.

I drove up a steep hill for about six blocks and made a few turns until I found the middle and high school complex on Gundlach Road on the outskirts of town. Then I turned around into the parking lot and went back down the hill two blocks before turning left onto Edwards. The house once occupied by the Quinn family stood at the edge of what looked like a well-kept, but ancient neighborhood. Like many of the surrounding homes, it had been remodeled many times over the years, with a two-car garage added to one side and a sun room jutting out on the other side. Clad in pale yellow siding, it appeared warm and inviting. A tricycle sat in the middle of the front walkway, waiting patiently for its little owner to return for another adventure. A new family had settled into Mary Jo Quinn's home, with the same hopes and dreams her parents had no doubt harbored—that their children would grow into happy, healthy adults. Someone else had had other plans for Mary Jo.

Chapter Three

I SAT STARING AT THE painting, but the more I stared, the uglier it got. Mick had decided she didn't want to haul it around the airport so she had pleaded with me to keep the thing until she returned with her husband's car for Thanksgiving in two months. There it sat on the floor of my apartment, propped against the sofa. Even Belle hated it and grumbled in low tones from her place on the rug at my feet.

"What the hell is it?" asked Charlie Baker, a detective with the Escanaba Public Safety Department and an old friend. He turned his head a notch to the left, stepped back and then sat down in an easy chair across from the wooden rocking chair where I sat.

"It's Lake Superior during a storm, an abstract depiction mind you, but Mick said the artist is gaining fame in New York. It is weird, though. I usually love water scenes, but not this one."

He got up and tossed an afghan over it.

"Put it in the attic later, will ya?" he said and cringed. "Now, tell me why you're so fascinated with some kid who disappeared before you were born?

It's not really all that uncommon. I remember a girl about six years ahead of me in school vanished when I was nine."

"Really, what year would that have been?"

"Seventy-nine. It was during the summer. She was walking home from this little grocery store in downtown Ishpeming after buying an ice cream cone one evening in July and just never showed up. Her family lived about two blocks from us. She and my sister were in the same grade, but they weren't friends. My sister was Miss Popularity, a cheerleader and all that. This girl was a mousey little thing who was into drawing." He reached over to scratch Belle behind a big floppy rust-colored ear.

"So she would have been about fifteen?"

"Yeah, fifteen. They were going to be sophomores in high school." Belle left me, waddled a few feet and plopped in front of Charlie. She was such an attention slut. *Traitor*.

"What was her name? Did they ever find her?"

He puffed his tanned cheeks and exhaled loudly through a little O his lips made. "I don't know, I can't remember her name. Isn't that sad? As far as I know, they never found a body or nothing."

"What about her family, what happened to them?"

His forehead scrunched, he ignored my question and stared into the distance.

"She had a president's name. Lincoln? No. Washington. No, that's not it." He screwed up his face in a bizarre expression of extreme concentration, which caused me to giggle. He scowled at me.

"Sorry, you just look so weird," I said and burst into gales of laughter.

"You're the one who's playing twenty questions. I don't have to take this abuse. I can go to work and get laughed at and at least get paid for the privilege."

"I'm sorry," I said, trying to keep my face straight while wiping tears from my eyes. Thunder cracked outside and I drew my bulky old sweater tighter and tucked my stocking feet under me. "Go on. You said she had the same name as a president."

"Mm-hmm. Ah, Franklin, that's it!"

"Benjamin Franklin was never president."

"No, but Franklin Pierce was a president," he said with a smug grin and then sat back in the chair with a sober face. "Lucy Franklin. As far as her family, I remember my parents saying that was the first place the police looked when she disappeared. That's standard operating procedure. They came up clean, though. I remember it was a really sad situation. I think she was their only child. They were an older couple, too, maybe in their late forties or early fifties."

I sat up in the chair and leaned toward Charlie. Even though the disappearances were five years apart, only about eighty-five miles separated them.

"Oh no, don't even go there," Charlie said. "I can see that little hamster working that wheel in your head. The two cases have nothing to do with each other."

"Did the police from Houghton ever compare notes with Ishpeming?"

"C'mon Robin, it would be a big stretch to link these two girls. You know as well as I do that communities in the U.P. are isolated from each other by more than just distance," Charlie said.

He was right. Yoopers, as natives of the U.P. are affectionately known, are territorial and tend toward pride in their little corner of civilization and aren't much interested in cooperating with the outside world, which could include people from the next town along the highway. It was unlikely the two police departments would have shared information unless there seemed to be an immediate threat to the public.

"Robin, I was nine when Lucy went missing. I was busy playing baseball and interested in nothing more than when the next "Star Wars" movie was going to come out. I didn't care about police investigations back then. I have no idea if they found any leads. Obviously, if they did, nothing came of them," he said and went back to scratching Belle's ears after she protested his lack of attention.

"Can you think of any other kids who disappeared in the U.P.?"

"Not off the top of my head. There was one over in Manistique about a dozen years ago, but they decided she just ran off with some carnie blowin' through town," Charlie said. He patted Belle's head, stood up and stretched his tall, lanky frame. "I've got to get up early tomorrow and so do you so I'm gonna hit the road. You want me to stash that masterpiece somewhere?"

He jerked his head at the painting.

"Please do. The entrance to the attic is in the hall. The stairs pull down."

After completing that task, with Belle trying to trip him several times as he carried the painting, Charlie left for his home on the far south side of Escanaba. I drank a glass of wine, leafed through Mary Jo's scrapbook for the hundredth time and waited for the storm to pass.

A scream shattered my sleep several hours later. At least I thought it was a scream. I had fallen asleep on the couch with the afghan thrown over me, but I was now wide awake, my heart thudding in my chest. Did something happen to my landlady, Rose Easton, I wondered. Belle growled softly from another room. I turned on a lamp and went to investigate. Belle was standing in the short hallway separating the bedroom and bathroom, staring at the entrance to the attic and shifting her weight from paw to paw in agitation. I felt cold and hot all at once, like every nerve ending was on fire, but my hands were ice.

"Belle, stop that. You're freaking me out. No one's up there," I said, more to convince myself than the dog. There was no way for anyone to get up there without my knowing it because the stairs could only be put back in place from below.

"We must have heard something outside," I whispered and went into my bedroom to one of the large windows overlooking Lake Shore Drive. I peeked around the blind and the road appeared empty, as was Ludington Park across the street. The rain had stopped and, in the glow cast by the streetlights, no people, no cars and no animals were visible. All was silent.

"This is nuts." I stomped back into the living room and let the television blast until it was time to get ready for work.

As soon as the newspaper's ten o'clock deadline passed, I pulled Bob Hunter, the managing editor, into his office and shut the door.

"What?" Hunter asked, his pale blue eyes wide with worry. "Don't tell me you're quitting. You can't quit. You just came back a few months ago."

"Bob, please, I'm not going anywhere. I just want to pick your brain." I filled him in on the story of Mary Jo Quinn's scrapbook and Charlie's own tale of Lucy Franklin's disappearance from Ishpeming. "You remember everything that's happened in the U.P. since the year one. What do you make of all this?"

He scratched his shaggy silver beard and squinted at me through his metal framed glasses.

"All what? Girls run away from home all the time, probably more often than you realize. I don't see the connection."

"Do you remember the Manistique case in the early nineties?" I persisted.

"Vaguely. The cops wrote that off as a runaway. There wasn't any reason to think otherwise. Oh, I see what you're getting at," Bob said and folded his hands on top of his heavily marked desk calendar. "You think these girls may have been murdered, maybe even by the same person. Now you know I'm the first one to jump at a juicy story, but you have to use some common sense here, Robin. These are all small towns we're talking about. Everybody watches everybody else, especially when it comes to kids. How could one person make three girls vanish without so much as a trace of evidence, and nearly twenty years apart at that?"

"My point exactly. It's too weird," I said.

"Mm-hmm. It's coming back to me now. The Manistique girl's name was Sabrina Danelli. We covered the story pretty extensively. Go check it out in the morgue. I don't think you'll find any connection, though."

I jumped up and opened the door. "Thanks, Bob."

"Hey, don't waste too much time on this. It's old news and we've got messes to deal with here and now."

"Sure thing, Bob," I called over my shoulder, already halfway down the stairs to the basement before he could reconsider.

The index, or morgue, was housed on three-by-five index cards in several tiny file cabinets atop full-size four-drawer units that lined the inside wall of the basement. The cards were arranged by number and corresponded with files full of clippings, notes and information in the larger cabinets. Scattered around the dimly-lit room were newspaper vending machines, plastic green distribution tubes for rural subscribers and a rack full of old circulation reports printed on reams of green-striped computer paper. Unlike most basements, this one smelled dry, albeit old thanks to the books of newspapers dating back more than a century stored in a small room at the bottom of a second set of steps. In the center of this room was a sturdy square wooden table where I sat with the Sabrina Danelli file. It was thin, just seven clippings inside. "Not very extensive, Bob," I mumbled as I leafed through them. No one seemed too excited about this girl's disappearance. There was no search of the nearby woods, no tearful parental cry for help. It was just assumed by police and family that the fifteen-year-old dark-eyed girl with a wild gypsy heart had flown the coop with a carnival worker after the Schoolcraft County Fair ended its three-day run in September of 1993. The newspaper ran a photo showing a beautiful young woman with eyes suggesting a fire burning deep inside. She looked restless, as if her soul wanted, needed, to be anywhere but the quiet little village of Manistique, Michigan. The reporter at the time, Tim Carter, had asked a few non-family members about Sabrina's personality. An English teacher described her as having a talent for poetry, dark, mystical verses that left the reader feeling haunted. A classmate just found her too much to handle. "She's a wild child, man. Too wild for this one stoplight town."

The assumption that Sabrina had run away sounded on target. Bob was right in that small town dwellers watch everyone else's kids like black bear sows protecting their cubs. Still, I found it odd that the girl never called home to say, "Hey, I'm okay. Don't worry." Of course, she might have and the reporter never caught wind of it. Perhaps I would try to find him and get his personal take on the story. The name Tim Carter didn't mean anything to me. He probably did a year or two at the *Daily Press* right out of college and moved to a bigger paper with a bigger paycheck and bigger stories, just like I had done.

"Robin, you down there?" yelled a distant voice.

"Yeah, what's up?"

"You've got a phone call, some guy named Alex Breyers. Do you want me to take a message?" It was our newsroom assistant, Amy Winklebauer.

"No, I'll be right up. Thanks." I snapped the folder shut and carried it upstairs to my desk. On the way up, I tried to figure out why the cabin owner would be calling me, unless we had left something behind. Amy transferred the call to my phone as I sat down.

"Alex? Hi, this is Robin. What can I do for you? We didn't leave anything behind, did we?"

"No, no, nothing like that. It's just, well, Christ, this sounds ridiculous, but I was wondering if maybe you could look into this deal with Mary Jo, you know, find out what happened to her."

His words came out as choppy as Lake Michigan during a November gale.

"I'll admit the case has piqued my interest, but I'm not a cop, Alex, just a reporter and not exactly Bob Woodward or Carl Bernstein, at that. I'm not sure what I can do."

"I know," he said and paused, sounding as though he hadn't slept well the previous night. "I've been thinking about our conversation the other night. It's not even so much about Mary Jo. You see, when she disappeared, I lost my best friend. Karl Maki and I never spoke again, ever. I don't understand why, but we just never seemed to know what to say to each other. Karen said it seemed like you had a real interest in what happened. I felt it too. Maybe you can come at this from a different angle. I know you're three hours away, but you and I both know anything happening in the U.P. is local news."

I let out a hollow laugh and stalled for a few seconds. I was already working on the story and had been since I'd picked up that damned scrapbook. Besides, what else was I doing with my spare time besides getting drunk on cheap wine more often and wallowing in my misery?

"I'll see what I can find out," I said and hung up the phone. What was that old saying about a cat? Curiosity killed it, but satisfaction brought it back to life. So I had a few more lives to spare.

Chapter Four

I MADE A COPY OF the articles in the Sabrina Danelli file, put it back in the basement and then called the news editor at the *Marquette Mining Journal*, the daily newspaper closest to Ishpeming. He hadn't been around when Lucy Franklin went missing, but he said he would check their files and fax me what he found. About twenty sheets of paper flowed out of the fax machine about an hour later, detailing the disappearance of the teenager. Unfortunately, more stories didn't mean more information. Like Danelli and Quinn, Lucy Franklin had vanished like a shadow on a cloudy day. I made a folder for the Franklin articles and set it aside. I had an interview scheduled in half an hour with the state attorney general, making his way through the Upper Peninsula on a rare trip away from Lansing. As I was pulling on my jacket, the receptionist passed by my desk and caught a glimpse of the Franklin file. Leafing through it, Amy said, "What is this all about? I grew up near Ishpeming, but I don't remember these stories."

"You weren't born yet," I said, pulling on a light blue cardigan over my white turtleneck sweater and grabbing my purse and notebook.

She looked at the dates and scowled. "Oh, yeah, 1979. Wow, I didn't know that sort of thing happened up here. I wonder why no one ever talked about her."

"Good question. I gotta run to the state office building. The AG is making his annual visit to town and I have to humor him by playing the eager young reporter dazzled by his power and prestige."

"You really don't like politicians, do you? Who knows, maybe he has something important to say," she chided.

"Uh-huh, and I have the solution to all the problems in the Middle East. If the president calls, tell him I'll be right back."

My cynicism toward anything political turned out to be on target. The attorney general gave the typical spiel about his cause of the moment, identity theft. I snapped a fresh photo, asked a few questions, got the standard rehearsed responses, tried a different approach on a few other subjects and finally gave in out of boredom.

I took my time walking the three blocks back to the *Daily Press* and thought about Alex's call. A large unhealed wound had been opened, a wound infected by a strong distrust of the police and even his childhood best friend. Viewed through the clouded lens of time, Alex may have looked back on Mary Jo's disappearance and seen something that was never there. The mind has a way of changing our perceptions of people and events as the years pass. Maybe Alex was remembering Mary Jo as his dream girl, not as she really was. The quiet artist he envisioned could have been living in a hell of abuse at home. Maybe she really did run away. Where does a fourteen-year-old run to, I wondered. It wasn't uncommon to find runaways working the streets of Chicago, trying to survive any way they could. Had Mary Jo or Lucy or Sabrina ended up on the streets? The blast of a horn shook me into the present. I turned to find myself in the middle of Sixth Street as a minivan tried to turn from Ludington Street, the main east-west thoroughfare in Escanaba.

"Watch where the hell you're going!" yelled the middle-aged soccer mom behind the wheel before speeding down the street.

Embarrassed, I ran into the *Daily Press,* situated in a century-old building on the corner of Sixth and Ludington. I scarfed down a container of microwave soup and set to work on the article about the attorney general's visit. By the time I finished, the rest of the staff were turning off their computers and heading for home. Taking their cue, I grabbed the Franklin and Danelli files, made dinner reservations with my father and left work.

I drove the six blocks to my apartment located in one of the many Victorian-era houses lining the west side of Lake Shore Drive. Stretching along the east side for nearly a mile was Escanaba's emerald jewel, Ludington Park. Beyond that was Lake Michigan, which sparkled like a sapphire as small waves glinted in the bright autumn sun. I hooked the brown nylon leash to Belle's collar, and we headed for the park. The air was warm, with the temperature around seventy, a perfect Indian summer day. We followed Jenkins Drive as it wound through the park, crossing a wide stone bridge to a man-made island that included a beach, small playground, fishing pier and walking trail.

"Beautiful day," I called to a neighbor walking her fluffy white Bischon frise.

"Yah. We better enjoy it now. It won't last long," she said as she passed us, leaving a cloud of perfume in her wake. The two dogs eyed each other warily, but Belle stayed on course. She didn't pay much attention to little dogs. Nope, it was the Dobermans and Rottweilers that brought out the fight in her. Once back home, I didn't bother going upstairs but helped Belle into the Jeep and headed across town to the house where I'd spent the happiest years of my life. The single-story ranch was built in the late 1960s and blended easily with the dozen or so like it in the neighborhood. Just a few blocks from an eighteen-hole golf course, it proved the perfect retirement home for my widowed father, who would never be bored as long as he had golf and other old firefighters and cops with whom to swap war stories and gossip.

Hank Hamilton met me at the door and invited us in to a house full of wondrous smells.

"Dad, have you been watching those Emeril Legasse shows again? Something smells awesome." I unleashed Belle, who barreled straight for the kitchen, waddling as fast as her muscular little legs could move.

Dad laughed and gave me a hug.

"No, but I am trying a new recipe from the church cookbook. It's a chicken dish with wild rice, herbs and vegetables. It's just about done," he said, pushing me into the kitchen. "What's with the pile of papers and stuff under your arm? It's too early for me to help straighten out your taxes."

"Ha, ha, ha. Actually, I'd like to dig into your memory vault concerning some teenage girls who've disappeared over several years in the U.P." I set the scrapbook and files on the counter and began to set the table. My dad hefted a large roasting pan out of the oven and set it on top, then turned to look at me, a pot-holder-mittened hand on each hip.

"You want to talk about girls who have disappeared? That's a strange topic for dinner conversation. What prompted this?"

Over a succulent dinner I filled him in on my find in the bookstore in Copper Harbor and where it had led me. After we cleared the table, he paged through the book and articles I had copied, emitting occasional guttural noises.

"Do you remember these cases?" I asked, draining my second glass of chardonnay.

"Of course I do. I was part of the team that went looking for that Franklin girl. They brought in law enforcement from as far away as the Soo and Iron Mountain. Don't you remember? I didn't come home for two days. As soon as we were done with our local shifts, we all went back up to Ishpeming. Sad story. The mom—a Gladstone gal, by the way—went nuts after that, wouldn't leave the house in case Lucy came home or called. She died a few years ago. The obituary listed the girl as a survivor. They just never came to terms with it."

"So you don't think that kid ran away?"

"I don't know that anyone seriously thought that. Obviously, I didn't know the girl, but from what I heard about her and what I saw of her parents, it wouldn't have made sense for her to run away."

"What about the Danelli girl?"

"I remember something about a girl missing right after you left for college, but no one got too excited because that seemed like a Romeo and Juliet case," he said and shuffled through the small pile of papers. "I notice you don't have anything in here about Caroline Baxter."

"Who's Caroline Baxter?"

"She was the daughter of a Kingsford Public Safety officer. She disappeared the summer your mother died, 'Eighty-five. She was supposed to ride her bike over to her grandmother's house one afternoon but never made it. They never found her or the bike," he said quietly.

I got up from the table and began loading the dishwasher.

"Okay, that's four girls over a period of nineteen years. Any boys?"

He thought for a minute then shook his head.

"Not that I can think of, at least none that just vanished. No kidnappings, either, except that one custody dispute a few years ago, but the cops caught the mother at a gas station near Milwaukee and the kids were fine." He turned in his chair and looked at me quizzically. "You know, I don't think anyone's ever tried to tie these four together. I can certainly see a pattern, though — all girls in their early to mid-teens, all disappeared during the summer when they were alone. This Danelli girl was never actually seen with the alleged carnie worker, according to these articles. She was supposed to go to a friend's house to study but never showed."

"But there's such a stretch of time between each one. Five, six, then eight years and there hasn't been another in more than twelve years," I said and groaned. If there was a pattern here, this story was way over my head. There was no way I had the time to research each disappearance and track down leads. I said as much to my dad.

"Maybe you could take your ideas to the state police and let them deal with it. I'll tell you one thing. Be extremely careful in what you say and do," he said, rising from his chair and placing a meaty hand on each of my shoulders.

"What do you mean?"

"Well, we're talking about kids here, maybe dead kids. As I said before, at least one of these families hasn't even accepted the fact that she isn't coming home. Second, if they are all related, we're talking about a serial killer and they are the most dangerous of all," he said and wrapped me in his still-muscular arms and planted a kiss on the top of my head, which landed at the middle of his chest. "You would've made a great detective, Kiddo."

"Is it too late for me to go to the police academy?" I mumbled into his red golf shirt.

"Thankfully, yes. You seem to find more than enough trouble lately without a badge on your chest and gun on your hip."

I collected the articles, scrapbook and Belle, said our goodbyes and started to drive home. A block from the house, though, I detoured to the newspaper office. Leaving Belle in the Jeep, I ran inside and found the sports editor typing furiously, the phone receiver clenched in the crook of his perennially-sunburned neck. I waved at him and darted down to the basement morgue. Articles from outside our coverage area, which included Delta and Schoolcraft counties and the northern tip of Menominee County, usually didn't make it into the morgue, but I hoped that Caroline Baxter's disappearance in neighboring Dickinson County might have been deemed important enough to clip and save, since Kingsford was only an hour away. I uttered a squeal of delight when I found her name in the index. Her corresponding file was thin but still held four articles, mainly because her aunt lived in nearby Bark River, a small town about ten miles west of Escanaba on the federal highway. I took the file upstairs, made copies and then returned it to the basement.

Once back in the apartment, I made a cup of hot apple cider, grabbed a legal notepad and spread out the stack of information I'd collected on the tiny kitchen table. Going through each file, I wrote down all the pertinent facts and then made a chart of any similarities. Other than being within a few years in age and having long hair, which certainly was the norm for a young girl, they didn't seem to have much in common. Lucy Franklin was quiet and shy, Sabrina Danelli was "wild," Mary Jo Quinn was a typical child of the seventies, earthy and friendly, while Caroline Baxter was an average kid with an above average aptitude for the violin. All were pretty and came from middle class backgrounds, as far as I could tell from the articles that listed the parents' occupations.

So what was it about them that might have attracted the attention of someone with evil intentions? I didn't have a clue.

Chapter Five

THE NEXT MORNING BEGAN WITH Belle whining. Squinting into the dark, I sat up in bed and listened. She was in the hall again. Padding to the doorway in stocking feet and groaning at the digital clock on the dresser that glared five-oh-five, I found the dog staring up at the attic door again. The apartment felt chilly. I shivered, retrieved my ratty old bathrobe and sat down next to Belle to pet her. Her muscles were taut with tension. Something was up there and it was annoying the hell out of her. With the nights getting colder, I figured it must be a squirrel or chipmunk seeking shelter for the winter. With all the massive oak trees in the neighborhood, there were plenty of the little critters around.

"I'll get Mrs. Easton to call the pest control people to live-trap whatever's up there and send it on its way, okay? Now stop fussing," I said and scratched her ear. She ignored me until I filled her dish with food and presented her with a bowl of fresh water.

I made a note to slide under my landlady's door, then got ready for work. Before I left, I stuffed the girls' notes, files and scrapbook into a tote bag resolving to talk my editor into letting me take some time to pursue my theory, such as it was, that someone had abducted teenage girls in the U.P. and slipped away unseen, unheard and unknown.

"I can see you're not going to let this go."

"Nope."

Bob Hunter sat behind his desk, elbows on the armrests of his creaky old chair, fingers forming a pyramid under his chin. Sitting across from him, leaning forward with elbows propped on my knees, I met his steely gaze without blinking.

"All right, here's my dilemma," he said, shifting forward to rest his hands on the desk blotter. "I know you're right. This could be one helluva story, maybe the biggest crime story in the state since the Michigan Murders. If you're wrong, I have to justify to Burns all those hours you spent on a wild goose chase in search of a serial killer." He tweaked middle and forefingers on each hand when he sneered the words "serial killer."

"C'mon, Bob, you know Sam is a reporter at heart. That's what makes him one of the last great publishers and one of the reasons I came back to this place. He'll understand, even if you obviously don't. Just give me two weeks. Let me clear my calendar of everything but essentials and give me mileage. I won't even charge you if I have to stay overnight somewhere. Please?" I smiled sweetly and batted my puny pale blond eyelashes.

"Oh, for Pete's sake, don't start that nonsense," he growled. "All right, but if you see this is going nowhere, drop it fast. If there is something to all this, you better hand me one kick-ass series of articles, got it?"

"Got it. Thanks, Bob. You're doing the right thing," I said, then laughed when he uttered an expletive.

My first step was a call to a psychologist I had interviewed for a feature story a month before. She agreed to meet with me at eleven. Until then, I busied myself with copy-editing and filing the past week's articles, meeting notes and correspondence. If I didn't keep up with the paper-shuffling, it threatened to bury my desk in sheaves of meaningless clutter.

Dr. Jennifer O'Connell's office was located on the third floor of the Ludington Centre, an old department store converted to offices on the corner of Ludington and Eleventh. I walked the five blocks, enjoying the sun on my face and the first hint of color on the young maples that lined the sidewalks. The street was empty except for two elderly women ahead of me, probably from the eighteen-story senior citizen apartment tower on the five hundred block, strolling past storefronts, stopping occasionally to peer in a window when something caught their eye. I couldn't help smiling as I walked by them, remembering how the elderly feared walking many of the streets of Chicago without an armed guard at their elbow, even in broad daylight. The worst problem these ladies had to deal with was speeding bicyclists and errant skateboarders.

Dr. O'Connell met me at the door to the stairwell on her floor, impeccably dressed in an emerald green tailored suit that made her light auburn hair gleam. She grinned at my raised eyebrows.

"I saw you coming. I must tell you, I'm intrigued by your call. Mind you, I'm not a forensic psychologist, but the field has always interested me," she said and led me down a wide long hallway to an ornate oak door with a large brass plate reading "Jennifer O'Connell, MS, PhD, Family Psychologist." We passed through a small lobby with four stuffed chairs, matching couch and an empty receptionist desk and into her large, classically-furnished office. She closed the door behind us and indicated I should sit down in one of the comfortable-looking cream suede chairs in front of her desk. Occupying the southeast corner of the building, the office had large windows that overlooked the intersection below and even offered a distant view of the lake, perhaps a relaxing site to a stressed patient.

I asked about her receptionist, whom I'd remembered as quite helpful in juggling the doctor's schedule when I needed to interview her.

"Carol's recuperating from a hysterectomy. In fact, I'm meeting her for lunch after we're through," she said, eyeing the calendar on her desk. "Now, tell me the details of this story you're writing."

I filled her in on the four missing girls and asked if the cases could be related. She leaned back in her chair, a large, expensive leather contraption with funky sloping arms, and squinted one eye.

"Hmm, they could be related. There's a pretty wide span of years between the disappearances, but that doesn't mean the same person couldn't be involved. What you're looking for is a criminal profile. What kind of person would go after girls of a certain age and why? It helps narrow down the list of suspects. Is there anything that ties these girls together at all? You know, like hair color, physical features, habits or hobbies?"

Pulling out the notes I'd written the night before, I scanned the papers quickly, then pushed them across the desk. The doctor studied them for several minutes then leaned back in her chair.

"You need more information before I can be of much help. Can you maybe trace the last few months of each girl's life? That could help determine if they might have encountered the same guy."

"Why do you say guy? Couldn't a woman be a serial killer?" I asked, not wanting to be accused of being sexist.

"Certainly. Eileen Wournos was just put to death a few years ago for shooting several men in Florida. But most serial killers are men, especially when it comes to young women and girls. Often, there's a sexual aspect, but not always. Sometimes something in the killer's past causes him to target a certain type of victim. That's what happened with Wournos. Men had always mistreated her so badly that eventually she snapped."

"What about the idea that some of these girls may have just run away from home?"

She shook her head. "I've seen lots of young girls from troubled families in the twenty years I've been in practice. There are plenty of warning signs before a girl just takes off, and she usually has help, say from a boyfriend who's a few years older, or a schoolmate. The girls in these cases were too young to get far on their own, especially coming from such an isolated rural area as the Upper Peninsula. They usually turn up in a few days, weeks or months, but they don't disappear forever without another word. We're six hours from Chicago and nine hours from Detroit by bus, for heaven's sake. If we were closer to a major city or the girls were sixteen or seventeen with a history of acting out, I might think differently."

"That's what I've been saying, although not as eloquently, but everyone from my editor to my friend Charlie at Escanaba Public Safety thinks linking the cases is fantasy," I said. It felt good to have someone agree with me, until one considered the fact that we were agreeing these girls were all missing, leaving behind few clues as to what happened to them. I looked up from the pile of files still in my lap to find the doctor studying me.

"What?"

"Why are you so interested in this anyway? I mean, it's not like you don't have enough work to do around here. I know the Press is chronically short-staffed."

I squirmed under her heavy gaze. I couldn't bluff my way through her scrutiny, it was her job to read people and see things in them they didn't want to acknowledge.

"It helps me to focus on other things right now, otherwise I wallow in self-pity," I said. At our earlier interview she had asked my marital status and I'd had to explain about Mitch, keeping it to a sentence or two lest I burst into tears. I wasn't ready to share more.

"I understand." She stood, straightened her suit jacket and handed back my notes.

Relieved, I gathered everything together and walked to the door leading to the stairwell, with the doctor in tow.

"One last question," I said, turning to face her. "I will have to approach the families, well, at least some of them, for information. How do I do it without sounding morbid? At least one of the families never accepted the thought that their daughter was dead."

She shrugged and shook her head slowly. "I can't imagine what it would be like to lose a child. My two kids are grown and on their own, but I still worry about them. I guess you just need to be honest. Tell them what you're doing and why. If they tell you to get lost, don't take it personally. But you must respect their wishes. If they want to be left alone, back off," she said. "I believe you have good instincts or you wouldn't have won all those awards. Robin, just follow those instincts and you'll get where you need to go."

Nodding, I stuck out my hand, which she took in both of hers, and I thanked her for her time.

"No problem. Keep me posted. I'd like to know what you find out," she said.

As I walked back to work, it occurred to me that maybe digging up old bones like these would only do more harm. Then again, what if their abductor was still out there, lying in wait for the next victim?

It was past five and the office was empty, but I continued to sit at my desk and stare at Sabrina Danelli's photograph. She was the last victim that I knew of, and her family was just an hour's drive down U.S. Highway 2 to the east. Her parents, Anthony and Susan Danelli, were listed in the phone book at the same address they'd had when their daughter had disappeared thirteen years before. What would I say if I called them? Hi, I'm interested in finding out who may have killed your daughter? I groaned and rubbed my temples. Maybe I'd be better off just showing up at their door. No, too aggressive. I picked up the receiver and dialed the first four numbers then slammed it down. It rang. I jumped, my heart thudding, then answered it.

"Hello?" I growled.

"Did I catch you at a bad time?"

"No, Dad," I said and exhaled. "I was just debating calling the Danellis over in Manistique. What's up?"

"That's actually why I called. Well, not about them, but about the Baxters over in Kingsford. I hope you don't mind, but I called a friend of mine who is close to the family and told him what you were working on. He thought the Baxters would be interested in talking with you so he called them. They want to see you."

"Really? Wow, when?"

"I'll give you the number and you can arrange it."

I wrote down the number on a piece of scrap paper, thanked him and hung up the phone. Did I really want to stir up bad memories and risk making a mess of things? All I had to go on were some vague suspicions that maybe these cases could possibly be related. My instincts as an investigative reporter had proven correct in the past, so I took a deep breath, dialed the Baxters' phone number and crossed my fingers in hopes that I wouldn't say anything stupid.

"Hello," a gruff male voice answered.

"Hello, my name is Robin Hamilton. My dad is Hank Hamilton. He's retired from Escanaba Public Safety and is a friend of, um—" I suddenly realized I hadn't asked my father for the name of his contact.

"Oh, right, Len called earlier. Yeah, my wife and I would be interested in hearing your thoughts on Caroline's disappearance. Can you come over tonight?" The hope in his voice surprised me.

"Uh, sure, but please understand, it's all just speculation," I said.

"That's more than we've gotten in over a decade," he responded curtly.

I jotted down the directions and thanked him for being willing to talk.

"I'm just thankful someone out there still gives a damn about what happened to my little girl," he said and hung up.

I swallowed hard, grabbed my jacket, stopped by the apartment to get Belle and headed for Kingsford. Located about fifty-five miles west of Escanaba, it was a working class town started by iron miners and loggers in the mid-nineteenth century. The area was now home to several small manufacturing companies and a large, proud Italian American community. It bordered another small mining town, Iron Mountain, and the two towns vowed to remain separate until hell froze over. The Baxters' house was on a quiet street in a relatively new subdivision of ranch-style homes with two-car garages equipped with basketball hoops over the stalls. The Baxter home was a sprawling red brick tri-level with white shutters. The lawn was freshly cut and well fertilized, the sidewalk and driveway lined with red, white and purple petunias. An American flag hung from a pole near the front door. The house was so Middle America I felt like saluting. I parked on the street, leaving the windows open a crack for Belle. She ignored me and focused on a beagle playing with two young boys a few houses down the street. Before I could knock, the front door was opened by a man of average height with broad shoulders and thick forearms exposed by rolled-up sleeves of a red plaid flannel shirt. He stuck out a meaty, weather-beaten hand and said, "Hi, you must be Robin. I'm Alan Baxter. C'mon in."

I shook his hand and followed him into the den where a plump woman with short dark hair sat in the middle of the couch, looking at a photo album. She stood when I entered the room and smiled tentatively.

"Robin, right?"

I nodded.

"I'm Shirley. I'm so glad to hear you've taken an interest in our daughter's case. Everyone, including the police, seems to have forgotten about us. Please, sit down. Can I get you something to drink?"

I sat in one of the chairs she'd pointed to facing the large-screen television that dominated one wall. Declining her offer of a drink, I pulled from my book bag a notebook and the rather paltry file on Caroline Baxter. Alan sat next to his wife and asked, "Well, where do we begin?"

"First, let me tell you how your daughter's disappearance came to my attention." I shared my tale of the scrapbook yet again and where it had led me. "I'm starting to think these cases might all be related, but I need more information."

"Caroline's dead." Shirley said it with finality as her husband nodded and took her left hand and massaged the palm.

"We've accepted that she's not coming back," she continued. "It's been more than twenty years. Believe me, she would have called. She loved being a part of this family. She adored her two brothers and little sister, her grandparents, cousins, even us, which is not always the case with thirteen-year-old girls."

She looked down at the album on the coffee table and pressed her lips together.

"Tell me about her," I said.

"She had an incredible ear for music," Alan said. "She asked to start taking piano lessons when she was four. I thought it was silly at first. I thought she got the idea from some cartoon or something, but she kept badgering us so we finally signed her up with a local teacher. This guy tried her on several instruments and, wouldn't you know, she fell in love with the damned violin. Oh God, those first few months were agony. It was like listening to a door with a rusty hinge that you couldn't oil. But she got the hang of it pretty quick. She had just gotten back from a music camp when she went missing."

There were no tears in his brown eyes, just the cold hard truth that his child was gone.

"How did the police handle it?" I asked.

"About as well as they could, I guess. I mean I was working for the department and those guys busted their butts searching for her. The state boys, the sheriff's department, even the Iron Mountain cops and the guys across the state border in Niagara, Wisconsin, helped out. They always figured it was a kidnapping because they never found her bicycle. She'd gotten this brand new pink ten-speed bike for her birthday that year and was riding that when she disappeared. For months, they put all their resources into finding her, but we just never got a break. We put her picture onto that Missing Children's Network, had artists do photo aging, everything we could think of, but no one ever came forward with a clue."

Shirley jumped in and said, "We got excited about seven years ago when a man over near Ironwood was arrested for the murder of a girl somewhere around there, but he denied everything. He was found guilty in a trial, but it never led anywhere with regard to Caroline."

I looked around the room for other signs of the girl, some memorial, but saw nothing other than a photo on the fireplace mantel. "It's always a parent's worst nightmare that something will happen to their child, yet you both seem to be doing okay. How did you come to terms with her disappearance?"

Shirley sighed and looked down at the album again, then pushed it towards me. "We went on living. We had the rest of the children to think about. Here, go ahead, look through that and you'll see."

The thick three-ring album began with the usual baby pictures, toddler antics and several photos of a beaming little brunette, with big brown eyes, pigtails and two front teeth missing, holding up a tiny violin. She was gradually maturing into a lovely young girl when the photos of Caroline stopped. The last one was of her and a younger girl, obviously her sister, standing with their arms around each other's shoulders while a slim boy of about sixteen towered behind them. Caroline sported a long curly hairstyle and a "Ghostbusters" t-shirt with a ghost bursting through a circle with a slash through it. The last half of the album held pictures of family gatherings, somber at first, as they coped with the emptiness, then more joyous as graduations, weddings and births followed.

"I'd love to show you Caroline's room, but it would mean nothing to you," Shirley said. "It's now the playroom where the grandkids stay when they come to visit. We kept it as it was the day she disappeared on July 24, 1985. Then, about five years ago, we all decided it was turning into a shrine and that would not be what Caroline would want. So we made it into a place of hope, happiness, joy, the future."

"Caroline would have turned thirty-five last week," her father said quietly.

"I'm sorry, I wish there was something more I could do," I said, feeling on the verge of tears at my helplessness. I certainly couldn't bring Caroline back to them, not unless she was still alive, and even her parents didn't believe that was possible.

"But there is something you can do," Alan said, his eyes wide, glowing with a fierce light. "As Shirley said, we know Caroline's dead, but we don't know why or who or how. The thing is, most of the cops who worked on Caroline's case have retired or died. God only knows where the file is or what condition it's in. Every once in a while, usually around the time of year she disappeared, I'll go down to the state police post in Iron Mountain and rattle a few cages, but it never gets us anywhere. Too much time has passed. They say it's still an active case, but I know they haven't looked at it in years. That's why we were so happy when Len called to tell us about your interest. Do you think you can help us find justice for our little girl?"

The hope shining in their faces left me with queasiness in my stomach. Was I raising expectations I couldn't meet?

"I'm going to try," was all I could answer.

Chapter Six

I GOT LESS THAN FIVE hours sleep total over the next three nights. By the time I dragged myself to work on Friday morning I was sorry I'd ever heard the name Mary Jo Quinn or any of the others. Their faded images danced in my head whenever I closed my eyes. Even my now-habitual glass or three of wine at night wasn't helping me fall asleep.

Belle was faring no better, thanks to whatever had taken up residence in the attic. Rose Easton, who owned the old Victorian house I called home and occupied the first floor, had called a pest control company to take care of it.

"Nothing, not a hole, not a dropping, not even a hair or a feather," she'd said Thursday evening over cups of hot buttered rum and fresh gingersnaps when I'd asked about the attic issue.

"Well, then, what on earth has got Belle so upset?"

"Maybe you should take her to the vet. Maybe there's something physically wrong with her. My late husband had a chocolate lab that went with him everywhere for thirteen years. One day she wouldn't leave the yard, wouldn't go for a walk, wouldn't get in his truck, nothing. She just wanted to curl up in the corner of our bedroom. Well, between the two of us, we finally got her to the vet, but it was too late — cancer. We had to put her down two weeks later. It was horrible," Mrs. Easton said, dabbing her eyes with a napkin. "That's why I don't have a pet; I don't want to get attached all over again. It's too hard when they're gone."

My heart felt like lead when I considered the possibility of losing Belle. It would be like losing Mitch all over again. She'd been a Christmas gift from him nearly two years before and was like our child, raised from a tiny puppy with ears and paws that were three sizes too big for her little body.

After getting permission from Bob Hunter to leave work Friday morning, Belle and I stood at the counter of the veterinarian's office on Stephenson Avenue as soon as it opened at eight. Of the three doctors, none seemed to have time for a hysterical owner and her bewildered, but otherwise normal, basset hound. Dr. Summer Johnson took pity on me, though, and ushered us into the examining room. I explained the trouble with Belle not sleeping and her fascination with the attic. Between pokes and prods and drawing some blood, she simply muttered, "Uh-huh, mm-hmm."

After about ten minutes of that, she threw her long blonde ponytail over her shoulder and said, "Robin, this is the healthiest animal I've seen all year. She looks better than you do."

"Thanks," I sneered. Summer had graduated a few years ahead of me in high school and had always kidded with me. "So what the hell's going on? Why is she acting so weird?"

"Sometimes pets pick up on the emotions in the house and react to that. Is there anything going on with you?"

She didn't know me very well and I doubted she knew about Mitch so I filled her in briefly on how he'd died and my return to Escanaba.

"When did he die, April?"

"Yes." I began scratching one of Belle's ears. "But this is the first time she's really had an issue like this."

"Then my guess is there's something else bothering her in the attic."

I thought about the bizarre painting Charlie had stashed there. That seemed to be when her behavior had changed.

"What about an object that's strange? Could that set her off?" I explained about the chaotic rendition of a stormy sea that Mick had left with me.

"Absolutely. There may be some energy tied with that painting that's upsetting her. Try moving it out of the house and see what happens," Summer said.

"No offense, but —"

She laughed. "Hey, I know, it sounds flakey. But there's a lot more to this world than our measly five senses can detect. Dogs and cats are very attuned to the paranormal. Just give it a try. In the meantime, spend a little time with her. Maybe she just needs some attention. I imagine she's left alone a lot."

After shelling out eighty-five bucks for the exam and blood test, we got in the Jeep and sat for a moment. Belle looked at me expectantly. She knew we weren't going home. I called Bob Hunter on my cell phone and told him I'd be back to work after noon and that I wanted to track down the Danellis in Manistique. Then I called my dad and asked him to get the painting and put it in his garage until Mick returned at Thanksgiving to retrieve the thing. I started the Jeep, gave Belle a pat on the head and pulled out my notes on Sabrina Danelli. I didn't know my way around Manistique but figured I could get directions once we got there.

"Ready to put that nose to work and do some private detecting?"

"Woof."

"Okay, Dr. Watson, the game's afoot," I said and headed for the highway. It would be several days before we would see Escanaba again.

The road north out of Escanaba is a four-lane divided highway until it reaches the tiny old lumber town of Rapid River, then the road turns east and narrows to two lanes for 126 miles to the Mackinac Bridge except for the occasional passing lane. Rapid River had one blinking light at the intersection of the highway and Main Street. A cluster of small businesses struggled to stay afloat against the tide of chain stores converging on

Escanaba about ten miles away. But the several hundred residents scattered across three townships, Masonville, Ensign and Bay de Noc, were loyal customers at Jack's Restaurant, the Dairy Flo and the Mini-Mart. My mother, Grace ("Gracie" to my father), had grown up in Rapid River and recalled fondly her childhood there. She'd wanted to settle in a home not too far from her parents on a country road a mile or so from town, but my father's employment required him to live within the city limits.

I hadn't spent much time there since her death, as her family seemed to not quite know what to make of my traditional ex-Marine father, who treated my mother like a queen but thought her relatives were "loopy." A forester with the U.S. Forest Service, my grandfather was an "environmentalist" before anyone ever coined the term, predicting earth's eventual destruction at the hands of men through materialism and war. My grandmother fed her family from an organic garden long before the rest of the world understood the dangers of pesticides, and the only meat ever served was fish caught fresh from the lake until even that became suspect due to pollution. The oldest of three, my mother, aptly named Grace, was the most "normal" of the bunch. Aunt Gina had run off to New York after college to help launch the women's movement and pile up numerous degrees in sociology. She had returned home, though, and was now an instructor at the community college in Escanaba, while Uncle George was a professor of marine ecology at the University of California in San Diego and caretaker of my grandmother, widowed for many years. Grace Hamilton, on the other hand, earned an associate's degree in secretarial science at the community college where her sister Gina now worked, and had found a job with the city of Escanaba. She soon met and fell in love with my meat-loving, flag-waving, Republican-to-the-core father. She had often told the story of Hank Hamilton's first trip to the Schmidt house in 1969. Her parents were horrified at his crew cut and tales of Vietnam and he was equally astonished at my grandfather's ponytail and revulsion for Richard Nixon.

As we approached the blinking light, a state police car turned in front of me and headed south on Main Street and woke me from my walk down memory lane. I considered following him, but he didn't look to be in a too much of hurry. *Probably in search of a barking dog,* I thought, and kept driving. As we neared the turnoff to Country Road 509 about a mile and a half east of town, I felt the urge to visit Mom. Making a left turn, I followed the bumpy old road about a quarter-mile until I found the sign for the Rapid River Cemetery. The cemetery was divided into two sections, Catholics on the left, Protestants and everyone else on the right. At my mother's burial, I had asked my dad why there was a separation between the religions.

"Um, well, um. Honey, don't worry about it. They all get together when they get where they're going anyway," was all my dad could come up with in reply. In retrospect, it was probably the most intelligent answer anyone could have given.

The Schmidt family plot was in the center, located near a large pine tree that probably wasn't much more than a sapling when my grandfather selected the site some 50 years ago. I got out of the Jeep, leaving Belle to watch me with curious eyes. A large polished granite headstone with "Schmidt" inscribed on it stood at the head of the section. To the right of where my grandfather rested was a smaller stone with my parents' names inscribed upon it, and my mother's side competed with dates of birth and death on the right. Kneeling at the foot of her grave, I tried to remember the last time I'd paid a visit. It had been many years. I never felt anything but sadness there. Even as a child I knew her loving presence wasn't in a coffin. I'd felt it many times in my life — at my high school graduation, when I'd won my first Associated Press award, even when Mitch had died. It was like a cool breeze against my face on a hot day, a reassuring touch on my shoulder, nothing I could ever explain to someone who'd never felt the pain of losing someone who loved you completely. Still, I wondered again why she had to leave so soon. I wanted to talk to her, to cry on her shoulder, to tell her all about Mitch. She would have liked him. Then again, maybe she already knew.

Belle barked and I looked up to see the caretaker start the lawnmower. The peaceful silence broken, I stood, said goodbye and left, waving to the elderly man clad in overalls and a John Deere cap as we passed each other on the main gravel road.

A half hour later Belle and I were in Manistique, a small city with a unique mix of modern industry, quaint Nineteenth Century charm and tourist getaways. It boasted a small paper mill alongside the Manistique River. Manistique's picturesque stretch of a few miles of Lake Michigan shoreline is home to several motels, restaurants, large gas stations which are as well-stocked as some grocery stores, and a Native American casino, one of several that dot the U.P. landscape. In the summer, its wide sandy beaches beckon to swimmers while its miles of backwoods trails draws snowmobilers in the winter. Today, the beaches were empty and the trails were traveled by nothing more than falling leaves and wildlife as a light drizzle hit the windshield. I stopped at a Shell station to let Belle relieve herself while I filled the gas tank, grabbed a cup of coffee and a box of dog treats and got directions to County Road 442, where the Danellis lived.

"Turn left onto M-94 up the road a bit, then when that turns north, you go straight. That'll lead you on to four forty-two," said a grizzled, middle-aged man in a dirty Ford Trucks cap standing at the counter chatting with the clerk, who looked about the same age as Mr. Ford Trucks, but less weathered.

"Thanks. Do you know the Danellis? That's where I'm heading," I asked innocently and handed the clerk a twenty. The two men looked at each other with raised eyebrows. Mr. Ford Trucks nodded and scratched his gray beard.

"They're an odd bunch. Keep to themselves mostly, especially after their daughter ran off about, oh, ten-twelve years ago. You with the government or something?"

The clerk handed me a dollar-thirty in change and sized me up.

"You don't look like a cop," he said.

"No, no. I'm not with the government, and I'm not a cop." I laughed uneasily. "I just want to talk to them about Sabrina. Will they be okay with that?"

"Is she dead? They won't like that, if that's what you have to say," said Mr. Ford.

"No, well, I don't know. Do you think she's dead?"

We were beginning to gather a crowd. I stepped aside to let a woman behind me pay her bill but she just stood and looked at me like I had grown a third eye in the center of my forehead. The clerk finally cleared his throat. Half a dozen pairs of eyes turned to him and stared.

"Well, uh, like Duke here said, the whole family has always been a little unusual, real radical, almost like those militia-types downstate. Hate the government, but they've never caused any trouble. Their daughter was the same age as my cousin Sheila, and she told me Sabrina was like a fish out of water with that bunch, real artistic and spiritual, almost like one of them hippies, I guess. It wouldn't surprise me if she got it into her head to run off," the clerk said and then turned to woman behind me. "Twenty-two, fifty-one in gas. Anything else?"

She tossed a bag of chips, bottle of Pepsi and a Visa card on the counter, and then looked at me.

"I think she's dead and has been since the day she disappeared. She baby-sat my two youngest kids that summer except for the month she was at that camp up north. She talked about becoming an English teacher, coming right back here to teach at the high school after she finished college at Northern Michigan University. She never talked about going anywhere else," she said, signed the credit card slip and stalked out to a green Chrysler minivan with a "Support our troops" yellow ribbon magnet on the rear door.

It was quiet for almost a minute until someone sneezed. Mr. Ford jumped a little and shook his head.

"Just be careful, young lady." He tipped his hat and walked to a dusty, late-model Dodge pick-up. The dealer should have thrown in a new hat for good measure.

I thanked the clerk and joined Belle in the Jeep. Taking a sip of coffee, I handed her a few jerky bits to munch and thought about the weird exchange in the store, especially the tension that filled the place when I'd asked about Sabrina. Manistique had somewhere between three thousand and four thousand residents, meaning it was small enough for everyone to know just about everyone else. If the Danellis made the locals nervous, it could mean bad news for an outsider like me. I picked up the cell phone and punched in Charlie's number at Escanaba Public Safety. A dispatcher answered and put me through to the detective after more than a minute.

"Hello?" said a muffled voice.

"What are you doin'? Stuffin' your face with donuts? Coffee hour's over, man."

"Bite me. What do you want, misplace your broomstick again?"

"Touché! Actually, I was wondering if you could run the names Anthony and Susan Danelli through your computer. I'm going to see them and the locals are giving me bad vibes."

"Danelli? You mean the parents of that missing girl? Are you in Manistique? Have you flipped? I could get in serious trouble doing this," he said.

"Please?"

"Urgh, hold on." He put me on hold, leaving me to listen to a recording about fire safety tips, followed by Halloween safety tips. Just as I was learning about how to use reflective tape on my costume, he cut in and said, "Nada. They're both clean as a whistle, not even a speeding ticket."

"Hmm, well, thanks for your help. I'll talk to you later."

"Robin?"

"Yeah?"

"Be careful."

"Always. Bye."

I felt uneasy and looked at Belle, but she was only interested in the bag of treats stashed behind the seat. I sighed, started the Jeep and pulled onto the highway. The turn-off to M-94 was close and led me through the southwestern part of town, then into the woods. I slowed until I found the fire number in black letters on a silver mailbox next to a winding gravel drive that disappeared into a thick stand of birch. The drizzle had turned to a light rain, creating puddles in the rutted lane, which gradually turned northeast and ended at a trio of buildings. I stopped the Jeep near a two-car garage detached from a one-story log home. A brown metal pole building larger than the garage and house put together was to the right of the cabin. The property looked deserted, like no one had been there for weeks. No tracks of any kind marred the gravel and mud. I shut off the engine and listened. The only sound was the rain hitting the roof. Belle whined softly and crouched down in the passenger seat.

"Shh, it's okay," I whispered and rubbed her neck. "I'll be right back."

I grabbed my purse, made sure the cell phone was tucked inside, although it probably wouldn't work this far out in the middle of nowhere, and walked to the cabin. A wide, covered porch stretched across the front. The logs had been painted a dark brown recently and looked to be in good shape. Green and white plaid curtains were open at a large picture window. I peeked around the edge of the frame, but the house looked empty. I knocked on the door anyway.

After hearing no answer, I started to walk back down the steps when a board creaked behind me. I turned to find myself staring into the black eyes of a double-barrel shotgun.

Chapter Seven

"WHO THE HELL ARE YOU?"

The strong smell of whiskey carried on the breeze with the voice of an ancient woman who sounded like she'd smoked a warehouse full of Camels in her lifetime.

"Ma'am, are you Mrs. Danelli?"

"I got the gun, I get to ask the questions," said the voice. The barrels moved up, then down again, leveling at my heaving chest. I swallowed, looked around the yard for a place to run and duck into for cover, but saw nothing except those barrels staring at me, unblinking.

"I'm Robin Hamilton," I stuttered and then swallowed hard in an attempt to regain my composure. "I work for the *Daily Press* in Escanaba and I'm doing an investigative piece on the disappearances of several teenage girls over the last thirty years. I was hoping to talk to you about Sabrina." The words came out so fast and high-pitched I could barely understand what I'd said, but the barrels fell and the door opened farther to reveal a tiny, aged woman with close-cropped silver hair and beady eyes the color of black coffee. She wore a gray sweatshirt underneath an unbuttoned red wool shirt and faded jeans.

"Sabrina? She's gone, never coming back either," she said in a softer voice than I would have believed possible.

"I know," I said and stepped back under the porch roof, risking getting closer to her, but she didn't raise the gun. "Are you Mrs. Danelli?"

"Yes, but not the one you're probably lookin' for. I'm Tony's mother, Sylvia. They're all gone to a gun show out West somewhere. They sell these things," she said and hoisted the shotgun in a brown wrinkled hand. She seemed to see me for the first time and looked at the gun, then back at me and cackled.

"Bet ya thought I was gonna shoot ya, eh?" She tried to laugh, but the guffaws quickly turned into wracking coughs that made her double over. I took the gun and eased her inside and into an overstuffed chair in front of a television with the sound turned down and some scantily-clad game show hostess flashing across the screen. I set the gun on the kitchen counter and filled a glass with tap water. She was still hacking when I handed it to her, but she managed to take a drink and gradually caught her breath.

"You smoke?" she asked when she could speak again.

"No, never."

"Wise woman. I smoked for sixty-four years. Quit last year. Too late now. I'll be dead within a year, doctor says."

"I'm sorry."

"Why? I'm seventy-nine. I've lived a good life. Frank died last year. Lung cancer. I miss him too much to stick around here by myself much longer." She emptied the glass and got up to retrieve a pint of Jim Beam from the coffee table. She poured two fingers of amber liquid, sat back in the chair and motioned to the couch nearby. I sat.

"What do you want to know about my granddaughter?" she asked after she had finished the whiskey in one gulp and cleared her throat. The sound reminded me of dead leaves swirling against a fence in a strong wind.

"Why do you think she's never coming back?" I responded.

"She was murdered, that's why. She was murdered because she was Frank Danelli's granddaughter."

I waited for her to explain, but she was lost in thought.

"Mrs. Danelli, I don't understand. Why would she be murdered because of your late husband?" I prodded.

She turned to me and looked as though I'd just asked why the sun rises in the east.

"Revenge, of course. Frank did a lot of work for Giancanna, then hid out up here beginning in 'Fifty-nine. They found us and got her," she said.

"You mean Sam Giancanna, the Chicago mobster?"

"Who else?"

"I see," I said and nodded, but the only thing I saw was a lonely old woman who really should not have been left by herself so far from town without people who could check in on her regularly. I thanked her for her time and let myself out, but she had already gone back to her memories.

Belle and I had been on U.S. 2 heading west toward Escanaba for about five minutes when the cell phone rang. It was Bob Hunter.

"What's up? I'm on my way back," I said and started to tell him about my adventure with Mrs. Danelli, a.k.a. wife of a former mobster, but he interrupted.

"Don't bother coming back right now. A fourteen-year-old girl has been reported missing from Rapid River. Get over there and find out what the hell's going on," he said through increasing static.

"When did she disappear? Where's the house located? Bob?" The line was dead, now out of range of a tower.

"Damn." I tossed the phone back into my purse. Another teenager missing. It was probably nothing. The last unsolved disappearance was Sabrina's in 1993, thirteen years ago. The Baxters had mentioned a case on the Michigan-Wisconsin border in the late Nineties, but that had been solved, the perpetrator sent to prison. No more than eight years had passed between the other cases so this would be a break in the pattern unless there was one I didn't know about, which was a distinct possibility since no one

— police, reporters, parents — seemed to communicate on a regional basis about the disappearances. Hunter had said this girl was fourteen, the right age and about the right time of year.

"This is nuts. Here I go jumping to conclusions. She probably just ditched school to hang out with some friends," I said to Belle, who looked at me with sad brown eyes.

It took about a half hour to reach Rapid River but felt like an eternity as the scenery changed little — thick woods broken only by the occasional field, house or motel. As we approached the community of Ensign a few miles east of Rapid River, I tried my cell phone, which now picked up a clear signal from a nearby tower, and punched the number of the *Daily Press*.

"Bob, where am I going? Who is this kid?"

"Just follow the cop cars. The house is somewhere right in town. The girl's name is Heather Stankowski. It's all over the radio, Robin. They have a search party in place already and they've put out an Amber Alert," Bob said.

The release of an Amber Alert, a warning to the public indicating a child has likely been abducted, meant the police were treating this as a serious disappearance, not a simple case of a kid ditching school. I noticed my heart beating as I pressed Bob for more information and silently cursed myself for not thinking to turn on the radio.

"You said earlier she's fourteen. Wasn't she in school? When did they discover she was missing?" I asked.

A burst of static cut off his answer, so I made him repeat it.

"Her parents are divorced, and she had spent the week at her dad's house. She was supposed to walk to her mother's, I'm guessing about half a mile away, and then catch the bus to go to school, but she never showed up at her house," Bob said.

"She's probably a freshman in high school. What makes them think she's not just playing hooky?"

"According to a press release and photograph we got from the state cops in Gladstone she's a sweet-looking kid and a straight-A student and, Robin, they found her backpack on the sidewalk a few blocks from the house. It had blood on it."

Bob was right about following the cops. They were everywhere, swarming over the little town, along with dozens of volunteers, criss-crossing back yards and front yards. I rolled down my window to ask someone where to find the girl's house and heard the name "Heather" floating on the damp breeze as searchers called for her. Just before the intersection of South Main and the highway, I pulled into a gas station and called to a man who was walking along the highway wearing a Masonville Township Fire Department jacket.

"Where can I find the home of the missing girl?" I called. Without a word he waved in the direction of the southwest side of town and then headed toward the Rapid River, which bordered the town on the east side and emptied into Little Bay de Noc. I turned left onto South Main Street at the blinking light, where I'd seen the state trooper turn earlier that morning, figuring I'd find a kaleidoscope of flashing red and amber lights at the girl's house. After cruising about four blocks, I spotted two Delta County Sheriff Department white Dodge Intrepids down a couple of streets to the right.

The deputies' vehicles, along with three state police cruisers, were scattered in front of a two-story red frame house on Ackly Street. I parked behind the dark blue sedan of the local television station and studied the scene. The TV reporter, a young man fresh out of college, was interviewing one of the state troopers. In the distance I could see the steeple of the Congregational church. From the look on the trooper's face, a little divine intervention was in order. Belle was antsy after being cooped up in the Jeep for a few hours so I took her for a quick walk in the direction of the trooper.

"We urge anyone who may have seen a girl matching Heather's description to call their local police department or nine-one-one as soon as possible. Time is a precious commodity when it comes to finding missing children. The slightest little piece of information could be critical," the trooper said into the camera, then turned a fierce glare on the reporter, who pulled away the microphone and thanked him. I walked over to the pair and introduced myself.

"My editor called me on my cell and sent me over here. Can I talk to you for a minute?" I asked the trooper. "That is, if you're finished here?"

"Yeah, I've got what I need," the reporter said. He was already dismantling the video camera's tripod and packing his gear.

The trooper led me toward the red house, adorned with hunter green shutters and a metal roof in the same shade. The grass in the front yard was trampled and the drapes were drawn in the front windows.

"I'm Bruce Grayson. You said your name is Robin?" he asked and then bent down to give Belle a scratch behind one ear. She wagged her tail and panted. "Who's this little bundle of energy?"

"My sidekick, Belle. Um, listen, I'm working on a story about a series of disappearances of young girls around the U.P. over the last thirty years or so. It's possible this one may be related or it may just be a coincidence. What's the deal with this girl?" I asked.

He straightened and stuffed his hands in the pockets of his jacket. "Well, we have nothing right now. Her father works at that big machine shop in Escanaba and his shift starts at seven, so he left his house over there on Pine Street," he stopped and gestured toward the northeast, "sometime around six-thirty this morning. He figures Heather was going to walk home to her mother's around seven, pick up a book she needed for school and then walk back to the bus stop on South Main. Her backpack was found against the fence in front of that playground across the street from the church."

He led me down the street past a few houses and pointed at the playground. Ominous yellow crime scene tape was tied around several stakes and attached to the fence. It looked out of place next to the multicolored slide, swings and jungle gym within the fence.

"So far, no one claims to have seen a thing," the trooper added, his expression grave. I frowned.

"That's odd. By six-thirty people are usually up and about on weekdays," I said. Belle was getting restless, pulling on her leash in the direction of some dogs barking. I shortened the lead, wrapping the thick nylon strap around my hand a few times.

"You're right. Except the backpack is right across the street from the church. Next to the church is the parsonage and you'd think the minister would be up and about. Unfortunately, he's visiting family out East," he said, then crossed him arms over his chest. "What was all that about other girls disappearing? Maybe you should talk to our new detective, Chris Parker. She just got up here a few weeks ago. She's in the house talking with the mother right now. Hang on."

He dashed back to the missing girl's house and up the sidewalk and disappeared behind a heavy oak door painted the same hunter green as the shutters and trim. The light was growing dim, and it was beginning to sprinkle again so I put Belle back in the Jeep and grabbed my purse and a notebook. She howled in protest as I crossed the street. Trooper Grayson emerged from the house with a trim woman with shoulder-length silver streaked brown hair pulled back in a low ponytail. Clad in a stylish navy blue pantsuit and black shoes that could only be described as "sensible," she looked like a cop.

"I'm Detective Sergeant Christine Parker. Trooper Grayson here tells me you're looking into some other disappearances in the area. I didn't know there were any," she said. She didn't smile, but I didn't sense any unfriendliness in her tone, either.

"Yes, it's kind of a long story, though," I said as the rain began to fall in earnest.

"Let's go sit in my car," she said and led the way to a lake blue Ford Crown Victoria with the state police shield emblazoned on the side and a single red strobe light on the roof. She opened the passenger side front door for me and then got in and started the engine, cranking the heater and turning her full attention to me.

"I don't want to put you on any false leads here," I said, suddenly feeling foolish. Maybe this was all my overactive imagination weaving a dangerous tale better suited for a late night movie than a current police investigation.

"Right now I have no leads, so you can't possibly do any harm," she said, and finally a smile played at the corners of her careworn mouth. Encouraged by her manner, I gave her the abbreviated version of what I'd discovered about the other four girls.

"Wow, you've really done your homework," she said as she took notes, then shook her head and sighed. "But other than the ages, I just don't see how they could be related. There's just so much time in between the cases, not to mention a lot of miles."

"I realize that, but please keep it in mind," I said, feeling she would. I hadn't dealt with too many female cops, especially in the Upper Peninsula, where law enforcement was still pretty much a men's club, but Parker didn't seem to suffer from an inflated ego that had the potential to limit one's viewpoint.

She confirmed what Bob Hunter had told me on the phone and gave me a few more details about the parents and the search before I asked about the girl's personality.

Parker shrugged and said, "Heather sounds very bright, very artistic. Her mother showed me some oils the girl had painted, nature scenes mostly, from her own backyard where the Tacoosh River runs past. They're phenomenal. She is obviously very talented, at least to my untrained eyes."

"Considering the blood on the backpack, do you think she's in serious danger?" I asked.

She sighed again, understanding the subtlety of my question. "On the record, we are treating this as a missing person's case until we have evidence that suggests otherwise," she said. Then softening her voice, she added, "Off the record, I don't like that blood. It's not a lot, but its mere presence is very troubling. There's also an additional complication. Heather has type I diabetes. She must monitor her blood sugar several times a day and give herself shots of insulin to keep it regulated. We found her insulin kit in the backpack. She can't go too long without that or she'll be in serious trouble."

"What kind of trouble?" I asked, not knowing much about diabetes.

"Without insulin, her blood sugar can fall to dangerously low levels. She can suffer from hypoglycemia, which would make her dizzy, drowsy and confused, which in turn would obviously make it more difficult for her to get away from her captor. If too much time passes without insulin, she'll develop a condition called diabetic ketoacidosis, which is basically where the body is so starved for energy that it starts feeding on itself, leading to a diabetic coma, organ failure and even death," Parker explained.

"Are you a nurse, too? How do you know so much about this?" I asked.

She grinned and shook her head, "No, but it runs in my family. My little sister was diagnosed with it when she was about seven so I had to learn about it."

"You used the word 'captor.' Does that mean you don't think either of the parents may have had something to do with the girl's disappearance?" I asked, scribbling notes as fast as she spoke.

"It's standard operating procedure to look at the family first, but the facts don't point to the parents. Heather called her mother shortly before six-thirty to say she was on her way out the door of her dad's place, which is at most a fifteen-minute walk from here, if she dawdled. When she hadn't shown up at her mother's by seven-fifteen, Mom went looking for her. She's the one who found the backpack. She ran back to the house and called us. Her boyfriend is a Gladstone Public Safety officer who's downstate at a training seminar. Dad, who doesn't seem to be dating anyone at the moment, was seen arriving at his worksite shortly before seven. The couple living in the house next to the playground where the backpack was found left yesterday for a weekend of fall color-viewing on the Keweenaw Peninsula. The woman on the corner is a respiratory therapist at St. Francis Hospital and left for work at about six-forty-five and saw nothing out of the ordinary. That's all we have. So far the volunteers, who've been out since about eight, have come up with zilch in the six hours they've been looking. I swear damn near every First Responder in the county is fanning out across this town as we speak.

"I'm sorry, but I really do have to get back to the parents. They went through a very messy divorce and are playing a pretty mean blame game right now. I do appreciate you sharing information with me. It may end up proving helpful. Do you have a business card so I can contact you with updates?" she asked.

I pulled one out of my wallet and wrote my cell phone number on the front underneath my name. We exchanged cards and then I ran for the Jeep in a downpour. I could barely hear through the rain drumming on the roof as I relayed my information to Bob via the cell phone.

"I'll stick around here and see if I can help in the search. I don't know how much help we'll be, but Belle's pretty excited. Maybe we can put that energy to use," I said.

"All right. No need to come back to the office, just keep in touch via cell. We've got Kevin Watkins on the scene shooting pictures for Saturday's edition," he said. "Hey, Robin?"

"Yeah?" I shouted over the driving rain.

"Do you think this is related to the others?"

"She's an artist, Bob. All these girls were artistic. It could be the key, but it could mean nothing. I just don't know," I said and hung up.

As I started the Jeep and cranked up the heater to try to get warm, I rolled down the window, stuck my hand out and flagged down a passing sheriff's deputy in his patrol car.

"I want to help in the search. Where do I go?" I asked.

He'd looked annoyed at having to open his window to the rain, but now softened his expression.

"Follow me to the truck stop. We're gonna search the other side of the Tacoosh," he said and drove toward the highway. I followed him about a quarter-mile where we turned into the Pantry Truck Stop. The deputy popped the trunk lid on his patrol car, jumped out and retrieved an extra rain poncho, which he handed to me through my open window.

"Is that dog trained to hunt?" he asked, nodding at Belle.

"No. She's the canine version of a housecat. She eats, sleeps and grumbles all day. But she'll keep me company," I said, pulling the poncho over my head.

He laughed and held open the door for me. Checking to ensure my keys and cell phone were secure in my pocket, I left the relative warmth of the Jeep with Belle in tow. We then spent the next five hours stumbling through woods, fields, swamp and assorted yards, calling helplessly for a girl that was not to be found that day.

Chapter Eight

BY SEVEN O'CLOCK THAT EVENING, my fingers were stiff as the limbs on a dead tree and about as useful, as I fumbled with my keys, trying to get back inside the Jeep so I could call the *Daily Press* and then die of exhaustion. Belle whined in the rain that had fallen all afternoon, now finally slowing to a drizzle. Eventually my frozen fingers made the proper key fit the lock and we deposited our wet, filthy bodies inside the Jeep. Belle shook the water from her thick white and rust-colored fur, drenching the interior in dog slop. Fat muddy footprints dotted the front seat, but I was too tired to care.

Bob was still in his office when I called. I relayed the update, which amounted to nothing, and dictated to him a second story about the searchers. Kevin Watkins, the *Daily Press* photographer, had managed to find me and had taken some pictures of the volunteers I'd interviewed. All in all, it was a horribly depressing scene, long faces on every one of the searchers as hope faded along with the daylight.

I tossed the phone into my purse and stared out the window at the approaching gloom, too tired to drive the twenty miles to my apartment.

Then I remembered my Aunt Gina lived just outside of Rapid River. She had been kind to me since my mother's death, but contact was sporadic partly because my dad had discouraged me from developing a close relationship with her. When I'd ask why, he would only shrug, frown and say, "She's scary." A mysterious and peculiar woman by small town standards, I saw her only when she made trips home from New York, where she had been a sociology professor at NYU. She'd returned home sometime in the last few years but I didn't know her phone number so I braved the rain again and limped to the truck stop where I ordered two hamburgers, one without a bun, and an order of fries to go, and then found a little-used year-old phone book. I looked up Gina Schmidt's number and address and scribbled them on the back of the detective's business card, then waited for my food. The talk around me was all about Heather Stankowski as volunteers and curious onlookers mingled together around the restaurant, sipping hot coffee and swapping gossip. No one seemed to know much about her except that her parents hated each other and did nothing to hide their animosity from the neighbors, but everyone was concerned, some even frightened at the idea of a child kidnapper in their midst.

After collecting my order, I stumbled back to the Jeep and fed Belle the plain hamburger. I wolfed down my own meal then dialed the number I'd found for my aunt. A cheery voice answered on the third ring.

"Aunt Gina? This is Robin."

"Robin? My goodness, it's so wonderful to hear your voice. It's been so long. Is everything all right?" she asked.

""Yes, fine, fine. I'm sorry I haven't been in touch, but I have a favor to ask. Can you put me up for the night? I'm really exhausted."

"Certainly, it's just me, Victoria and Albert here. We have plenty of room," she said.

"Victoria and Albert?"

"My Yorkies. I got them after Darren died, for company, you know."

"Oh, yeah," I said lamely. She had come back to Rapid River not too long after her longtime love had died of cancer. Not knowing what else to say about that, I told her about Belle.

"I have my basset hound with me. Will that be okay with them?" I asked. This could bring on World War III if Victoria and Albert weren't keen on having a houseguest.

"They've been through obedience school and are pretty used to other dogs, they just don't like cats too much," Aunt Gina said with a loud guffaw. She then gave me directions to her house and said she was anxious to see me again.

After stopping at the nearby mini-mart for some dog food and biscuits, I drove about five miles up U.S. Highway 41 until my headlights came upon the head of a gravel driveway marked with orange reflectors that formed a giant "S."

The first thing I noticed when Aunt Gina threw open the front door to welcome two soggy sorry-looking guests was the smell of incense. I deposited my wet jacket and shoes in the mudroom that led into the one-story nineteen-twenties-era bungalow while she applied a thick dry towel to Belle's damp fur. Her two Yorkshire terriers charged into the room, yipping at Belle, who let out a few deep woofs and then trotted after them as they darted to the kitchen, completely ignoring me.

"Well, I guess they all made fast friends," Aunt Gina said and laughed, her blue-gray eyes crinkling at the corners. She turned to me and smiled warmly, clasping her hands together as she surveyed me.

"You look so much like your mother. She was tiny and blonde, like you, but not as tough," she said, her head cocked to one side.

"Tough?" I asked. No one had ever told me I was tough. Stubborn, yes, but never tough.

"Oh, come here." She wrapped her arms around my shoulders and drew me to her breast. She smelled of rosewater, the same scent my mother had worn. The smell brought back a flood of memories — watching my mother spritz herself with fragrance and apply makeup before a night on the town with my dad, snuggling next to her in my bed as she read me a story. Tears stung my eyes. I stiffened and Aunt Gina pulled away before I could hide my moist eyes.

"Robin, what's the matter? Did I say something wrong?" she asked, rubbing a freckled hand on my arm.

"No, no. I'm okay, just tired," I said, then sighed, feeling compelled to tell her the truth. "It's your perfume. My mother wore the same thing. I'd forgotten."

"Yes, Grace loved the smell of roses. She looked and smelled so wonderful when she was a teenager while I was this gawky little kid who followed her around and tried to imitate everything she did. It drove her nuts. Besides, I'm a poor imitation," she said and smiled again. She must have outgrown the gawkiness at some point because she now was beautiful, really and truly beautiful. Her eyes sparkled with mirth, her face was open and flush with good health, and her strawberry blonde hair fell in ringlets to her shoulders. The curls were natural, something my mother had said she'd envied, but I suspected the color may have been doctored, considering she was in her early fifties.

"I'll tell you what, you take a hot bath and then settle down in the living room in front of the fire while I make us some chamomile tea. Okay?"

"Sure. Do you have a bowl I can use to feed Belle?" I asked and followed her to the kitchen where Belle had taken up residence next to two tiny empty food dishes.

Gina presented a small white bowl for Belle and made a gesture pointing to the bath.

"I get the message," I told her as I filled the bowl before Belle's eager black nose.

The bath felt like a momentary trip to heaven. The aches melted into the steaming water, relaxing me to the point of nearly falling asleep until Belle nudged open the door and sniffed my hand. I pulled on a pair of flannel pajamas and a terry cloth robe Aunt Gina had laid out for me on the vanity.

We then settled in the small square living room filled with book cases and jewel-toned mismatched furniture. Sipping a large cup of hot tea, I felt the stress of the day seep from my bones. I felt comfortable in a way I hadn't for years. There was something about Aunt Gina that just felt like home.

"What are you thinking about?" she asked. She sat in a jade Queen Anne chair with her legs tucked under her, clad in magenta silk pants and a multi-colored long-sleeve smock of the same material.

"How come you and my dad never got along well?" I asked.

She set her cup down on the little mahogany table next to her chair and studied her short, unpolished nails for a minute. Her eyes were moist when she finally looked up and spoke.

"A lot of years have been wasted, haven't they?" she said and sighed. "I'm different, Robin. Unconventional. Your father is a good man and your mother loved him dearly. He doesn't understand different, though. When your parents married, I was attending grad school at NYU and marching down Fifth Avenue in support of women's rights. I have a doctorate in sociology and write books about things like the role of women in religion. I lived with a man for fifteen years and never married him. Your father and I have different beliefs when it comes to spirituality, politics, you name it. Hank just never 'got' me. Frankly, he was always afraid I'd be a bad influence on you. Your mother would never admit it, but I could sense how he felt when I'd come home occasionally.

"I don't have any hard feelings, though, and neither should you. He was entitled to raise you as he saw fit, without any interference from me or anyone else." She waved a hand at me. "And just look at the result. I'd say he did just fine, for the most part."

I smirked.

"Well, I haven't murdered anyone and I try to do right by people, even if I don't like them," I said in a feeble voice.

Aunt Gina sat back and scowled at me. "You aren't happy, though. That's obvious."

I gulped down the rest of the tea and put the cup down harder than intended.

"No, I'm not happy. Most of the time I alternate between feeling tired, angry, sad and confused because I'm always looking for ways to not think about what's really wrong. But when I try to think about it or talk about it, about Mitch, nothing good seems to come of it." Just mentioning his name brought the sting of tears to the inside of my eyelids. I blinked and faked a smile.

She gave me a genuine smile, then nodded and said, "I understand. So let's not talk about Mitch. Why don't you tell me what brings you to my doorstep."

Sighing with relief, I said, "That missing girl in Rapid River. I feel like I'm in some bizarre maze where I make a little progress then run into a wall."

"What's at the end of the maze?"

"I'm not sure. A killer maybe?"

She looked startled and said, "Why don't you start at the beginning? I know about the missing girl from watching the six o'clock news, but you lost me after that."

Starting with the scrapbook in Copper Harbor, I laid before her the whole web of missing teenaged girls as the wind blew rain in sheets against the house.

When I was done, Aunt Gina shivered and studied the bottom of her cup.

"It sounds so sinister, the lying in wait until just the right victim comes along, the rest of the world completely unaware of what's about to happen," she murmured. "I'm sure you're right in that the cases are all related. The fact that they're spread out over time and distance just shows the character of the killer. The U.P. is not so isolated that we can't have the occasional lunatic on the loose, but it is isolated enough for one person to wreak havoc in several different communities over a couple of decades."

She stood and collected both tea cups.

"I'll make some more tea and pop some popcorn. Why don't you get those notes you put together and we'll map out what you have so far. I'll bet we can find a connection between them."

An hour later, with papers strewn across the thick purple living room carpet and three dogs staring at us in bewilderment from their perch on the couch, we had the five disappearances outlined on a large piece of white poster board. The board was divided into five columns, one for each girl, and six rows for age, location, parents, personality, academics and interests. It was that last row that got my attention.

"Look here," I said, pointing at it. "Amanda was into fashion design. Lucy's square is empty because I don't know about her interests except that she liked to draw. Sabrina was a poet, Caroline was a violinist and Heather was a painter. These are all creative things. I bet Lucy had some real artistic talent as well. I'll check with the Ishpeming High School Monday and see if anyone remembers her. I bet that's important."

Aunt Gina chewed her lower lip and studied the board.

"That's all you've got, besides the fact they're all in their early to mid teens and all disappeared in the summer or early fall. What do you suppose that means?" she asked.

"The killer hates winter?" I said in a lame attempt to lighten the mood, which was as somber as a wake.

She frowned and said, "Maybe it's a matter of opportunity. People are more likely to be outside and accessible when the weather is nicer." Looking at the clock on the mantle, she added, "It's almost eleven o'clock. Let's watch the late news and see if there's anything new developing."

She dug the remote control out from under a pile of newspapers and clicked on a thirteen-inch television tucked atop a large oak bookcase.

"You don't watch much TV, do you?" I asked.

"Nah, waste of time other than the news, PBS and a good Sam Elliott movie," she said with a devilish grin.

Unfortunately, watching the news turned out to be a waste of time as there was nothing new concerning Heather Stankowski. The same young guy I'd seen earlier was reporting live from the mother's front yard, the red house as a backdrop. He looked beat. The rain was still falling heavily, the trail now most assuredly cold as a January morning. Heather's school photograph flashed on the screen, followed by the reporter interviewing Detective Christine Parker. He asked her if the police had received any tips from the public.

"Not yet, but we're hopeful." The look on her haggard face said otherwise.

The detective was followed by film of Heather's father making a statement just before dark. Louis Stankowski read from a piece of notebook paper with a jagged edge that flapped in the wind while his shaking hands tried to keep it straight. His voice trembled as he pleaded for help.

"Heather is my only child and the center of my world," he began, his voice trembling. "She's a diabetic and needs insulin injections several times a day or she'll die. Not knowing where she is or what's happened is terrifying. If someone has any information about where she is, I beg you to let the police know. They need your help. Heather, I love you. Please come home." The poor man broke down in tears before the clip ended, and the reporter turned the broadcast back over to the anchor. The next story was about the Marquette school board, so Aunt Gina clicked off the set.

Leaning back and propping herself on her elbows, she shook her head.

"Can you imagine what that father is going through? He leaves for work thinking everything's fine and then his daughter disappears into thin air when she tries to walk a few blocks. He can't help but feel it's his entire fault," she said.

"Maybe it is," I said. She shot me a look of disbelief, but I continued. "Look, I know it sounds cynical, but I covered a couple missing children cases in Chicago. Both of the kids were found dead, one killed by a neighbor and another by the mother. She was a real nutcase. She went on all the TV and radio stations, crying that someone had stolen her baby. It turned out she had bludgeoned the kid, who was about four, with a claw hammer, wrapped him in plastic, stuck him between two wall studs in her apartment, and then used the same hammer to nail a sheet of drywall over him. She was acting out some storyline on a soap opera where a little kid had disappeared and she wanted the attention."

"So you think maybe the father killed this girl?" Aunt Gina asked as I began to gather and organize my notes.

"The cops don't seem to think so, but it's possible. It's too soon to tell. All I'm saying is it's way too soon to write him off as a suspect. That detective told me it was a nasty divorce. Maybe he got sick of paying child support. Who knows?" I said.

"That's a pretty harsh assessment. You don't have much faith in humans, do you?"

"No, I don't," I said and began scratching Belle's ear. "Animals are much more predictable. You know what motivates them — survival. Humans are ruled by their passions — love, money, power. I can understand killing for food. I can't understand killing someone for money."

"Is that what happened to your fiancé?" she inquired softly.

"Yes, I think that's exactly what happened."

"I'm sorry," she said as she sat up and reached out her right hand. I just looked at it for a few seconds and then grasped it. We ended up in a hug. It felt strange at first to be held in such a familiar way by a woman. I was so used to my father's strong arms and chest. Aunt Gina felt soft, like a plush stuffed animal, except she was warm. I pulled back and looked into her gray-blue eyes, so like my mother's.

"I'm glad I came here. It feels good to connect with someone from my mom's family again. Thank you," I said and smiled.

"Me too, Kiddo."

We finished straightening the living room and headed off to bed. The spare bedroom was furnished with a full-size bed, dresser and small desk, all painted white. The bedspread and pillow shams were covered in white tulips on a black background—attractive but not overpowering. Like everything else in the house, it seemed to symbolize peace and beauty. I climbed between the cotton sheets and petted Belle as I went over the events of the day, from the shotgun aimed at my chest by a crazy old woman to Aunt Gina's warmth and kindness. It dawned on me that growing up without a mother deprived me of that feminine touch of empathy. How much was she like my mother? I realized I missed not getting to know my mother as a woman, learning how she felt about men, children, politics, work and the world in general. I had never asked my dad such questions because I feared I'd remind him of what he'd lost. Now I wondered if not talking about her had created a worse void. I finally fell asleep sometime around one and dreamt of two young blonde girls wading in a narrow, shallow river on a bright sunny summer day.

Chapter Nine

THE MUFFLED MECHANICAL TONES OF my cell phone shook me awake. I pulled it out of my purse and flipped it open, keeping my eyes closed all the while.

"Mm-hmm," I mumbled.

"Where are you?" It was my dad, sounding almost as frantic as Louis Stankowski had last night on the news.

"Oh, Dad, I'm sorry. I forgot to call you. I'm in Rapid River at Aunt Gina's," I said, sitting up and searching the room in vain for a clock. I found the watch he'd given me as a college graduation present on the nightstand next to the bed and blinked several times before its face came into focus. Ten after ten. I hadn't slept that late in months. Looking around the room again, I said aloud, "Where's Belle?"

"Your aunt probably boiled her for dinner," my dad snapped.

"Would you stop that? You're talking nonsense. Aunt Gina's not like that at all. She's very nice. She's just a little different than what you're used to when it comes to women," I said.

"Humph," was his only response.

"Dad, we'll talk about Aunt Gina later. Right now I need to focus on this missing girl. Her disappearance might be related to the others. Would you do me a favor and look up Bob Hunter's home number in the phone book, please?" I asked and got out of bed to pull open the heavy drapes. Sunlight blinded me as it flooded the room.

"Wouldn't he have an unlisted number, being the editor of the paper and all?" my father inquired.

"No way. Bob loves it when people call him at home with news tips, gripes and threats. He even makes jokes about it."

There was a pause and a distant shuffling of paper. "Yup, here we are. Bob Hunter, Willow Creek Road, Escanaba. He lives near the wastewater treatment plant? Must go through a lot of scented candles."

"Nah, he says you can't smell a thing, Dad," I said and jotted down the number on a notepad stashed in my purse. "Thanks. I'll give you a call later, I promise. I love you."

"I love you too. Just don't turn into one of them feminazis, okay?"

"Dad!"

"Bye."

I groaned, put the phone away and looked out the window. The sky was a brilliant blue, swept clean of any residue of stormy weather. Aunt Gina was in the backyard with Belle, Victoria and Albert dancing around her as she picked up some apples that had fallen on the ground and placed them in a basket. While she worked, I took a quick shower and contemplated my next step. What troubled me most was the huge gap between Sabrina Danelli's disappearance and this latest event. The Baxters had mentioned a disappearance somewhere near Ironwood on the western end of the Upper Peninsula. Someone had been convicted, but it was possible the person was innocent. Several death row inmates in Illinois had been freed in recent years after new evidence had surfaced that cleared them, even after juries had decided they were guilty beyond all reasonable doubt.

When I emerged from the bathroom, the smell of waffles and fresh-brewed coffee blended pleasantly. Aunt Gina greeted me with a bright smile as she stirred some cinnamon-scented concoction in a pot on the stove.

"What is that?" I asked as I poured myself a cup of coffee.

"Apple syrup for the waffles. I make lots of things with apples since I have about a dozen trees in the back yard. They're one of the reasons I bought this house, those and the space for a big garden. I don't eat red meat and I don't have a lot of time to shop, so my garden is pretty much my store," she said.

"I appreciate this, but I hate to see you go through all this trouble for me," I said.

She laughed. "Don't flatter yourself, honey. I love food and treat myself to a good breakfast on the weekends because I teach four classes during the week this semester. So, what's next for the intrepid reporter this morning?" she asked as she poured her creation over two stacks of waffles.

"I'll stop at Heather's house and see what's happened overnight. If there's nothing new there, I'm going to drive to Ironwood to look into that 1999 case to see if it fits with the others. Then maybe I'll go up to Houghton on the way back and probe that first disappearance a bit more. I'd like to talk to Karl Maki," I said.

"Oh, the artist who was friends with the cabin owner. Doesn't sound like he'll be too friendly."

"Tough. If he's got nothing to hide, then he has no reason to be worried," I said and delved into a divine breakfast.

After some hugs and promises to stay in touch, Belle and I departed from the warmth and comfort of Aunt Gina's refuge in the woods and headed back out onto U.S. 2, one of the many desolate two-lane highways that cross the Upper Peninsula. Ironwood was a good three hours away, but before embarking on that trip I drove back to Heather Stankowski's house. There were even more media types in the neighborhood now, with trucks from both television stations in Green Bay, Wisconsin, the closest major city to the U.P., on scene. I spotted Dave Holmes, the Associated Press reporter based in Traverse City, leaning on a car parked behind him. Climbing out of the Jeep, I followed his gaze to the house where Heather's mother lived.

It was eerily quiet, despite about a dozen reporters, cameramen and police milling about.

"Dave, what's up?" I called.

He turned to me and waved, then stuck out his right hand as I drew closer.

"Robin, how are you? Glad to hear you're back. The Press needs your experience," he said, then jerked his head at the red house. "Nothing new. She's still missing."

"Is this story that big that the Detroit office would send you up here?" I asked. Traverse City was a five-hour drive, making Dave a rare sight in Delta County.

He chuckled and said, "No, I was up here working on a piece about a proposed mining operation up north and caught this story on the six o'clock news last night so I figured I'd stop by and see what was happening. Child kidnappings and murders are thankfully few and far between in the north woods."

"What's going on in there?" I asked and waved at the house.

"The cops are in there right now, updating the parents. I talked with that Detective Parker and got the feeling they think the kid's dead. There've been no phone calls, no tips, nothing. A bunch of people are searching the woods again, but it sounds pretty hopeless," Dave said with a shrug. He'd been a reporter for nearly twenty years and had seen enough of man's inhumanity to man to have forged a protective shield around his soul. I doubted he ever got personally involved in the stories he pursued.

The myriad members of the media were scattered about the block, most looking restless, a few even looked bored. The sun was high but the wind still howled, blowing gold, red and orange leaves off trees and swirling them in mini-cyclones down the quiet street. The effect was reminiscent of tumbleweeds down the streets of Tombstone — out of place in a town that was known for its grand Memorial Day celebrations, church holiday bazaars and Lions Club barbecues.

"Dave, how long have you worked in the Traverse City bureau?" I asked.

"About fifteen years. Why?"

"Have you noticed any other disappearances of teenaged girls up here?"

He adjusted his glasses, folded his arms over his chest and thought for a minute. "Well, now that you mention it, I remember one somewhere around Manistique more than a decade ago and then another one on the western end by Ironwood some years back. You think maybe they're related?"

"I don't know. Supposedly they caught the guy on the western end, but I've come up with some pretty strange coincidences," I said and relayed the highlights of my investigation so far.

"Geez, I don't know, Robin. That's one hell of a span of time. You're talking thirty-two years. I just don't see it," he said.

"Yeah, you may be right. Listen, I'm going to head west anyway and see what I can find. Here's my cell number. Would you call me if something changes here?" I said and handed him my card.

"Sure. No problem. Hey, if you do come up with a solid pattern, let me know. I won't tread on your territory, but, if your theory turns out to be true, I bet the story would run statewide, if not nationally."

"You got it," I called over my shoulder and hopped back in the Jeep. He saluted as I drove by and I tooted the horn in response. I didn't see much point in hanging around Rapid River when there was clearly nothing happening. No fan of ambush journalism, I waited one more day before I approached Heather's parents for a one-on-one interview.

It was almost noon by the time I hit Marquette and merged onto M-28, the state highway which spans the northern Upper Peninsula from just east of Ironwood on the western end to Sault Ste Marie on the eastern end of the state, a distance of more than three hundred miles. The twin cities of Ironwood, Michigan, and Hurley, Wisconsin, are almost three hours west of Marquette. One thing you get used to living here is the driving — everything seems to be at least an hour away. High school sports teams routinely travel more than a hundred miles for games, even on school nights. The only major hospital, in Marquette, is a one or two-hour drive for most people. The largest mall in the U.P. was also located in Marquette, along with Northern Michigan University, the largest college in the area.

During a quick stop for gas and a bathroom break for Belle near some cedar bushes, I called Bob Hunter. He answered on the second ring.

"What are you doing inside on such a beautiful day?" I snarled.

"You sound like my mother. She just called wondering the same damn thing. Where the hell are you, Robin?" he asked in a crabby voice, probably calculating the overtime and mileage expenses I was incurring as we spoke.

"At a convenience store in Negaunee and getting ready to drive to Ironwood," I said.

"Ironwood! What on earth for?" he yelled. I pulled the phone back from my ear and cringed. Belle even grumbled at the noise.

I gave him a brief rundown of what was happening with the Stankowski girl and how the case near Ironwood might be related. Hunter wasn't convinced.

"But there's already been a conviction in that case. What's the point? What's next? Will I be flying you to Florida for an interview? First class? You're costing me a fortune. The publisher's pretty understanding, but even he has limits," he said.

Burns would be thrilled if I was able to pull this together, but if it did turn out to be a wild goose chase there would be plenty of grief.

"You'll have to trust me. I'll see you bright and early Monday morning," I said and clicked the phone before Hunter could register a retort.

Fortunately, fall color made the drive west along the two-lane highway entertaining. Ironwood sits at the edge of Michigan's Iron Range. Although the iron mines that brought the town to life have been deserted for several decades, it remains a bustling little community of a few thousand residents thanks to a small hospital, community college and year-round tourism. Belle and I rolled past the business district, complete with a Kmart and McDonalds, just past two o'clock. I pulled up to the newspaper office on East McLeod Avenue and bought a copy of the *Daily Globe* from the machine in front of the building. I found the name of the managing editor listed on the Opinion page, then called information and got her home phone number.

Evelyn Smith finally answered after what seemed an eternity. I explained why I was in the area and needed her help.

"Wow, I wish I had a reporter as enterprising as you. Tell you what, I live just a few miles from the office. I'll be there in about ten minutes and we can see what we've got in the files. I remember that case very clearly. It's one of the few serious crimes we've had in the last few decades," she said.

While I waited for Evelyn to arrive, I took Belle for a walk around the block. She enjoyed rides, but she was restless and fussed when I tried to put her back in the Jeep. As I was trying to wrestle a forty-five-pound ball of fur into the truck, a red Oldsmobile coupe pulled up behind us. A petite blonde with glasses hopped out of the car and laughed at my situation.

"Are you Robin?" she asked.

"Yes," I grunted and tried to remove Belle's hind leg from the side of the Jeep.

"That's okay, you can bring her inside. We're getting new carpeting in a few weeks anyway," she said.

I put Belle back on the ground and she immediately dashed to Evelyn Smith's feet, wiggling and panting with joy. The woman knelt and gave her a good scratching.

"How did you know Belle is a girl?" I asked. Most people referred to animals as "it" or "he".

"I know dogs, especially basset hounds. We have three at home, all rescued from various animal shelters around the area. She's so pretty, she's obviously a girl," she said to which Belle woofed her agreement. "I'm Evelyn. It's nice to meet you."

She shook my hand and asked how I came to be in the Upper Peninsula while she unlocked the front door of the newspaper building.

"Actually I'm a Yooper born and bred. After college I worked at the *Daily Press* for a few years, won a few awards, attended a conference in Chicago and stopped by the *Tribune* office on a whim. They had an opening in their research department, so I grabbed it. That was about six years ago," I said and then swallowed hard. "Well, then my fiancé died and I came home at the end of this past May."

She rubbed her jaw and uttered a "huh" sound before leading me to her office, a tidy little room with papers stacked around the floor by her desk. She directed me to a chair and then went in search of the file, which turned out to be quite thick. The first article in the pile had the headline "Bessemer man sentenced to life for death of Ironwood teen." Accompanying the story was a photo of a Native American man in his late thirties or early forties being led away in handcuffs. He towered over the two deputies, but rather than looking fierce, he seemed as though he were sleepwalking. Next to his photo was the image of a bright-eyed girl with flaming red hair and freckles and a bold smile. The article described Crystal Jensen as a high-spirited girl with a flair for the dramatic.

"What happened to her?" I asked Evelyn, who had settled behind a cluttered desk.

She leaned her head back and closed her eyes, as if searching the files in her mind for the right folder, among the hundred she had compiled in her career as a reporter and editor. Her voice was low and strained as she began the story of Crystal Jensen.

"I've been with this newspaper since I returned home from college thirty-two years ago. As I'm sure you know, this is a small operation. If you stay here long enough, you cover every kind of story. By the time I saw

Crystal's bloody, beaten form in the road that summer, I'd been a reporter for almost twenty years. I'd seen a few decomposed bodies of hunters lost in the woods and a couple of bad accident scenes, but nothing tore at my heart like the sight of that little girl. I knew her and I knew her family. She deserved better. Her family was nothing but human garbage — drunks, abusers, liars, thieves. You name it and at least one of the Jensens had been arrested for it. Her mother didn't even have to change her name when she married because Crystal's father was a third cousin."

Evelyn shook her head and sighed.

"But Crystal was different. I always made it a point to get to know the names of every single kid in school from the time they hit kindergarten. It's not that hard since we're not talking thousands of kids here and it has paid off in many ways over the years. They tend to trust you and the newspaper more if they've grown up around you and know you think of them as more than juvenile delinquents. Anyway, Crystal had charisma. She smiled at everyone, talked straight, acted a little precocious, but showed no disrespect. She just had a lot of questions. Despite the hell at home, she somehow saw the good in life and embraced it. Sometimes when I'd be at the school covering a story she would stop and ask me questions about things she saw on the news. Within a few minutes she'd have me laughing so hard at her jokes I'd forget what I'd come there for. She was never mean, though, never made fun of people. Others weren't so kind. The other girls were terrible to her, making fun of her thrift store clothes and her red hair. But if it bothered her, she didn't let it show. I was there on the last day of school the year she died and she told me she was going away to camp for a month, that she'd received a scholarship. She was going to be a freshman in high school that fall and was hell bent on getting straight A's so she could get into Northwestern and study theater. 'I'm going to be a star someday, just like Lucille Ball.'"

Evelyn wiped a tear that had escaped down her right cheek. "See? Damn kid broke my heart."

She stopped talking for a moment and stared at her desk. Belle took the opportunity to sniff around the office and began pawing in a small cardboard box in the corner. Snuffling heavily now, she noised through the contents and came up with a green box and dumped it on the floor. Evelyn looked startled, then laughed.

"My goodness, you are a nosy one. You found my stale Girl Scout cookies. I think it's time I tossed those in the trash," she said and wrestled the box away from Belle. Placing the soggy container on the desk, she smiled warmly. "That's why I love animals so much; they know how to have fun.

"Well, back to Crystal. I got a call at home shortly after eight on a Tuesday late in August, just before school was to start. One of the Gogebic County Sheriff deputies is a close friend of my family and he told me Crystal had jumped from a speeding car and had been run over by another vehicle on M-28 just outside of Wakefield. I drove to the scene as fast as I could, all the while trying to understand why she had taken up joyriding with the local punks when she had such big dreams. When I got there, she was near death."

Evelyn choked on the word death, then took another deep breath and continued.

"I told the ambulance crew I knew the girl and they let me talk to her. I asked her what happened. She kept saying something that sounded like man eater. I asked if she had been with a bunch of kids and she shook her head no. Crystal had been stabbed once in the forearm so deeply it cut into the bone and there was blood all over her. They let me ride with her to the hospital so she'd have a friendly face to, to, well, look at while she died. Good lord, look at me, I'm bawling like this happened yesterday."

She swiped some more tissues, dabbed her eyes and blew her nose.

"Anyway, no one saw the car she had jumped from. It happened on a curve and it was getting dark. The poor woman who hit her didn't know what was happening until it was over. No one saw a damn thing. It didn't matter, though. The cops immediately thought of Peter Rawlins, a local bum who had a history of problems with alcohol and young girls," she said, shaking her head. "They arrested him that night at his dump of a trailer near Bessemer. He had no alibi and he had in his possession a knife that could easily have sliced Crystal's arm. They never found any blood in his car, which was full of junk. You'd think they would have found a blood spatter. Anyway, the jury took the lab results from the knife — a perfect match to the wound in her arm — and his lack of an alibi and his different answers to the same questions and hostility to the cops, and convicted him of manslaughter."

"Wow, that's quite a story," I said, stunned at her show of emotion, rare in a veteran journalist who ordinarily would have developed an armor against getting too involved in a story. Then again, we both worked in small towns where it was hard not to get involved when the story concerned your neighbor, friend or distant relative.

"Yes, well, as I said, Crystal deserved so much better. You said on the phone you are looking into some other disappearances. Do you think they involved Rawlins?"

"No. I don't think this guy is old enough," I said, leafing through the heavy file. "The cases I'm investigating go back to 1974 and have some striking similarities with Crystal's case, except no bodies were ever found."

I filled her in on the information I had gathered so far, including Heather Stankowski's disappearance the day before.

Evelyn was silent for several minutes as she mulled over the facts laid out in the chart Aunt Gina and I had prepared. Suddenly the color drained from her face.

"Ohmygod. Maybe they were wrong," she said and shuddered. "Dear God in heaven."

"Wait a minute. You said they had the knife. That sounds like fairly straight forward evidence," I said.

"Robin, do you know anything about forensics?" she asked.

"A little. Why?"

"Because the defense attorney argued that the knife could be purchased at just about any sporting goods store in the country. But we had Crystal's words that sounded like Peter Rawlins. It was weak, but enough to convict him," Evelyn said in a quiet voice.

"How would she have been on a first-name basis with this guy? Was he a friend of the family?" I asked.

"No. Her parents knew him from hanging out in the same bars, but they weren't friends," she said and tore her fingers through her short hair. "Christ, what if he was innocent?"

"Listen, if we can piece this all together and prove he really is innocent, we can get him out. It happened in Illinois just a few years ago, thanks to some college kids," I said.

"You don't understand. Rawlins is dead. He was stabbed to death two years ago in the rec room of the prison."

"Oh." It was a pathetic response, but I didn't know what else to say. "I'm sorry."

"Damn. All I can say is I hope you're wrong. I hope none of the cases you're working on have anything to do with Crystal. I'd hate to think they sent an innocent man to prison and got him killed," she said. "That goes against everything I've worked for in this job."

"I know."

She sat back in her chair and studied me for a minute.

"Robin, may I offer you a piece of advice from an old reporter who wishes she had been at least half as good as you when she was your age?" she finally asked.

"Of course, I can always use a little mentoring," I said, wondering where she was going with this.

"Don't spend too much time in the U.P. You don't have to go back to the *Tribune*. In fact, I'd advise against it, but don't let yourself get stuck here. You're too talented, too much of a real journalist to be happy at one of these rinky-dink dailies up here. Go to Minneapolis or Detroit or Indianapolis, if you want to stay close to home, but don't stay here. Whatever brought you home, take care of it and then get back out there before the fire in your belly dies."

I knew what she was saying. I was hiding, running from the pain of Mitch's murder that threatened to engulf me three hundred miles from the scene of the crime. Some day I would have to turn and face it, but not now. Besides, that was none of the editor's business. I thanked her for her help and made a quick exit. I pointed the Jeep toward Houghton and Mary Jo Quinn's young Lothario, Karl Maki, my number one suspect in her disappearance.

Chapter Ten

ALEX BREYERS HAD SAID MARY JO QUINN had taken a shine to Karl Maki and the two had become a couple, likely the first love for each of them at fourteen. He'd also said he figured Mary Jo knew her abductor since she wasn't the type to behave recklessly and get in a car with a stranger. But, back in 1974, the world wasn't quite as scary as it was now. Ted Bundy was not yet a household name. BTK had yet to terrorize the women of Wichita, Kansas. The Hillside Strangler had yet to strike in California. People simply weren't as cautious. They didn't think they had to be. Yet, I was inclined to agree with Alex that all these girls probably knew their abductors. How else could they have been whisked away without anyone noticing anything out of the ordinary? They must have gotten into the vehicle without making a scene.

Houghton was a two-hour drive east then north of Ironwood and by the time I reached the western city limits on M-26, I felt like an over-the-road truck driver must feel after a long trip—road weary. I found a gas station and grocery store at the intersection of the highway and Sharon Avenue and stopped to fill the Jeep's tank and let Belle empty hers. The gas station was one of those unstaffed outposts that only take credit cards so after parking the Jeep in the grocery store's lot, I went in search of a clerk who could direct me to a phone book and Karl Maki.

It turned out that the "family business" Alex had said Karl ran was the Maki Funeral Home and it was just down the street on Sharon Avenue about half a mile. A funeral director who was a nationally-known artist? No wonder the painting Mick had bought struck me as weird. It held the essence of the dead.

The Maki Funeral Home, however, looked anything but dead or funereal. It was built to look like a Georgian manor with thin white columns holding up a second floor balcony that extended over the front entry and driveway, sheltering attendees from the weather. The white trim and shutters gleamed against the red brick. It was elegant yet understated, like some of the antebellum homes Mitch and I had toured on a trip through the southern United States two summers ago. Upon ringing the doorbell, I fully expected to see a trim elderly woman with her hair pulled back in a bun, welcoming me in a soft accent and inviting me inside for a mint julep. Instead, a harried-looking middle-aged woman with shoulder-length brown hair answered the door.

"May I help you?" she asked, looking over her shoulder into the far reaches of the building toward muffled yelling.

"Um, I was wondering if Mr. Karl Maki is available. I'd like to ask—"

"I'm sorry. Could you please wait a minute?" she asked and stomped down the hall, leaving the front door open. I stepped across the threshold and shut the door behind me.

"Knock it off! You two have been arguing all day and I'm tired of it. You, upstairs and get your homework done. And you, outside and clean up that mess you made this morning. NOW!"

Two girls, one about fourteen and the other maybe three years younger, flounced into the hall and turned and stuck out their tongues at each other before the oldest headed up a flight of stairs and the youngest turned toward the rear of the building. The woman reappeared around the corner, took a deep breath, exhaled and smiled.

"I apologize for that. They're at that age when even the slightest little transgression instigates World War III. I'm Lily Maki, Karl's wife. Now what can we do for you?" she said.

"Well, this may sound a bit strange," I began, wondering how I was going to finesse asking about the disappearance of her husband's teenaged girlfriend some thirty years ago. "You see, I came across this scrapbook about a young girl who vanished in 1974 and, well, um, I'm a reporter by trade and it intrigued me and, well, it led me here. I just have a few questions for Karl. Is he around?"

"Oh, you must be talking about Mary Jo Quinn. He really doesn't like talking about that. Maybe I can help you; I was in the same class with Karl and Mary Jo. She was a friend, not a close one, but we hung out together once in a while," she said. "Why don't you come upstairs and we can talk. Karl is at the cemetery right now for a graveside service, but he should be back within the hour."

Lily led me up the stairs to the living quarters, which were beautifully furnished in a French country style, with floral upholstered wing chairs and sofa occupying the living room. We sat in the wing chairs opposite each other, Lily looking much more relaxed than just a few minutes ago. I told her about Astrid Heikkinen's scrapbook and my conversation with Alex and Karen Breyers. At the mention of Alex's name, Lily smiled sardonically.

"Alex," she whispered and shook her head. "He's such a complication. He's right, though. He and Karl have never been friends since. I'm not sure why either. I've asked Karl about it a few times, you know, if he thought Alex was involved in Mary Jo's death, but all he says is he doesn't want to talk about it."

"So you believe Mary Jo's dead?" I asked.

"Of course. My god, she's been gone for thirty-two years. I would think if she had just run away, someone would have spotted her or she would have contacted someone back here. It's not like she had any reason to run away. Her parents were wonderful. I found her house an oasis from the crazy cacophony I lived with. I have ten brothers and sisters and I'm smack-dab in the middle. My house was a zoo, no privacy whatsoever. But Mary Jo's house was calm, peaceful."

Light footsteps sounded on the stairs and a trim, athletic man with steel gray hair and blue eyes that seemed to look at nothing and everything all at once appeared in the doorway.

"Oh, Lily, I'm sorry, I didn't realize you had company. Please excuse my intrusion," the man said, his voice almost feminine in its pitch and theatrical in its elocution.

"No problem, Uncle John. This is, oh, I'm sorry, I don't know your name."

"Robin Hamilton," I said.

Uncle John strolled over to me, took my hand in his and shook it gently and bowed his head.

"It's a pleasure to meet you," he said with a smile, then turned to my hostess. "Lily, I just wanted to let you know I'm done with Mrs. Williams if you'd like to come take a look when you get a moment."

"Okay, I'll go downstairs in a bit. I'm sure she looks wonderful, though," she told him with a tender look, then turned to me. "You know when people attend a funeral and say the deceased looks alive, like they're just sleeping? John's the one responsible for that in this operation. He's marvelous. It's one of the things we're known for."

John smiled shyly and said, "I'm just thankful I've found a use for my God-given talent. Excuse me. Again, I apologize for the intrusion."

He seemed to glide out of the room, moving like a dolphin through water. He fit in perfectly with the atmosphere of the house, graceful, elegant.

"What a gentleman," I exclaimed when I thought he was out of earshot.

"Uncle John is an amazing man with quite a history," Lily said. "He has a very old, artistic soul. The whole Maki family is like that, but John is special. He served in Vietnam as part of the Mobile Riverine Force and was there for the Tet Offensive. It was tough on him; he wasn't able to go back to his old job in New York, so he came home and took Karl under his wing and really encouraged him in his artistic pursuits. My husband paints these fantastic oils that are selling for quite a bit of money now."

"Yes, a friend of mine just bought one. About Mary Jo, are her parents still around?" I asked.

"No, they moved to the Nashville area about ten years ago to be closer to their son and his family. He's a pediatric neurosurgeon, one of the best in the country, I hear. Mary Jo would have been like that, too. I have no doubt she would have reached the top of her field, no matter what she went into career-wise. It's such a waste."

"What do you think happened to her?"

Lily stared out the large window overlooking a wooded area behind the building and exhaled through her mouth.

"I guess I agree with Karl. I think Alex had something to do with her disappearance. He was very jealous of Karl. I know that sounds crazy considering we were all fourteen years old, but I can't come up with anything better," she said and then looked at me through narrowed eyelids. "Are you writing an article on Mary Jo?"

"No, not really. I'm just curious. Actually, there have been other disappearances of girls about Mary Jo's age in the Upper Peninsula over the last several decades and I'm wondering if there's any correlation," I said. "Don't worry, I won't quote you. I'm just collecting background information."

A car door slammed from somewhere within the house and I jumped.

"That's Karl bringing the hearse back. The garage is underneath us," she said and stood. "I'll take you down to see him, but I don't think he'll tell you much. It's still very painful for him. The cops questioned him extensively for more than a year after her disappearance, but he knew nothing."

We went downstairs through a painted steel door and into a three-stall garage that held a pick-up truck, large sport utility vehicle and the black Cadillac hearse, it rear door now open. A man who looked to be in his late sixties stood next to the hearse for a moment as if trying to figure out where he was and then smiled and breezed by us with a bemused expression on his pale but relatively unlined face. He disappeared down the hallway without a sound as I stared after him in wonder.

"That's Karl Senior. He's a bit lost these days. Dementia," Lily whispered and made a swirling motion with her finger next to her head. In a louder tone, she called, "Karl?"

"Yeah?" answered an agitated voice.

"We have a visitor," Lily said.

"In here?" Karl asked and poked his head out from rear of the Cadillac. I had to giggle at the horror in his voice.

"It's okay, Mr. Maki, I'm not a client. My name's Robin Hamilton. I was just talking with your wife about a scrapbook I found in Copper Harbor last weekend," I said, extending my hand, which he took.

"A scrapbook? What kind of scrapbook?" he asked.

"I'll leave you two alone. Uncle John wants me to check on his handiwork with Mrs. Williams," Lily said and left.

I again explained about the scrapbook and what Alex Breyers had recalled about Mary Jo's disappearance.

"Good Lord, why would Ms. Heikkinen keep such a thing? Well, I guess I can understand it. She always was a bit off the beam, but she cared about her students and worked as hard as the rest of us in the search for Mary Jo," Karl said. He eyed me wearily with his hands on his hips and shook his head. "Listen, there really isn't anything I can tell you. The last time I saw Mary Jo was shortly after school let out for the day, for summer, actually. We were standing at the edge of the block at school and agreed to get together late the next morning for a picnic down by the canal. We lived in opposite directions from the junior high school so we each went our own way, fine and healthy as can be. I was shocked when her parents called that evening wondering where she was. I never saw her after that. Now, if you'll excuse me, I have to prepare for a funeral tomorrow." He slammed the back door of the hearse, brushed some invisible dust from his dark blue suit and stalked past me to the steel door leading into the house, his long grayish-blonde ponytail swinging across his upper back.

"Just one more question, Mr. Maki," I pleaded.

He stopped and looked at me with the same ice blue eyes Uncle John possessed, only Karl's held no gentleness.

"What?"

"Are you aware that five other girls about the same age as Mary Jo have disappeared under similar circumstances around the western and central Upper Peninsula since Mary Jo vanished? In fact, one just went missing yesterday in Rapid River," I said.

Karl's face turned white, then red, then purple, then back to white in about fifteen seconds.

"Are you saying they're all related? That's ridiculous. Are you saying I'm responsible, that I'm going around abducting young girls? That's even more ridiculous. What are you trying to do to me? This is all about Alex, isn't it? It's always about Alex. I suggest you leave and tell Alex Breyers to stay the hell out of our lives," he sputtered and stormed out the door, slamming it behind him.

I stood alone in the garage, just me, the pickup, SUV and hearse, listening to Karl's angry footsteps echo as he stormed up the stairs.

"That went well, don't you think?" I said to the empty garage and quietly let myself out the front door.

Chapter Eleven

I LEFT THE MAKI FUNERAL HOME in Houghton feeling like the scum at the base of a toilet in a gas station. Not only had I ruined Evelyn Smith's day by making her dredge up terrible memories, but now, she questioned the community role in possibly the death of an innocent man. If that wasn't enough, Karl Maki thought I was accusing him of murder on a mass scale. Then again, was I?

I stopped at the Burger King in L'Anse about thirty miles south of Houghton, ordered a chicken sandwich and stopped at a downtown park overlooking Keweenaw Bay to eat and figure out my next move. I gave Belle some food and water in two bowls on the back seat then scarfed down my sandwich. There was a clue somewhere in the mess of papers and information I had accumulated, but it resisted revealing itself to my befuddled mind. I ran through the list of similarities again. All the girls had disappeared in the summer or early fall, all were between thirteen and fifteen, all were creative in some way and there were no witnesses to any of their disappearances. Six girls in thirty-one years and not one damn thing directly linking them, other than death, and I wasn't even sure of that.

"Crap!" I yelled and slammed my hand against the steering wheel. I was tired and emotionally drained, but I wasn't ready to go home. The freshest case probably held the best clues so I headed back toward Rapid River, taking M-28 again. Belle and I had registered more than five hundred miles on the odometer in the last two days but she seemed to be enjoying the adventure, perched in the passenger seat, alternately napping and watching the scenery flash past her window. I wasn't having nearly as much fun.

It was dark by the time I reached Beth Stankowski's house. There was just one vehicle parked in the driveway in front of the detached one-car garage. The media onslaught was apparently over for the day, except for me, of course. I parked in front of the house, grabbed my purse and notebook and strolled up the front walk. The blinds were drawn, but lights were on in the front room. Ringing the doorbell, I took a few deep breaths and prepared my speech. The door opened abruptly and a tall, slim woman with short blonde hair eyed me suspiciously and snapped, "Yes?"

"Hello, are you Mrs. Stankowski?" I asked, trying to sound non-threatening.

"No, I'm her sister, Bonnie. May I help you with something?" she asked. She was tired and probably sick of people asking questions.

"My name's Robin Hamilton and I'm a reporter with the *Daily Press* in Escanaba, but I'm not here just to do an interview. I'd like to get some background information for another article I'm writing about some other disappearances. It won't take more than a few minutes," I said.

She considered me for a moment then held the door open.

"Okay, c'mon in. Beth, there's another reporter here looking for some background on Heather," she called over her shoulder.

I caught a glimpse of the kitchen counter stacked with casserole dishes. The residents of Rapid River were doing all they could to support the Stankowskis.

Footsteps thudded down hardwood stairs toward the back of the house, and then a woman who could have been a model walked into the living room. She was tall and thin like her sister, but her features were softer, prettier. Bonnie introduced us and we shook hands and sat in the living room.

"I'm sorry I have to come here under these circumstances, but maybe I can help by keeping people informed. Is there any word on Heather's whereabouts?" I asked.

Beth exhaled, looked at the ceiling and gripped her denim-clad knees with both hands. "No, not yet."

"I'm so sorry. I don't pretend to know what you're going through because I don't have children." I said.

"Thank you," she said and seemed to relax a little. She put her hands in her lap and asked what sort of information I needed. Choosing my words carefully so as not to alarm her, I said, "I'm working on an article about several young girls who have disappeared in the U.P. since 1974, with the last one occurring in 1999, until now. One or two were thought to be runaways, but we just don't know. Is there any chance Heather ran away?"

"I guess there's always a possibility. The police asked that, too. If she did, she never gave any hint that such a thing was on her mind. She seemed to love school and her friends. Then there's her diabetes. She was diagnosed about five years ago. I'll tell you, that kid has dealt with it better than me. I know she wouldn't have left her insulin kit behind if she had planned to run away," Beth said and swept her page-boy-style hair from her face. "I can't see any reason for her to even think of running away from home. She's an only child and she had a tough time with the divorce when it happened a few years ago, but it got easier when her dad bought the house on the other side of town. I wasn't crazy about it, although I have to admit he can be a good dad, even if he was a lousy husband."

Bonnie snorted and added, "The pig ran around on her like a race car at Daytona and the only reason he bought that house was so he could have Heather half the time and avoid paying child support. You know that, Beth."

"Bonnie! Please!" she chided, her cheeks red.

"I talked with Detective Chris Parker earlier and she said Heather is a talented artist," I prompted.

"Oh yes, just look around. All these paintings are hers," Beth answered with a wave of her hand.

Parker was right. The canvases were quite advanced, full of detail down to the blades of grass and individual leaves on trees. Even Michaela, the New York art connoisseur, would have been impressed. I took another deep breath and plunged ahead to the tough part.

"So far, the only thing these missing girls have in common is that they're all creative in some way, writing, drawing, acting, playing music, painting, but I don't know if that means anything. Most girls at that age use some form of art to express their emotions. I remember writing some of the absolute worst short stories imaginable as a teenager, but it helped me through some difficult times," I said.

Beth turned to her sister and said, "I never thought of it like that. She always loved to draw, but she didn't take up painting until Lou and I split. Maybe she was hiding her unhappiness in her art. Maybe she has run away, but where?"

Bonnie enveloped her sister's hand in her own long fingers, and then fixed her piercing hazel eyes on me. "What about these other girls? What were their lives like?" she asked.

"As far as I know, most seem to come from fairly normal backgrounds except the last one. Her family sounded pretty dysfunctional. She had earned a scholarship for some month-long camp and was looking forward to getting more scholarships to college so she could build a better life for herself," I said, remembering the Ironwood newspaper editor's account of Crystal Jensen's short, tragic life.

Beth's demeanor was starting to crumble. She was under an impossible strain and I was only adding to it. I stood up and took out a business card. After writing my cell phone number on the back, I handed it to Bonnie and left just as Beth started to cry.

By eleven that night, Belle and I were nestled back in Aunt Gina's spare bedroom, not really wanting to go home and be alone with my thoughts. After calling my dad to let him know we were alive and kicking, I had filled her in on the events of the day while she listened intently. Not since Mitch had someone just listened to me without offering advice or a lecture. Aunt Gina was concerned about me, that much was obvious by the look on her face, but she kept her concerns to herself. I didn't need someone to tell me I looked exhausted. I could feel it in my bones as I tried in vain to sleep.

What would Mitch have done in this situation, I wondered. He loved being a cop, especially investigative work. Whenever the opportunity arose to help out the four detectives on staff, he jumped at it. His dream had been to take over as chief of a small department so he tried to learn every facet of police work. Just thirty-two when he was murdered, he had already been a sergeant for about a year and was highly respected for his ability to see patterns where no one else could and use them to solve tough cases. I could have used his help now because I sensed there was a thread linking Mary Jo to Lucy and Caroline to Sabrina and possibly even Crystal to Heather, but I was damned if I could see it.

At some point I fell into a fitful sleep where I dreamt that an unseen force was pulling me below the surface of an icy cold lake. I didn't awaken until someone softly called my name. Through one half-open eye I saw Aunt Gina sitting at the edge of the bed. I groaned and pulled the pillow over my head. She laughed softly, the sound not unlike a warm summer rain pattering on a tin roof. It brought to mind visions of safety, warmth, comfort.

"You know, you'd make a great mother. You've got that way about you. You're patient and kind," I said, throwing off the pillow and sitting up in bed.

This time she threw her head back and cackled. "No one has ever said that to me. Your cousins think I'm a hoot. Crazy Aunt Gina, they call me," she said and slapped my leg through the covers. "C'mon, it's nearly nine o'clock on another gorgeous day. Let's enjoy it before you have to go home. Get dressed and I'll take you to breakfast at Jack's."

After a shower, I pulled on the same clothes I'd worn all weekend, although they smelled freshly washed, and saw that Belle's dish was full. For once, she was too busy playing tag with her new friends, Victoria and Albert, to worry about eating. I, on the other hand, was famished. We climbed into Aunt Gina's Toyota Prius and headed toward the main gathering place in Rapid River, Jack's Restaurant. Located on the corner of Main Street and the highway, it was full of diners when we stepped inside. The young dark-haired waitress sat us in a recently-vacated booth overlooking the highway. After clearing the table, she left us to peruse the menu, which was full of fattening, delicious-sounding choices. I ordered a platter of eggs, ham, hash browns and toast, then turned my attention to watching the traffic on U.S. 2. Several trucks passed by the window and I began to fantasize about what life would be like living in the cab of a truck for days on end, isolated from the problems of the world, focused only on keeping it between the lines.

"Yoohoo."

I looked across the table at Aunt Gina and grinned. "I do that a lot, drift off, I mean. Please don't take it personally," I said.

"I don't, but I notice that you do live very much within yourself," she said.

"What does that mean?" I asked, bracing myself for a lecture.

"It just means you're introverted. It's not necessarily a bad thing, but it does make it tough for people to get to know you. I imagine it's a way of protecting yourself," she said, resting her chin in her hands and gazing at me with those soft blue-gray eyes that reminded me of an approaching thunderstorm, full of power to cleanse or destroy those who stared into them too long.

Fiddling with my silverware, I said, "Wow, you're very perceptive. Are you sure that doctorate isn't in psychology? You seem to have me figured out."

She put her hand over mine to stop the jangling of the spoon, knife and fork and said, "It's simply called wisdom and comes with age and experience. If you just sit back and watch and listen, you can learn a lot about people, even if they never say a word about themselves."

I pulled my hand away and rearranged the silverware a few more times before revealing, "The reason I push myself so hard is that I don't want to think about Mitch."

"I know."

"It's not so much that he's gone, but the way it happened. He was shot in the ...." Suddenly I was crying. I struggled to keep from sobbing, aware that diners at three other tables around us were alternately staring at me and anything but me. Aunt Gina pulled a packet of Kleenex from her purse and handed one across the table. I blew my nose and chuckled nervously.

"You see, that's what happens when I talk about him," I said.

She smiled knowingly. "Do you know how long it was after Darren died that I was able to laugh? Six months. He had lung cancer. Never smoked a cigarette in his whole life other than a few joints in college. It took two years to kill him and it was agonizing to watch this vibrant mountain of a man waste away to a hundred and twenty-five pounds. Then one day I pulled out a photo album of a trip we had taken to the British Isles. I saw myself smiling with Darren in the photos and remembered how much he loved hearing me laugh. I knew he'd be disappointed if I allowed grief to stifle my laughter so I began to look for the joy in life again. I moved back to Michigan and started over. I still miss him, but I also treasure those warm feelings, even the sadness, because it means our love was real."

She reached for my hand and squeezed it. "The same thing will happen to you when you're ready, but it will probably take longer because there's so much you have yet to resolve. When the time is right, you'll turn all that passion and energy you now put into your work toward finding Mitch's killer. Until then, just accept the love and support of those who care about you."

The waitress delivered two steaming plates heaped with food, diverting our attention from grief to gluttony. The rest of the meal was spent discussing our work—my journalism adventures and her teaching at NYU and Bay College and writing articles on feminism and religion. We discovered a shared interest in helping life's underdogs, albeit through different means. She studied how certain groups were marginalized because of superstition or ignorance and I rooted out corruption and deception and revealed it to the public via the newspaper. I was telling her about how I got involved in solving the murder of a prominent accountant in Ludington Park the previous summer when my cell phone rang. Figuring it was Bob Hunter looking for an update, I answered it with a casual "Yo."

"Hello, is this Robin Hamilton?" It was a woman's voice.

"Yes. Hello, who's this?"

"Beth Stankowski, Heather's mother. I've been thinking about something you said last night about one of those girls. You said she'd been to a month-long camp that summer. My daughter attended the Great Lakes Summer Institute for four weeks in June and July. It's a camp for kids interested in art, theater and music."

Chapter Twelve

MY ADRENALINE WAS PUMPING AS I loaded Belle and my briefcase into the Jeep, kissed Aunt Gina goodbye and sped back to Rapid River and Beth Stankowski's house. I parked in the driveway and met her on the front porch where she handed me a pamphlet with the words Great Lakes Summer Institute emblazoned in blue letters arching over a drawing of a lake and scattering of log cabins.

"I called Detective Parker, but she said it probably means nothing. She said it's unlikely these cases are related. I don't know what to think. Is Heather in the hands of a madman or is she dead?" Beth asked, squeaking out the last word.

"It won't help to worry yourself into a frenzy. Parker's probably right. Heather could turn up at a bus station in Milwaukee this afternoon. Anything is possible so please try to relax," I said.

"You're right, of course. Well, I have to go inside. You never know when the phone might ring," she said and tried to laugh, but it sounded hollow and frightened. "You can keep that, but let me know if, well, if you find anything."

I nodded and watched her shuffle into the house. I waited until pulling into the parking lot of the Dairy Flo, a little ice cream shop located on the highway, but closed for the season, before leafing through the pamphlet. The first section outlined the history of the Institute, which began in the nineteen fifties when the head of a Detroit advertising firm saw a need for intensive education for rural students who showed some talent in the arts. William Murdoch purchased one hundred acres of land bordering Lake Independence in northern Marquette County and built dormitories, classrooms, a gallery and even a small theater. The camp offered an opportunity for sixty boys and girls to spend a month studying under some of the country's finest artists and musicians, recruited by a board of directors that managed the camp and its multimillion dollar endowment.

This had to be the link between the six girls, if we counted Heather. I considered driving to the camp, then realized that would be futile. It was undoubtedly shut down for the year. Besides, the phone number for the director had a Marquette exchange. I resolved to pick up the lead from home and headed south to Escanaba.

The message light on my answering machine was blinking when Belle and I walked into the apartment. After giving Belle some fresh food and water, I pressed the button and waited. There were three messages. The first was from my dad and was left on Friday ("Hi, I just called to remind you to let me know when you're home. The cell phone was out of range. Just want to make sure you're not dead in a ditch somewhere. Bye.") The second was from my editor telling me I'd better be at work on Monday or he'd move my desk onto the sidewalk. The last message, left this morning, was from Charlie. His voice sounded bewildered and strained as he said, "Hey, I tried your cell but it wouldn't connect. We got a strange phone call today that I think you should know about. Call me."

I threw together a sandwich with almost stale bread and borderline edible smoked turkey, Swiss cheese and mustard, and called my dad. Naturally, he wasn't home, probably out golfing, so I left a message indicating I was not dead in a ditch, at least not yet. I would deal with Bob Hunter in the morning. Charlie picked up his home phone on the first ring.

"Hey, what's up?"

"Oh, Robin. I'm glad it's you. I've been a little worried," Charlie said, that bewildered sound still evident in his voice.

"Worried about what? I've just been traipsing around the U.P. digging up dirt on those missing girls and upsetting a few people's apple carts. I've found out some interesting stuff, too. I may have a lead that ties all these kids together, even that girl in Rapid River who disappeared on Friday," I said between bites of my sandwich.

"Hold on a minute. That's what the phone call was about, these missing girl cases," he said.

"I don't understand. Did the cops call you?"

Silence.

"Charlie?"

"I don't know if it was the cops, Robin. It was weird," he said and paused. I was getting impatient. What the hell was he trying to say? Finally he blurted, "Someone called the station at about six-thirty this morning and asked the dispatcher if she knew you and if you were a reporter for the paper. She said yes and asked what of it. This person — she couldn't really tell if it was a man or woman — tells her you're interfering in a police investigation and need to be reined in. Those were the words the person used, 'reined in.' I listened to the tape."

"So the cops want me to back off. I've heard that one before. Although that is a bit odd because the detective handling the Rapid River case didn't seem to have a problem with me. In fact, she's pretty much dismissed my theory as improbable. Besides, if it was someone from the state police post at Gladstone, why wouldn't he just say so? I don't get it," I said.

"That's just it. It wasn't the state cops that called. It was from a payphone in Ishpeming. Why would a cop call from a payphone, especially one way the hell up there?" he said.

Now my voice sounded bewildered as I whispered, "I don't know." I felt a chill, like someone walking across my grave, as my grandmother used to say.

"Robin, you'd better tell me what exactly happened this weekend," Charlie said.

We agreed that I would pick up a pizza and meet at his house in an hour. In the meantime, I took a shower and mulled over the strange phone call. My first guess was Karl Maki, but he'd said he had a funeral today. Ishpeming was about ninety minutes from Houghton, which would mean three hours out of his day just to tell the cops to "rein me in." Wouldn't his wife question his absence? Then there was Alex Breyers. The Makis certainly weren't among his admirers. Lily had said something about him being a complication and that Karl possibly suspected him in Mary Jo's disappearance. Then Karl had said, "It's always about Alex." Was Alex's request for me to probe Mary Jo's case simply a ruse? Had Karl confronted him after my visit Saturday?

"Here I go again," I said to my reflection in the mirror as I toweled my hair. I was jumping to conclusions. For all I knew, it could have been Louis Stankowski who bumped off his own daughter to escape paying child support. It had been done before. What I needed was more information about that camp. After dressing in clean clothes and applying a touch of make-up, I sat at the kitchen table and updated my notes with what I'd learned about the Crystal Jensen case in Ironwood, the Makis and Alex Breyers and the camp Heather had attended this past summer. I studied the pamphlet again, but no contact name was listed, just a phone number, which I dialed and got only a recorded message. I next called Alex Breyers. His wife answered with a cheery hello. After reminding her who I was I asked for Alex.

"He's not home yet. He went to an art show downstate. I don't expect him back until late tonight," Karen said.

A blip appeared on my radar screen.

"When did he leave for the show?"

"Hmm, let me think." I could almost imagine her biting her lower lip as she thought. "It was Thursday afternoon because I had school the next day."

"Is he looking for art for the cottages?" I asked.

"No, no. He's a painter, really abstract stuff. I don't understand any of it, but he usually sells three or four canvases a year for several hundred dollars apiece," Karen said wistfully. "He's so talented. It's that artistic side that drew me to him, you know, what with me being a writer and all."

"Yes, how is that book coming along? Was Michaela able to help you?" I asked, anxious to get back to the subject of her husband's whereabouts yet not be obvious about it.

"Oh, she was very helpful. She gave me the names of a few agents in New York. I'm polishing the manuscript right now so I can send it out to one of them tomorrow," she effused.

"Well, good luck with that. By the way, do you happen to know if Alex ever attended a summer arts camp for a month or so when he was in junior high?" I asked.

"Do you mean the Great Lakes Summer Institute? He never mentioned it. Why?"

"How do you know about the Institute?"

"I sent one of my students there this past summer — a boy with the soul of Lord Byron, mad, bad and dangerous to know. He came back from the camp a little less mad, not quite as bad and much less dangerous. I think he might actually have seen a future for himself," she said.

"Sounds like Crystal Jensen," I mumbled.

"Excuse me?"

"Nothing. Did you say that art show was in Traverse City? I have a friend who weaves and might be interested," I said, lying through my pearly whites.

"No, I'm pretty sure he said Grand Rapids, but I'll have him call you tomorrow, if you like," she said.

"I'd appreciate that," I said and hung up the receiver.

I was getting a bad feeling about Alex Breyers. Between his vagueness to his wife about his whereabouts and the Makis' disdain for him, I suspected he was up to something no good. Unfortunately, the devoted, romantic woman he married seemed to have the common sense of a whitetail deer trotting alongside the highway. At any second she could dart onto the road of life and get squashed, if she wasn't careful.

Belle was asleep in the corner of the couch when I dashed out the door shortly before five. After picking up a large pizza with everything but anchovies, I pulled up to Charlie's house on the far south side of town. It was a newer ranch-style home, small but tidy. The foundation had been laid for a two-car garage the week before and the framing was nearly finished thanks to a few weekends of sweat and hard work on the part of the detective and some friends handy with hammers. Charlie had indicated that his homeowner's insurance didn't carry enough coverage for people as clumsy as me, so I hadn't been invited to help.

I heard banging coming from the shed around back. He was trying to find room for the lawnmower in a structure crammed with garden implements, a snowblower, two bicycles and other assorted junk including a Radio Flyer red wagon. I snickered and he turned around and glared at me.

"Going to take your dollies for a ride later?" I said with an innocent grin and pointed at the wagon. He growled and gave the mower one last shove, slid the door shut with a slam and secured the padlock.

"For your information, that wagon is a family heirloom, passed on to me by my father," he snarled.

"Some heirloom. You've got it stashed in there like a screw at the bottom of a junk drawer," I said.

"Smartass. Let's eat. I'm starving," he said and led the way to a cedar picnic table near the back door. I opened the pizza box while he went inside to retrieve some paper plates, napkins and a beer for himself and a wine cooler for me. Once settled across from each other, soaking up the early evening sun, I asked him about the strange phone call to the public safety department that morning.

"After I got off the phone with you I got in touch with that Chris Parker," he explained. "She said she met you, thought you were nice — for a reporter — and that you had shared some information with her that you thought might be helpful." He shook his head in mock disgust. "She has no idea what a pain in the ass you are. She certainly didn't think you were interfering with anything, although she did have a concern that you might get that girl's mother riled up about nothing. Robin, what exactly have you gotten into now?"

I put down my slice of pizza, finished chewing and took a drink before answering.

"This is just speculation, but I think it's the same guy responsible for the disappearance and possible murder of at least six girls. I may even have a suspect or two," I said and filled him in on the events of the last two and a half days.

"So you think this Alex Breyers or Karl Maki may have killed the girl in Houghton thirty-some-odd years ago and then killed five others? How are they connected to this summer camp?" he asked. The sun was setting and the night air had grown cold and bit into my skin. I shivered.

"I don't know if either one of them has a connection. According to Alex, he and Karl haven't spoken in years so, if he's telling the truth. It's unlikely they both are instructors at the camp. Only the camp personnel can answer a lot of these questions. I'll try to contact them first thing in the morning," I said and wrapped my arms around my chest. "It's cold and I'm tired so let's call it a night, okay?"

Charlie collected the garbage on the table and stood. "Okay, keep me posted, though, and be careful," he said as he walked me to the curb where the Jeep was parked. Before I climbed inside, he touched my shoulder. I stopped and turned to face him.

"I don't like this. That call this morning wasn't from a cop. If you're right about all these cases being connected, you're dealing with a psycho. Keep your eyes open."

"I'll be fine," I said. He looked worried as I drove away. He was beginning to remind me of my father, always worrying about me.

Back at the apartment, Belle greeted me at the door, tail wagging furiously. After we took a walk around the block for her nightly constitutional I called my dad. Too tired to get into a long conversation about my work or Aunt Gina, I agreed to visit him after work the next day. As I wiggled between the flannel sheets, I remembered the painting that my dad had taken from the attic and stashed in his garage and wondered if Belle would finally be able to sleep through the night again. For once, we both did.

Chapter Thirteen

BOB HUNTER WAS ATWITTER WITH anticipation when I walked through the door Monday morning at seven-thirty. I'd made my routine stops at Escanaba Public Safety and the Delta County Sheriff's Department in search of other news from the weekend, but the only news was about Heather Stankowski. Hope was growing dim.

"Well?" the editor drawled as I sat at my desk. He reminded me of an undertaker at an Old West hanging, his eager expression almost ghoulish.

"Well what? It was a quiet weekend, just a few bar fights but no one even ended up in the hospital," I said. "They were all too busy looking for that girl."

"Who cares about bar fights?" he snapped. "What did you find out about all those missing girls, including this latest one?"

I stared at the blank computer screen in front of me. Did I have enough to write an article, to go public and tie everything together? No, not yet. I needed to explore the summer camp angle first. Besides, my gut told me it was too soon to write off Heather Stankowski as dead. I was certain Mary Jo, Lucy, Sabrina and Caroline had long ago welcomed Crystal into the ranks of the murdered, but somehow I suddenly felt Heather was still among the living. Maybe it was the Ironwood *Daily Globe* editor's recollection about Crystal still being alive when she jumped from her captor's vehicle. That meant this guy didn't kill his victims immediately. Crystal had a defensive wound, but was it because she was trying to escape?

"Robin? Hello? Are you there?" Bob leaned over my desk and called loudly.

"Yeah, yeah, I heard you," I said and heaved a weary sigh. "I have to tread carefully here, Bob. I believe there are six girls, including this last one, who were kidnapped by the same guy, but I have a few leads I need to track down first. Let me do an update on this last one for today's paper and then I'll make a few phone calls after deadline. Maybe we can put something together to run later in the week."

He drew up to his full height of just over six feet, folded his arms across his chest and began to nod his silver-haired head slowly. "All right, I can do that. Keep me posted. The more I think about this, the more I feel in my bones that you're on to something," Bob said and shuffled into his office. I was thankful to have him for an editor. The man knew exactly when to push and when to back off a reporter.

I made a quick call to the Ishpeming High School to see if anyone there remembered Lucy Franklin. A secretary curtly informed me that no one at the school was authorized to give out information on prior or present students without parental permission, period. No amount of cajoling, pleading or sidestepping made the secretary budge, so I gave up and turned my attention to churning out the few brief news items on miscellaneous misdemeanors that had occurred during the weekend before calling Detective Christine Parker in Gladstone for an update. She had nothing substantially new to report but did ask about Charlie Baker.

"I haven't met him in person yet. He sounds handsome. Is he single?" she asked.

I couldn't help but giggle. "Yes, single and good-looking. Tall with sandy brown hair and blue eyes. Are you available?"

"Nope. Happily married with two little girls, but I do have a younger sister who teaches school in Gladstone and she is in search of a tall, dark and handsome man to enslave in wedded bliss," she said wickedly.

"Well, at least you're honest," I said.

"Men just think they want to be free. They'd be miserable without us," she declared. I wasn't sure Charlie would agree, but I let it slide and drew her back on point.

"What about the Great Lakes Summer Institute? A girl who died about six years ago under suspicious circumstances not far from Ironwood attended that camp the summer she died. Are you going to look into Heather's attendance there at all?"

"We are looking at every possible angle, especially since the longer Heather is without her diabetes treatment, the more likely this will have a bad outcome. That worries me more than anything at this point. Since we haven't found a body, I suspect she is still alive," Parker said.

"I agree. Please let me know if you find anything out," I said.

"And you do the same. You may even be a step ahead of us on this case. I don't mind that; just don't get yourself into trouble. Leave the policing to us," she said and hung up.

I moved on to the next task of putting together an update on Heather's disappearance and then set about confirming Alex Breyers' whereabouts over the weekend. A quick search on the Internet yielded a calendar of events for the Grand Rapids area, but showed nothing about an art festival. I tried the community college and nearby Grand Valley State University but neither website revealed anything art-related happening the previous weekend. I cautioned myself not to jump to conclusions. There were a number of possibilities for the cottage-owner's activities other than kidnapping a teenage girl. Karen could have gotten the location wrong, or perhaps Alex was having an affair. I gave the art fair search one last attempt and called an acquaintance at Escanaba's William Bonifas Fine Arts Center.

"I don't know of anything major going on there, but let me do some checking. There could certainly be a small festival or gallery opening I don't know about," she said, agreeing to call me back in the afternoon.

That left the Great Lakes Summer Institute lead to follow. I dialed the number listed for the director on the pamphlet Heather's mother had given me the day before. A young woman, who turned out to be the director's secretary, answered the phone in nasally voice with a thick Yooper accent. ("Yah, I believe she's here. Let me see if she's available for calls.") She finally put me through to the director after leaving me on hold for about five minutes. ("Yah, she said she can talk to you. Here ya go. You have a good day now.")

I was still smiling when a very different-sounding woman's voice came on the line.

"This is Audrey Gaston. How may I help you, Ms. Hamilton?" she said in a voice as smooth as vanilla pudding, with diction so precise I immediately pictured a stereotypical New England prep school dean, hair pulled into a tight bun, glasses perched low on an aristocratic nose and a gray wool suit that hit below the knees. This wasn't a woman interested in small talk so I got right to the point and asked how I could find out about prior camp attendees.

"I'm sorry, that information is confidential," Ms. Gaston said.

"Why?"

"We are dealing with children. How do I know you aren't a person of nefarious character with dubious intentions," she said.

Nefarious? Dubious? I chuckled.

"I understand your dilemma, Ma'am. Perhaps it would help if I explained why I'm calling. Have you heard about the disappearance of Heather Stankowski?" I asked.

"Of course. Everyone's talking about it. Heather's a delightful child, full of spirit and talent," she said, not realizing she just broke her own rule.

"Ms. Gaston, I believe Heather is one of six girls to mysteriously vanish in the last thirty years and the other five may have attended your summer camp, but I need your help," I implored, adding, "As you know, Heather's a diabetic. She left her blood sugar test kit and insulin behind when she was grabbed Friday morning."

"Oh my, I see, well, perhaps you could give me the names of these other girls and the years they would have attended. Then I can look them up on our computer database," she said.

One by one, going backwards from Heather, Audrey Gaston confirmed that each one had indeed attended the camp the summer she went missing. With each name and confirmation, Gaston's voice grew shakier, as the horror of what may have happened sank into her mind. Then we came to Mary Jo Quinn and June of 1974.

"I know that name. She was a friend of my brother's," she said, her voice flat. "I know Mary Jo never made it to the camp. It's always been the last two weeks of June and the first two weeks of July. She disappeared early in June, the day school let out for the summer, I think."

Startled that she knew Mary Jo, I asked, "Is your brother Karl Maki or Alex Breyers?"

"Karl is my half-brother. We had the same mother," she said, her voice still flat.

Something was wrong. She had been so animated earlier, but at the mention of Mary Jo's name, Audrey Gaston had turned into an automaton. I tried a different route to break through, ignoring the connection between her and Maki for the time being.

"What about 1973? She would have been thirteen that year," I said.

"I'll look," she said. The click of her fingernails on the keyboard sounded like Belle walking across the kitchen floor when her nails needed a trim. "Nope, nothing," Audrey finally said and the clicking stopped.

"Tell me about the camp staff. Who are these people and how do you select them?" I asked.

"None of our people could possibly be involved with these girls. They all undergo extensive background checks. In fact, most of them are teachers in the public school system or they're university professors. Others are highly successful artists recruited as presenters. What you are suggesting is reprehensible and I won't let you slander the name of this institute. It's crazy." She was nearly screeching into the phone by the time she finished.

"If Karl Maki is your brother then you must know a painter named Alex Breyers," I said.

"Of course, I know Alex. He was a friend of Karl's for a while, then they went their separate ways, but I've been in touch with him often over the years. He's been a judge of the juried exhibit that is the capstone project for the institute. He's done it for several years. We were so happy when he and his wife moved to the U.P. It made it so much easier for him to fit us into his schedule," she gushed.

"How long has he been a judge?" I asked. Lucy Franklin had disappeared in 1979. Alex would have been nineteen, certainly old enough to show some talent as an artist.

"I don't like the direction this conversation is going, but I'll answer that because no one here has anything to hide. I took over as director of the Institute in 1989 and personally recruited Alex as a judge that same year when one of our long-time judges fell seriously ill. It took a lot of work to get him on board because of his busy schedule. He had to travel between here and Massachusetts," she said curtly. "Certainly you don't think he's involved in all those disappearances, as you call them. I happen to know he searched for Mary Jo right along with half of Houghton. He had nothing to do with her death. He's a kind, gentle soul with a deep, abiding love of nature."

"Your brother doesn't think so highly of him," I said.

"How do you know that?" she asked, surprise evident in her voice, which had grown strong again.

"I met with him a few days ago. Let's just say he doesn't share your opinion of Alex. What about the other staff or judges? Do you have anyone who's been around since the late seventies?" I asked.

"There was Helen Steinhausen. She was the first director, and then stayed on as a judge and advisor after I took over, but she died in May. She was an amazing woman, she kept painting until two weeks before her death at the age of ninety-one," Audrey said.

"That's it, just that one woman stuck around for more than twenty years?" I asked. If the Institute was the institution Audrey Gaston made it out to be, one would think the staff would be a bit more dedicated.

"Yes, that's it. People retire, move or have other commitments the month of the Institute. Teaching is an honor. It doesn't come with much in the way of a paycheck. Some people can't afford to do this year in and year out. Besides, you can grow stale in sticking to a routine. The Institute is always fresh and cutting edge because we are always recruiting new talent," she said.

I blew out a deep breath in frustration. Talking with the Institute's director wasn't helping as much as I'd hoped. I hadn't counted on her being related to Karl Maki, either. It might mean I could eliminate both Karl and Alex as suspects, but I wasn't even certain of that. I gave her my number at the newspaper and asked her to call me if she thought of anything that might be relevant. She agreed, albeit reluctantly. I certainly hadn't made a friend of the high-toned camp director.

Leaning back in my chair, I focused on a nail hole in the wall above my computer and let my mind digest what it had been fed so far. Mary Jo Quinn didn't fit the pattern of the other girls. That meant one of two things —either the killer knew her from somewhere else or her disappearance had nothing to do with the others. If the latter turned out to be true, the irony would be astonishing considering she was the one who'd provoked my interest in all these cases in the first place. For now at least, I decided to eliminate her case from consideration and focus on the five girls who had attended the Institute. Audrey Gaston said she'd been the director for sixteen years and that no one other than the old woman had been around when Lucy Franklin had attended the camp. Yet there had to be someone who'd had contact with the attendees through all those years.

It occurred to me that it could be someone who only taught at the Institute sporadically, but it was time for lunch and I didn't feel like calling Audrey back and getting the runaround again. Perhaps Bob would let me go to Marquette tomorrow to talk to her in person and maybe see the camp firsthand. In the meantime, Belle needed a walk and I needed sustenance. We took a brisk walk around Ludington Park under a clear blue sky and bright sun, although the air still had a bite to it, thanks to the stiff northeasterly wind blowing down from Canada. Belle stopped to sniff around various tree trunks and assorted metal garbage cans while I watched the seagulls dive-bomb a few hearty souls eating at picnic tables. Once back home, I downed a mediocre microwave lasagna that resembled, and tasted like, two slabs of vinyl flooring smeared with ketchup and topped with processed cheese.

A message from my artist friend awaited me upon my return to work. "The only major art fair in that part of the state was the weekend before last in Charlotte," she'd said. That was more than an hour from Grand Rapids, closer to Lansing, the state capitol. Besides, it wasn't even on the right date, so where exactly had Alex Breyers been over the weekend? Rapid River?

Because the *Daily Press* is a small newspaper with a miniscule staff, I couldn't devote all my time to what I was beginning to think of as "The Institute Case." I put it out of my mind long enough to make a few phone calls and write an article for the next day's edition about a proposal to cut funding to the area's undercover narcotics squad, which was seeing more and more work and getting less and less financial help.

When Bob got out of the monthly department head meeting around two, I followed him into his office and shut the door.

"I need to go up north tomorrow. Can I have the afternoon to follow up on a lead?" I asked.

He rolled his eyes and threw his head back against his chair.

"Robin! I gave you all day Friday, plus you spent the whole weekend working. How am I going to justify all this mileage and the hours to the publisher, let alone the fact that you aren't here writing stories for the daily paper?" he asked in exasperation.

"I wrote you a story for tomorrow and I think I can come back with something for a story for Wednesday. I want to visit a summer camp that five of the six missing girls attended," I said, adding, "Besides, I told you I wouldn't charge you for the hours over the weekend. That should help."

"Uh-huh. Are you talking about the Great Lakes Summer Institute?" he asked.

"Yeah, what do you know about it?"

He scratched his scraggly gray beard and looked thoughtful.

"Both my sons went there for writing. Bobby went in Eighty-two and Jason in Eighty-six. Now one's an accountant and the other's a corporate lawyer. Go figure," he said and shrugged. "But what about these girls? Are you thinking someone on the staff killed them?"

"That's the logical explanation, but I need more information, which is why I want to go up there. I'd like to talk to the executive director face to face. She's kind of snooty and has some very personal ties to a few people connected with the first girl who disappeared so she jerked me around on the phone this morning. I think I'll have better luck in person. Plus, I want to see this place for myself," I said and shifted in my chair. What I was about to say next sounded weird, even to me, but I wanted to bounce the idea off my venerable old editor, who had the news sense of Mike Wallace.

"There's something else. I feel there's a good chance Heather Stankowski is still alive, if her diabetes hasn't gotten her yet. There's something about the previous cases that makes me think this guy doesn't kill them right way. Where are the bodies? How come not a single one has turned up in the last thirty years? Then there's this Crystal Jensen in Ironwood. He put her in the car while she was still very much alive and she managed to escape, only to be run over by someone else by accident," I said and filled him in on some of what I'd learned over the weekend.

"If you're right, this girl could be dead by the time you find this guy. Do the police know about the Summer Institute angle?" Bob asked.

"Detective Chris Parker is the state police cop in charge of the investigation. I talked with her Friday evening and this morning. She said she doesn't think it matters but that they would look into it. Do you want me to talk to her again and tell her about the connection between the camp director and Karl Maki and Alex Breyers?" I asked.

He bit his lower lip and squinted at me. The effort made him look like a near-sighted old chipmunk. He finally heaved a sigh, groaned and threw up his hands.

"Of course. We have an ethical obligation to share information if it could save a life. She probably won't listen to you, but you have to try. Now, about tomorrow, leave right after deadline. Now go call that detective."

Unfortunately, Parker was out of the office along with every other trooper assigned to the post. I left a long voice mail, got cut off, called back again and left a second message explaining my conversations with Karl, Alex and Audrey and left my cell phone and work numbers. I had no idea if she'd take me seriously. For Heather's sake, I hoped she would.

Chapter Fourteen

I HADN'T BEEN OFF THE phone more than five minutes when it rang but it wasn't Chris Parker.

"Hi, Robin. Alex Breyers here. My wife said you called yesterday before I got back from Grand Rapids. Did you find out something about Mary Jo?" he asked, his voice full of hope.

I didn't answer right away, knowing I had to speak carefully lest I tip him off to my suspicions about his whereabouts over the weekend.

"Well, I thought I had made a connection with some of the other girls who disappeared but I'm not sure," I said. "A bunch of them attended a summer arts camp on Lake Independence, but Mary Jo never did, at least according to the camp's records."

There was silence on the line for an uncomfortably long time. Finally, Alex said, "I know the one you mean. For years I've been a judge for the juried painting exhibit they hold at the close of the camp. I'm not sure Mary Jo knew about the camp. I know Karl Maki never went and look what a famous artist he is now."

There was a hint of contempt in his voice at the mention of Karl's success.

"Yes, Karl has done quite well for himself. I met him on Saturday," I said, but got no response from Alex so I continued. "About the camp, did you attend as a student?"

He laughed. "No way. I didn't even get into painting until my freshman year at Michigan Tech. I took an art class as an elective and discovered I actually had a little bit of talent, but I loved history and math so much I stuck with industrial archeology as my major. I've never regretted it. In fact, my paintings reflect history. I didn't start selling my work until the mid-Eighties, beginning with starving artist sales. I'm no Dietmar Krumrey or Paul Grant, but there is a small market for my art. "

He sounded sincere, but something didn't add up. It was time to ask the tough question and hope he told me the truth. I really didn't want Alex to be a cold-blooded killer.

"Alex, your wife said you went to an art festival in Grand Rapids. Out of curiosity, I asked a friend of mine about it and she said the only major art festival anywhere within a hundred miles of Grand Rapids in the past two weeks was in Charlotte," I said, leaving the question implied.

The pause at the other end told me he had lied to his wife. Would he cook up a fairy tale for me?

"Look, I don't care if you're having an affair or something like that," I finally said. "I want to know where you were this past weekend because it would sure ease my mind if I knew you weren't anywhere near Rapid River on Friday morning."

"Wait a minute! Do you think I killed Mary Jo? I was fourteen! I certainly had nothing to do with any of the others," he squealed.

"Alex, I'm just covering all the angles. I'm not accusing you of anything. Do you understand my job as a journalist?" I asked.

"Robin, you sound more like Colombo, minus the cigar and rumpled trench coat, than Diane Sawyer," he said, the octave of his voice returning to normal. "All right, here's the truth. I was in Grand Rapids, but not for art. I was visiting my son."

"Your son? I thought you didn't have any kids," I said.

"I don't have any with Karen. Eric is a product of a short-lived relationship with a woman I encountered several years before I met Karen. I didn't even know he existed until about three years ago when his mother called me at work. Eric was having some health problems and she wanted me to undergo some genetic tests. I was in shock. I didn't tell Karen a thing. The tests showed he is indeed my son, and they were able to treat him so he's fine now. He's a sophomore at Davenport College in Grand Rapids. I was visiting him over the weekend, one of about two or three I try to sneak in each year."

"I don't get it. Why the big secret? Karen shouldn't be too upset considering the relationship occurred before the two of you met," I said. There was something Alex wasn't telling me.

"I know it sounds crazy, but Karen always wanted children, but she had breast cancer when she was thirty-two, the kind that runs in families. She had a double mastectomy and a hysterectomy. It threw her into premature menopause. We've talked about adoption over the years, but with her medical history, well, it's just not that simple. Knowing I already had a child would be very hard on her. She already suffers from depression. I don't want to make it worse," Alex said. "Besides, Eric's life has been tough. His mother was married when Eric was conceived. The man he thought was his father was elderly and died many years ago. Having me enter his life now has been, well, upsetting. We're just starting to build a relationship."

"Alex, why do I get the feeling you're hiding something?" I asked.

"Hey, I've told you the truth. What you do with it is your business, but please keep Karen out of this," he yelled.

"I've no intention of bringing Karen into this. By the way, what does Karl Maki have against you? He still harbors some pretty angry sentiments toward you," I said.

"How should I know what Karl's problem is? Maybe he thinks I killed Mary Jo. Maybe he's just nuts. The whole damn family is cracked. His old man was a twisted old grouch even when he was my age and now I hear he has dementia; his uncle suffers from shell shock or some nonsense from his time in Vietnam and makes his living making corpses look pretty since he can't handle the stress of working on Broadway. How's that for an unusual occupation? Why don't you ask Karl yourself why he hates me so much?" Alex snarled.

"I tried. He threw me out. Alex, I'm sorry I've upset you. But remember, you asked me to look into Mary Jo's death. That's all I'm doing. I have no prior issues with you or Karl or anyone else in this case so far," I said.

Alex exhaled loudly into the phone and said, "Don't apologize. You're right; you're doing what I asked you to do. Boy, you are good at it, too. You've made more progress in a week that all those cops have in more than thirty years. Besides, to be honest with you, it's good to finally get this all off my chest. I haven't been able to tell anyone about Eric yet, not even my parents."

"Your secret is safe with me, but you might want to consider getting some counseling. You're carrying a heavy load," I said and hung up the phone. It never ceased to amaze me how people's lives appeared one way to the outside world, but were often very different in reality. Everyone has a secret, even the sweet old man next door.

I left the office at three and drove to Rapid River, parking in the driveway of Louis Stankowski's faded blue one-story cottage just off the highway on Pine Street on the north side of town. The property, including a large old double-door shed beyond the gravel parking lot, looked tidy but old, as though the occupant was concerned about maintenance, but not grand appearances. His appeal on the late news Friday night had been heart-wrenching, but I had to consider him a suspect in his daughter's disappearance. From what Detective Parker had told me, I knew the shift he worked at the plant and figured he'd be home soon if he didn't make any stops between Escanaba and his house. After about five minutes, he arrived in an older dark grey Chevrolet pick-up which he parked next to my Jeep. I got out, extended my hand and introduced myself.

He wore a puzzled expression as he said, "My ex-wife is handling all the media stuff. I'm not very good at that sort of thing. My TV appeal didn't do no good."

"I'm sorry. I know this must be very difficult, but I just have a few questions for you, Mr. Stankowski. I'm not only working on the story of your daughter's disappearance, but that of several other girls around her age over the last few decades."

"Well, okay, what do you want to know?" he asked, setting his aluminum lunch pail on the hood of his truck and eyeing me with curiosity.

"Were Heather's activities normal Friday morning? I mean, did she have an established pattern that someone could watch and determine an opportune time to grab her?" I asked.

He crossed his arms and knitted his sparse brown eyebrows together and considered my question for a minute.

"Yeah, I see what you're saying. Yeah, every other week, Heather was at my house. She always walked back toward her ma's in the morning to catch the bus. It was less confusing that way, and she tended to be a bit on the plump side, which wasn't good for her diabetes, so it was good exercise for her," he said as he shifted his feet. "Are you saying somebody watched my kid for a long time and then took her?"

"It's possible, even likely, that she was targeted by someone she either knew or who knew of her through someone else. Can you think of any friends or relatives who have shown an unusual interest in your daughter in the last few months?"

He shook his head and said, "No, the cops asked me that, too. I don't really let my friends around Heather. I know how guys are and she's growing up and, well, I just don't do it. It's not like I hang with lowlifes or nothing like that, but you gotta protect your own, you know what I mean?"

"Yes, I understand what you're saying. My dad was the same way. Just one more question. I get the feeling the divorce was bitter. Is that true?" I asked.

"That's a pretty nosy question. You're not going to put that in the paper, are you?" he asked, shuffling his feet again.

"No, it's just background."

"Humph. Yeah, it was 'bitter'. There's two sides to every story, though. Believe me, Beth ain't no saint. We manage to be civil for Heather's sake. Look, I want to get in and see if there's anything new from the cops. Are you helping them?" he asked, his brown eyes softening, filling with tears.

"Yes, I'm trying," I said and left him to stand alone in his driveway, waiting helplessly for his only child to return.

Belle was waiting for me at the door when I stopped by my apartment to retrieve her and take her to my dad's house. She knew she was guaranteed a multitude of treats and tummy rubs from her old buddy, a man who had rescued more than a few cats and dogs from burning buildings and treacherous trees over the years.

To my surprise, Aunt Gina's Toyota Prius was in the driveway when I pulled up. She was helping my dad unload his golf clubs from the back of his classic Chevy Stepside. They both waved when I tooted the horn and Aunt Gina grinned and winked when dad went to set the clubs by the utility sink in the back of the garage. I let Belle out of the Jeep and she toddled first to my aunt and then to my dad, anxious for a good scratching.

"Oh, how's my girl?" he said, massaging his fingers over her ears and down her muscular shoulders. She wiggled in ecstasy, tail wagging and nose snuffling his face. He sat back on his haunches and let her slobber over his clean-shaven tanned visage.

"That dog makes a bigger fuss over you than she does over me," I said in mock jealousy.

"You just have to know how to treat a lady," he said with a wide grin and went about tickling her.

I laughed and turned to Aunt Gina. "What are you doing here?"

She sat on the bumper of my dad's truck and studied her nails for a moment, then gave me a solemn smile. "Robin, I've been thinking about you and Hank all weekend and realized that you are both a big part of the Schmidt family. Actually, we three are the only ones left in the U.P. It's time we acted like a family. Monday is my light day at the college so I called your dad; we played a round of golf —"

"She stinks!" a voice yelled from the garage.

"— and we talked," Gina continued after rolling her sparkling grey eyes. "We agreed to a truce for your sake."

"My sake? You guys sound like a divorced couple agreeing to be nice for kids. I just got done hearing the same thing from Louis Stankowski," I said.

She straightened and her eyes flew open. "You talked to him? What did he say?"

I filled her in our conversation and added, "There's no way he harmed her in any way Friday morning. He's just a simple man who lives a simple, unencumbered life. I don't know what the deal is with his ex-wife, but he loves Heather."

We walked inside the one-story ranch in search of food. Since my mother died there twenty-one years before, the house where I grew up had changed little. Decorated in earth tones, it was full of thickly-padded comfortable furniture and family photos, awards and honors on the walls, including a cadre of medals my dad had earned proudly serving in Vietnam as a young Marine, an experience he was always willing to talk about. I had enjoyed growing up here, even after my mother's death, because it was a place of love and refuge. Hank Hamilton, despite his military background and physically demanding occupation as a firefighter, had raised me with a firm but gentle hand. He never uttered an insult about me or my friends, even the one or two who lived on the edge of society's limits. After I graduated from college he had morphed easily from authority figure into the role of the wise mentor, experienced in the ways of human nature. He'd been there for me when Mitch was killed, holding my hand through the funeral and trying to help me find a way to deal with my grief. So I couldn't understand the rift between him and my aunt. Was it really all about religion and family values?

As I was about to further question Aunt Gina, who was taking in the décor of the house, my dad bounded into the kitchen. "What do you ladies feel like eating?"

Before we could answer, Belle began barking and whining, as if excited and frightened all at once. The three of us exchange startled looks and then dashed into the garage through a door in the laundry room. Belle was in the far corner growling at a cloth-draped slab.

"What the hell is wrong with her?" my dad yelled above the howls.

"It's that damn painting!" I said and picked up the squirming basset hound and deposited her safely inside the house. When I'd returned, the cloth had been removed. My dad and Aunt Gina stared at the artwork in bewilderment and horror, respectively.

Shaking his head, my dad said, "I don't get it. I mean, sure it's ugly, but it's not *that* bad."

"Hank," Aunt Gina said, "don't you see it? There's death in that painting. I can feel it."

My dad cast a weary glance at her and then at me as I stared at the swirls of blue, gray, green and brown. There was a face in the clouds hovering above the lake. Concentrating, I drew close and lightly traced the eyes, nose and mouth with my fingers.

"It's a woman," I whispered to no one in particular.

"What? I thought it was supposed to be Lake Superior." my dad said.

"Yes, it is, but see here—" I pointed at a place where the clouds parted high on the canvas and rays of soft moonlight shone through. Below, between the eyes, was another cloud shaped like a nose, straight and finely chiseled. In the waves, lips seemed to be trying to smile — or scream.

"You're right, I see it now. Who painted this? Karl Maki? My god, do you suppose that's Mary Jo, his girlfriend? That would explain the extremely dark emotions emanating from the painting," Aunt Gina said.

"Blech! That's awfully morbid," he said with a groan and shook his shoulders in disgust.

Ignoring him, I said quietly, "Yes, I believe it is Mary Jo," and visualized the photograph pasted at the beginning of the macabre scrapbook detailing her death. The nose was the same. "Mick told me it's not uncommon for artists to paint a picture within a picture. The subconscious picks up on it and feels the emotion the painter is trying to evoke, but the conscious mind doesn't comprehend it. The person looking at the painting may feel haunted by it without ever realizing why."

"Uh-huh. Well, I'm with Belle. It's hideous. When is Michaela going to get this thing out of my garage?" my dad asked, tossing the old bed sheet back over the painting.

"Thanksgiving. You're stuck with it for another month and a half," I said and followed both of them into the kitchen.

"Great. Maybe I'll put it out on the front porch on Halloween and scare off all the little trick-or-treaters. I could save myself a small fortune in candy this year," he said and opened the refrigerator door. "I'm hungry. What'll it be? I have salmon steaks, turkey breasts or frozen pizza?"

"I vote for salmon," Aunt Gina said. I seconded and the three of us worked on various parts of the meal while I laid out all I'd learned in the last few days about the missing girls.

"So Karl Maki is a funeral director. That's an unusual profession for an artist," my dad said.

"Actually, his uncle works there, too, and is apparently quite talented with making the dearly departed look beautiful," I said. "Alex said Karl's dad is manic-depressive and that John, the uncle, has some sort of mental issue going back to the Vietnam War. He served on some mobile river force. I wonder if he has post traumatic stress disorder. Dad, what do you think of that? You came back from the war okay. You've never talked about having any bad memories or flashbacks. Is all that PTSD stuff real?"

He scratched his chin and thought for a moment.

"He was what's called a river rat, part of the Army-Navy Mobile Riverine Force. He probably saw some pretty bad stuff, but that doesn't necessarily mean anything. Most of us saw some pretty bad stuff," my dad said, then he sighed heavily, put down the glass of white wine he'd been sipping and studied the kitchen floor tile. His voice was low when he spoke again. "I went over to that hellhole with my head screwed on straight thanks to a good solid upbringing that provided me with a map for getting through tough times. Wars are terrible things, but people do terrible things to each other all the time. They don't need a war for an excuse to hurt others. You know that better than I do, I suppose, what with losing Mitch the way you did."

I swallowed hard. Yes, I knew.

"But not everyone goes into a war with all their puzzle pieces in place. In those cases, the horrors of war, the things you see, the friends you lose, the people you kill, they can haunt you and drive you to drink or insanity or both. That's not to say the memories never bother me, though," he said. His voice thickened and he swallowed. "Every once in a while, an old song will come on the radio or I'll hear a name and I'll remember the ones who didn't come back. There were far too many."

He wiped a tear that had escaped from his right eye and looked at the ceiling. I wrapped my arms around him and said, "Oh Dad, I'm sorry for bringing it up."

He smiled, his eyes wet, but full of love. "No, that's all right. Sometimes it's good for an old Marine to cry. It proves we're human. We tend to forget that sometimes. I'm just thankful I came home. I try to live my life to the fullest, for all those guys who didn't get the chance," he said.

"Hank, I've never said it before to your face, but you really are a great guy," Aunt Gina said and moved tentatively to give him a hug as well. My dad cleared his throat and Aunt Gina studied the toes of her black lace-up boots, hands behind her back, cheeks slightly red.

"Listen, Hank —"

"Gina, I —"

They both smiled, Gina through tears in her gray eyes, my dad with chagrin. "Let me go first just this once," he said.

Aunt Gina held up her hands and said, "Okay."

"I'm sorry. I guess you're not as bad as I thought."

Aunt Gina blinked a few times and cocked her head to one side. "That's it? I'm not 'as bad' as you thought?"

"Yup."

"Oh, heck, apology accepted. The least we can do is be nice for her sake," she said and waved a hand at me.

"Thanks for making me feel like a five-year-old, guys," I sneered. "Now, can we eat? I'm starving."

The dramatics over, we set the table in the dining room, a little-used alcove that overlooked the back yard. As we ate, the discussion returned to potential suspects, mainly Karl Maki and Alex Breyers.

"I say it's Karl Maki," my dad said. "It would certainly explain that awful thing in the garage. Are the rest of his paintings like that?"

"I don't know, but I'm inclined to agree with you. He's at the top of my list. I have to confirm his whereabouts, though. It would be difficult for him to spend days on end away from the funeral home, scouting potential victims, without someone noticing something odd," I said.

"I agree that it's probably one of those two, but what about Alex?" Aunt Gina said. "We know he's capable of lying, and don't you think it's odd that he asks you to look into this girl's death, and then gets huffy when you start asking questions? I'd look a little more closely at his whereabouts when all these girls disappeared."

"I don't have the resources to do that," I wailed. "Besides, time is running out for Heather. If her kidnapper hasn't killed her yet, she's in serious trouble from lack of insulin. She could go into a diabetic coma and suffer permanent kidney damage." I got up and started clearing the table. "What I need to do is put all of this into that detective's lap and get her department to look into the backgrounds of these two guys. This has gotten way too big for one measly small-town newspaper reporter to handle."

They both nodded glumly and helped me fill the dishwasher.

After leaving my dad and Aunt Gina engaged in a conversation about "emanations," Belle and I went home, tired and stuffed with food, but I had one more phone call to make before going to bed.

It was seven-thirty Chicago time when we got back to the apartment. I dug through one of the many catch-all drawers in the kitchen and found my old address book full of the names, numbers and addresses of friends and sources from my days at the Tribune. I wanted to know if there was even a kernel of truth to Sylvia Danelli's story about her late husband's enemies taking her granddaughter. Niccolo Granati, or Nick, was a homicide detective with a downtown precinct of the Chicago Police Department and had gone through the police academy with Mitch, although Mitch had left the department after a few years, hating the bureaucracy. Nick — young, gorgeous and a brilliant investigator — knew more about organized crime than John Gotti's consigliore. I had never been able to determine if Nick was a wise guy himself or just an attentive, street-wise bystander. It didn't matter to me because he had proved to be a friend and a reliable source many times over the years. It was Nick who had helped me pack up the apartment after Mitch was murdered, and it was Nick who had promised to never rest until the shooter was found, even though it didn't happen on his turf.

He picked up on the fourth ring, his thick ethnic accent, belying an agile mind.

"Nick, it's Robin. How's life treating you these days?" I asked.

"Robin, how ya doin'? I was just thinking about you and wondering if you were okay. What've you been up to up there in the north woods?" he asked.

"Well, let's see, last Friday a little ol' lady named Sylvia Danelli pointed a shotgun at my chest. I broke my ankle jumping from a burning building this summer, and I'm on the trail of a possible serial killer. Other than that, nothin' special," I said.

His laugh was full and loud. "Sounds like normal to me. You've always been a pisshead. Your parents should have named you Buzzard, not Robin. You're always swooping in and causing trouble," he said.

"Buzzard doesn't quite have the same ring to it. Hey, I didn't call to be insulted, I called to pick your brain," I said.

"And how is that not like a buzzard?" he asked, his smile coming through the phone.

"Funny. Have you ever heard of a guy named Frank Danelli? He would have been active some time during the Fifties maybe," I said.

"There's lots of Danellis down here. What was his racket?" Nick asked.

"His wife said he did some work for Giancanna and then moved to the U.P. to hide from some people," I said, trying to recall Sylvia's tale of her late husband's unusual activities.

"Sam had a lot of soldiers in the Fifties. Those were kind of his heydays until Bobby Kennedy started breathing fire up his ass. I can't say the name Frank Danelli sets off any bells. Why?"

"His granddaughter vanished in August of Ninety-three. I'm thinking she's a victim of that potential serial killer I mentioned earlier, but her grandmother, Sylvia, said she was taken away and murdered by enemies of

Frank as revenge for something he did. You know how it is, I have to rule out a thousand other things before zeroing in on the real suspect," I said, doodling little circles in the space next to his name in the address book.

"Sure, but I can tell you right now the old lady's having delusions of grandeur. Too much time had passed if he left Chicago in the Fifties and had nothing more to do with the Outfit. Nobody would haul ass to the sticks to snatch his grandkid three decades later. Him, maybe, but not the kid. They don't have time for that. Hell, by then, most of his enemies were probably dead or in prison," Nick said.

"Right, that's what I figured," I said and looked down at my doodles. In the margin was Mitch's name. My hand gripped the pen as I asked, "Nick, anything new on Mitch?"

"Um, no, not that I know of. Look, I gotta go. I'll let you know if I hear something," he said, and hung up before I could say goodbye.

Chapter Fifteen

NICK'S UNCHARACTERISTICALLY ABRUPT ANSWER to my question about the investigation into Mitch's death led to a nearly sleepless night as images of my dead fiancé flashed in my weary mind. I finally fell asleep sometime after two-thirty, only to be jarred awake by Belle's frantic barking. Actually, basset hounds don't bark so much as yodel loudly — aroof-woof-roooo-ruh-roooo — when they're upset.

"Not again," I grumbled, throwing off the covers and climbing out of bed. I cursed when my bare feet hit the cold hardwood floor. The colorful rag rug that was usually next to my bed was now in a ball underneath it, probably kicked there by Belle when she'd jumped off the bed to investigate whatever was bothering her now. She was standing in the kitchen, barking at the window above the sink. With the lights off, I peered into the back yard, dimly lit by a few light fixtures attached to garages along the alley. All appeared quiet, but Belle was not in the habit of barking about nothing. I tried to hush her and detect any sound or movement. Nothing but stillness. I was tempted to get dressed and go outside for a look. Then I remembered how easily all those girls had disappeared without anyone seeing a thing.

Had he come for me? Perhaps he was out there now, crouched behind a fence or a garbage can, lying in wait for his prey to make her naïve appearance. No, I thought, I'll leave this one to the police. I dialed 911 and scratched Belle behind an ear as I explained there was an intruder in the neighborhood. Five minutes later, an Escanaba Public Safety cruiser turned off Fifth Street into the alley. The officer stopped by the garage after shining a spotlight this way and that down the alley and into back yards. A second car pulled in behind him while a third arrived from the north. All three men got out and stood in front of the garage, out of my line of sight.

"What the hell is going on down there?" I asked aloud. Pulling on a pair of jeans, sweatshirt and sneakers and grabbing a coat, I dashed down the stairs and out the back door. One of the officers came around the corner of the garage when he heard the door slam.

"Are you the one who called us, Ma'am?" asked the young man with close-cropped dark hair and a trim, yet powerful figure.

"Yes. Did you find something?" I asked in return.

"Follow me, please," he said, crooking a long finger at me.

I wasn't sure what I expected to see as I rounded the corner of the garage, but it definitely wasn't an eye dripping three bloody-looking teardrops. The spotlight mounted on the driver's side of the patrol car parked in front of the garage cast a blinding beam at the white slab of steel that served as the door for the two-car garage Mrs. Easton and I shared. Someone had painted, in thin red strokes, an eye, complete with pupil, lashes and flecks in the iris, that turned up slightly at the far corner and dripped teardrops from the inside corner. I sniffed the air but didn't sense the usual chemical smell associated with spray paint. The eye had a garish sheen that blazed out at us in the cold night under the glare of the spotlight.

"What is that? It doesn't smell like paint," I said.

One of the officers approached the eye, dabbed his thumb in the pupil and sniffed the red residue. "I don't know. It doesn't really smell like anything, but it feels greasy," he said, appearing confused.

I stepped forward and looked at his thumb.

"It's lipstick," I said.

The three officers stood behind me in stunned silence. Every hair on my body felt like it was standing at attention. I could feel the killer's eyes boring down on us from some secret hiding place. I scanned the alley and back yards that surrounded us, but, of course, saw nothing. He, or she, was too smart for that.

"Any idea who did this?" a thirty-something blonde with sergeant's stripes on his jacket finally asked.

Logic dictated it could have been the work of a couple of bored kids with nothing better to do than deface other people's property. But kids would likely use spray paint, not cosmetics. No, this drawing was personal, meant to convey a message, most likely to me. Should I bother to explain all this to three young cops with no idea who I was or on what I was working?

I shrugged and nodded my head all at once. "Yes and no. It's a long story. I don't have a specific person in mind, unfortunately," I said in a low voice, afraid *he*, or *she*, might hear me. Had I been wrong all along to assume it must be a man behind the disappearances simply because they involved girls of a certain age? But if it was a woman, who was a potential suspect?

"Audrey," I whispered to myself.

"What?" the sergeant asked, leaning toward me.

"Nothing. I don't know who did this, but I can guess what it's about. I'm sure it's related to the stories I'm working on about Heather Stankowski and some other missing girls," I said.

"You're the cops-and-courts reporter with the Press, aren't you?" the sergeant asked.

"Yes, I'm Robin Hamilton." I stuck out my hand and he enveloped it in his large cold grip.

"Keith Daniels. That's Craig Johnson," he said, nodding at the dark-haired cop who had first approached me, "and this is Scott Mattson." A tall, thick-set guy who looked like he'd been a linebacker in high school waved a gloved hand at me.

"So you think this has something to do with your job, like maybe the guy who snatched that girl from Rapid River is now after you because of what you've written?" he asked. He sounded skeptical.

"Yes, that's my guess, and I'm not sure it's a guy. Most guys don't walk around with a tube of lipstick in their pocket. Can you take a sample of that and have it analyzed at a lab to find out the manufacturer? I would be willing to bet the person responsible for taking Heather Stankowski and a bunch of other teenage girls over the last thirty-two years has that same lipstick in their possession," I said, pointing at the glistening eye that mocked my every word.

The three officers stared at me in disbelief.

"Look, Charlie Baker knows all about it. I've been looking into the disappearance of six girls, the first one vanishing in 1974. From the looks of this fine piece of graffiti, I'd say I've kicked a hornets' nest," I said.

"It would seem so," Officer Mattson said drolly, pushing his dark saucer cap back on his head and eyeing the garage door with curiosity.

The back door slammed again causing all four of us to jump, and then Rose Easton appeared around the corner of the garage.

"Is something ... Good lord! What on earth is that all about?" she shrieked and pointed at the eye.

"I'm sorry, Mrs. Easton. This is meant for me, not you. I'll take care of washing it off later," I said and put my arm around her shoulders.

She pulled her terrycloth bathrobe tighter around her stout frame and swept a strand of silver hair off her face.

"Robin, I don't care about the door. I want to know who did this and why. Are you in danger?" she asked, encircling an arm around my waist. I didn't answer, but instead looked back at the eye, which seemed to be watching us, taking in our fear of the unknown, unseen, unheard artist, and laughing.

After taking several digital photographs and statements from me and Mrs. Easton, who had heard nothing, not even Belle's barking, the officers left. It was almost five, so I showered, fed Belle, walked her around the block (with my cell phone tucked in my pocket and a long heavy flashlight in my hand) and ate a bowl of cereal. I made the rounds of the police stations early and was seated in front of my computer by six-thirty. There were no messages from Detective Christine Parker, which I found odd. Was she simply not going to take me seriously? There was a message from Beth Stankowski, though, wondering if I'd found anything to connect Heather's disappearance to the summer camp. What could I say? There was only scant circumstantial evidence and a gut feeling that someone involved with that camp was also responsible for snatching all those girls. Magistrates didn't issue search warrants based on gut feelings.

I pulled out a sheet of notebook paper and divided it into three columns, with the names Karl Maki, Audrey Gaston and Alex Breyers at the top of each section. Karl and Alex were in close proximity to Mary Jo Quinn the day she went missing. Plus Karl had easy access to lipstick since it was required for preparing the bodies for viewing. Of course, Alex, or anyone else for that matter, could easily obtain a tube of lipstick. As far as Audrey, I had no idea about Audrey, not her whereabouts, her age, or even her size in relation to Mary Jo at the time of her disappearance. And if she did kill Mary Jo and the others, why? What would prompt such action? I groaned. Those last two questions applied to any suspect, not just the Houghton triumvirate, as I was now thinking of Karl, Audrey and Alex.

I dialed the number for Heather's mother, figuring she'd be up and about, even at this early hour. Her voice was tired but awake when she answered. I filled her in on my conversation with Audrey, with whom Beth had never spoken, and told her of my plans to go up to the camp later in the day. There was no news on Heather, not a phone call, sighting or even a tip.

"Beth, as a mother, what do you think happened to Heather?" I asked, knowing there are intangible bonds that link souls in ways that reveal things the eyes cannot see. Caroline Baxter's mother had said she sensed that her daughter was dead; perhaps Beth had some inkling in her bones about her child as well.

"Oh, Robin," she sobbed. "I had the most awful dream last night. She was in a dark room surrounded by dead bodies and they were all staring at her. She was crying out for me, but I couldn't touch her. It was like I wasn't there. She couldn't hear me or see me. It was horrible. My God, I'm losing my mind. I can't live like this. I have to know where she is!"

She was screaming by the time she finished. I knew how she felt. My nightmares of late had been enough to make Wes Craven or Stephen King squirm in their skin.

"Beth, is there anyone with you right now?" I asked.

She sniffed and choked out, "Yes, my boyfriend came home yesterday and is staying here. He's upstairs asleep."

"Go wake him up and tell him what you just told me. It'll help you get a handle on reality," I said. It occurred to me how funny it was that I was able to dole out advice but never seemed to take it very well, remembering my dad's many admonitions to get counseling after Mitch was killed.

Beth agreed, though, and we hung up after I promised to stop by after meeting with Audrey. By then it was seven o'clock so I tried calling Parker's office again at the state police post in Gladstone. A desk sergeant answered and informed me in a staccato tone that she was expected in at eight and would call me "if she has time." I felt like telling him to stick his phone somewhere unpleasant and then thought better of it. No one cares about pissing off a reporter, but pissing off a cop can have long-term inconvenient ramifications.

I typed a quick e-mail to Mick in New York and asked if she knew much about Karl Maki's background, hoping she would check her messages before heading to work. Then I tapped my fingers on the desk and stared at the clock. I really didn't want to wait around the office for Parker to call back. I felt like time was slipping away; time for what, I wasn't sure. Time to find Heather alive? Time to catch the kidnapper? The person seemed to strike every six or seven years so there didn't seem to be much danger of him, or her, snatching another girl any time soon. Of course, the kidnapper, if that was who drew that picture on my garage, obviously knew where to find me since the person had left his or her bizarre calling card. I considered the strange painting on the garage door while I waited for Bob Hunter to get into the office. He was running late.

I felt the eye was a warning that the culprit was watching me. But what about the tears dripping from the corner, as if the eye was crying? The symbolism confirmed in my mind that whoever was behind these disappearances was creative, intelligent, maybe even gifted. The Upper Peninsula is a little known haven for all sorts of artists, from painters to potters. Its rugged landscape and hundreds of miles of lakeshore inspired the soul, calling out to the primal nature in all of us, urging us to get back in touch with the earth. I'd felt it myself many times watching one of the

Great Lakes lap the shoreline and lull me into a trance, feeling at one with the water and its cycles. There were places in the far reaches of the region where, if you sat quiet as the grave, you could almost hear the voices and soft footfalls of the natives who had traversed the forests, echoes of the miners who had toiled in the ground in search of iron and copper, and the shouts of sailors who had ridden the waves of Lake Superior during a November gale. This killer had a soul that understood all of that, albeit a very old, damaged soul.

Bob Hunter kicked my desk, startling me from my daydreaming. "Anything new?" he barked.

I followed him into his office and told him about the masterpiece drawn on my garage door.

"Lipstick graffiti? This guy must be a real whack job, Robin. I don't like this. You just healed up from one encounter with a criminal. You sure you want to keep pursuing these cases? I'd understand if you turned all this over to the cops and let them do with it what they will," he said as he peeled a banana.

"Bob, honestly, I'd love to do just that. This is too big for me. We don't have the resources to track down the whereabouts of people or the skills to handle 'whack jobs,' as you call them," I said and swiped a large paper clip from his desk and began pulling it apart. "The problem is, I can't get that damn detective to call me back, and no one else over there seems interested in anything I have to say. That means I'm the only one following these leads."

He lifted his bushy gray eyebrows. "Really? That's kind of odd. The state cops aren't usually so dismissive of reporters. They almost always tell us to buzz off rather than just ignoring us."

"Yeah, well, I'm not waiting around for Parker to call. Is it all right if I hit the road now? I've got a lot of things to look into today."

"Sure, but keep in touch. Check in with me at lunch and then again when you head back this way. If I don't hear from you by eight this evening, I'm calling the cavalry," Bob said.

I checked my e-mail and was happy to see a reply from Mick. After wading through three paragraphs about how wonderful her new husband Miguel was, I finally got what I wanted. Karl Maki began painting in high school, winning a national competition as a senior. He could have gone to any of the top art schools in the country, but chose to attend Northern Michigan University in Marquette, about a hundred miles southeast of Houghton, to be close to his family. Apparently, he'd always planned to take over the business because immediately after earning his bachelor's degree, he attended mortuary science school for two years in Lower Michigan and returned home. He'd married, had children, run the business and kept painting, gradually building a reputation for his oils despite missing the big art shows in New York or Los Angeles. His paintings were often described as somber, soulful and powerful. The *New York Times* featured him last winter, the reporter traveling to Houghton to interview him, describing him as a "brooding individual, seemingly full of secrets, dark secrets that you and I could never understand."

I dashed off a quick reply thanking her for the information and promising to update her later. Then, after leaving the phone number for Audrey Gaston's office with our receptionist "just in case," I drove back to the apartment and hefted Belle into the Jeep. She'd be cooped up in the car for several hours, but a voice whispered from a corner room in my mind that I needed to bring her along. I'd learned not to question those voices.

The sky began to lighten gradually, although it was obscured by thick clouds that threatened more torrential rain as we made the turn onto the highway toward Rapid River. A continuous trail of vehicles, their headlights providing more illumination than the meager daylight, headed into Escanaba, the center of commerce locally, in what amounted to "rush hour" for Delta County. Before going to Marquette to see the mysterious Audrey Maki Gaston, I wanted to check out the place where the cops found Heather's backpack, to get a feel for what she might have seen, how the kidnapper could approach her and how no one else had seen anything out of the ordinary. The bag had been found near the fence surrounding a small playground at the corner of South Main and Cleveland Streets. I got out of the Jeep and walked around the place where I'd remembered seeing the yellow crime scene tape. Standing in the approximate spot on the sidewalk where her bag had been found, I surveyed the neighborhood. At least five houses had a clear view of the playground. Whatever happened to Heather must have been quick and quiet. I closed my eyes and tried to picture the scene as it would have looked around six-thirty Friday morning. She would have just turned the corner from South Main on to Cleveland. A responsible girl who liked school, she was probably walking at a swift pace to make sure she wouldn't be late. Someone pulled up next to her, someone she recognized. Perhaps they spoke to her. Unable to hear, she might have readjusted her backpack, probably slung over one shoulder as opposed to secured on her back, and moved closer to the vehicle. That's when hands reached out and grabbed her.

"She not der no more."

I jumped and whirled around at the sound of the slurred voice behind me. A short man, who I estimated to be somewhere around twenty-five, stood on the sidewalk about ten feet away from me. His thick horn-rimmed glasses magnified soft blue eyes spaced much too far apart over a small nose and cheeks flush with the morning chill.

"I'm sorry. What did you say?" I asked.

He huffed and jerked his hands inside the pockets of the tan coat that hung loosely on his chubby figure.

"She not der no more," he said.

"Who's not here? Heather?"

"Yes, Heather." It sounded like "header." He couldn't enunciate the "th" sound.

"What happened to her?" I asked, taking a step toward him. He stood his ground and eyed me with interest.

"She nice. I miss her. She was nice to me," he said, his voice dropping.

"Yes, Heather is very nice. Nice people are pretty cool, aren't they?" I asked.

"Yeah," he said and beamed. He was a good two inches shorter than me, but his diminutive body held a humongous heart.

"Where did Heather go?" I asked.

"In da van," he stated.

"What van?" I asked, my heart thudding in my chest. Did the cops know he saw something? Did the kidnapper know?

"Da van dat was over der," he said and pointed at the parking lot of a church on the other side of Cleveland Street.

"Did she go over to the van at the church?" I asked.

"No, no, no," he said, shaking his head as if I were being silly. "Da van was der when she left."

He was now pointing at where Heather's backpack had been found.

"What's your name?" I asked.

"Danny."

"Danny, my name's Robin. I want to find Heather. Will you help me?" I held out my hand for him to shake. He looked at it a moment and then smiled and took it one of his sweaty, soft palms.

"Okay."

"Great. Danny, what color was the van?"

"Brown, like dat," he said, indicating a two-story frame house on the corner with deep tan siding and black shutters.

"Did you ever see who drove the van?" I asked. Please, please, please say yes, my mind screamed.

"Sure. It was an ugly woman," he said. An ugly woman? Was Audrey ugly? How could he have seen her — it was still quite dark when Heather was taken. Perhaps Heather had opened the door, causing the interior light to come on and cast a glow on the driver.

"How do you know it was a woman driving, Danny? Did you hear what she said to Heather?" I asked.

He started to answer when a silver-haired woman with a kind face stuck her head around the screen door of a one-story ranch across the street on South Main and called, "Danny! Honey, it's time for breakfast, c'mon inside." She stepped onto the small cement front porch when she spotted me.

"Gotta go. Dat my mom," he said and trotted across the street, taking care to look both ways several times. I started to follow but stopped when his mother gave me a stern look. As soon as Danny was inside, she slammed the door behind him, making it clear there would be no further discussion. At least I had another solid clue — a brown van had been parked nearby, its occupant waiting for just the right time to make a move on the young girl unaware she was walking into a trap.

Chapter Sixteen

I GOT BACK IN THE Jeep and tried calling Detective Chris Parker again, feeling like an old scratched vinyl record that repeated the same line over and over. I could tell the desk sergeant was as tired of me as I was of him. No, she hadn't come in yet. Yes, he would have her call me. I told him to tell her there was a possible witness to Heather's disappearance, a young man who probably had Down Syndrome, and that he had seen Heather get into a brown van, possibly driven by a woman.

"I'll tell her, but that whole neighborhood was canvassed numerous times and nobody told us a damn thing. The guy probably imagined the whole thing after seeing the media reports. You can't rely on someone like that," the sergeant said.

I wanted to say, "Are you always this much of a jerk or did you just feel like making a special effort today?" Instead, I thanked him for his insight, debated asking for the post commander and then disconnected the line. What would be the point? Where the hell was Parker? She would be able to talk to Danny. I got back out of the Jeep and slammed the door with enough force to rock the truck. Belle looked at me with wonder.

"I'll be right back," I told her and walked across the street to the Rapid River Congregational Church where Danny had said the van had been parked at some point.

The small white wood-sided chapel reminded me of the sort shown on postcards of small towns in Vermont, idyllic and quaint. A parish hall was located behind the structure and the parsonage, a modern two-story white house, was west of the church. The chapel was locked, so I tried the parsonage next, knocking on the door, but received no answer. Walking around to the parish hall, I met a woman with short curly brown hair and sensible shoes coming out the front door.

"Excuse me," I said. "I'm a reporter with the *Daily Press*. I was wondering if I could ask you a question or two about the disappearance of one of your neighbors."

Recognition flashed across her pudgy face as her hand flew to her chest.

"Oh my, yes, Heather Stankowski. She and her mom attended services here occasionally. Such a nice girl. I'm afraid I wasn't here when she was kidnapped. I'm the church secretary and I usually don't come to the church until about nine, so I won't be much help," she said.

"That's okay. Actually, what I'd like to know is whether you ever saw a tan or light brown van parked in front of the church in the days before Heather was taken," I said.

She thought for a moment and then shook her head and frowned. "No, I can't recall anything like that. I'm sorry, but we're a small congregation and I know everyone who walks through our doors. I also know their vehicles. I can't think of a single member of our church that drives a van that color. I see lots of green minivans and blue ones and white ones, but no tan or brown ones," she said.

"Well, this wouldn't have belonged to a member, but it sounds like you would have noticed something out of the ordinary. Thanks for your time," I said and walked back to the Jeep. It had been a long shot, but I was still disappointed she hadn't seen the van. I was hoping the kidnapper had parked there a few times in the week leading up to Heather's disappearance, scouting her every move in search of an opportunity to grab her.

Once inside the Jeep I pulled my cell phone out again and called Dr. Jennifer O'Connell's number. Her secretary, back from her medical leave, answered. She put me through to the psychologist after a short wait.

"Robin, what's new with these girls? I've been following the news and see another one has gone missing. Is it related to what we talked about last week?" she asked breathlessly.

"I'm certain it is. I wanted to bounce a few things off you," I said and told her about the drawing on the garage and the link to the summer arts camp. Dr. O'Connell pondered these items briefly, asked me a few detailed questions and then gave me her diagnosis.

"There's a gender issue here. I still think you're dealing with a man, but I would say he has some gender confusion. Perhaps he is fascinated by girls around age fourteen because that's when he started having problems with his own identity," she said.

"That's kind of a stretch, isn't it?" I said. "I mean, I went to a few bars in Chicago where I ran into people I knew who turned out to be cross dressers. They were otherwise perfectly normal people who wouldn't harm a soul. They were just living out some fantasy or having a good time." I told her about the time I had been shocked to see one of the Tribune's award-winning city reporters, a rather macho-looking Latino, wearing a daring hot pink wrap dress and high heels one evening at an upscale club downtown. Not knowing how to react, I tried to avoid eye contact, but he spotted me, came over and sat down and explained his startling appearance quite simply. "I'd rather be a girl. It's more fun, but God made me a man, so I come here to play. Some people play golf; I dress up like a chica," he'd said.

Dr. O'Connell laughed and said, "Of course being a homosexual or transsexual doesn't make you a murderer, but just as there are warped heterosexuals, there can be warped people struggling with gender issues. You're obviously straight as an arrow so you never questioned who you are as a person, but it can be a tough thing to handle, especially for men raised to be tough."

"Okay, what about the eye? If this person has gender issues, as you say, perhaps he's running around with tubes of red lipstick. I took the eye as a warning that whoever drew it is watching me, but what do the tears dripping from the eye mean?" I asked.

"Sorrow, regret, fear, anger. Tears can mean lots of things. Humans are a strange lot in that we cry when we're laughing, grieving or sharing a beautiful moment with someone we love. I'd say the eye is a combination of an expression of sorrow and a way to let you know he knows who you are and where you live. Robin, I urge you to be very, very careful. This man is not someone with whom you can reason," she said.

I thanked her for her help and flipped my phone closed. Great, I thought, a confused psycho who knows just where to find me. Droplets of rain were starting to dot the windshield. I hadn't noticed the clouds rolling in, so intent was I on Dr. O'Connell's assessment. After writing down the psychologist's thoughts and the vague description Danny had given me of the van and its occupant, I thought about calling Parker's office yet again. Something was wrong. Why hadn't she called me back by now? She had not been enthusiastic about my theory of one person behind all the disappearances, but she hadn't treated me like a crackpot either. The last time we spoke Monday she said she would follow up on the Great Lakes Summer Institute lead. Had she gone up there, only to fall into the clutches of the killer? I tried to think of any contacts I had with the state police other than Parker and the desk sergeant, but my old sources from my first stint at the *Daily Press* more than six years ago had either retired or transferred to other posts, as was normal in a statewide operation. I'd always had a high opinion of the state police. State troopers were well-trained, well-paid and usually highly-dedicated cops, especially the detectives, so her handling of the case seemed out of character for the department.

Rather than waiting until I returned from the camp, I decided to stop by Heather's house and check on her mother now. The driveway was empty and the house looked dark, but the front door opened before my foot hit the first step to the porch. Beth Stankowski emerged from behind the screen door, looking bedraggled and bedeviled.

"Have you found anything out?" she asked, her eyes red and swollen.

"Possibly. Have you heard from the cops?" I asked and followed her into the house.

"Someone from the state police post called about an hour ago asking if that detective had been here, but that was it. I haven't seen her or anyone else for that matter," she said and plopped onto the couch. "This is maddening. What the hell's going on? Has the detective disappeared, too?" She picked up a bracelet from the coffee table in front of her. Made of sterling silver, it held several little charms including a red ladybug and bejeweled butterfly. Beth fingered a tiny cross, closed her eyes tightly and drew a deep breath before exhaling.

"I have prayed and prayed and prayed, but all I hear is silence — from the police, my neighbors, God ... from Heather. Where is she? Why can't someone tell me where she is?" she said through gritted teeth.

I sat next to her and held out my hand for the bracelet. She understood and let it slip from her long slim fingers. It was hot, full of a mother's energy. Wrapping my fingers around the chain, I said, "Beth, right now, only two people know what's happened to your daughter — Heather and her abductor. If we are going to find her alive, we have to focus on what we know and how it fits together."

I opened my hand and studied the bracelet, all the while listening as Beth's breathing evened and she grew calm. One charm struck me as particularly fitting the young artist. Dangling on the link before the clasp was a pallet of paint like those used by oil painters. Each dab of paint was a different colored stone.

"This is lovely. Where did she get it?" I asked, caressing the tiny pallet.

"Isn't it nice? That was a gift from someone at the camp," Beth said.

"Did she say who it was who gave it to her? Maybe there was someone there who took an inordinate interest in her," I said.

Beth scrunched her forehead, then shook her head. "No, she didn't say anything specific. If it would have bothered her, I think she would have confided in me. She just acted like it was no big deal, and I didn't think anything of it," she said.

I returned the bracelet to her and told her about my conversation with Danny. Her eyes lit up and she rose from the couch.

"My God, he saw something? Why didn't he say so earlier? I know the police went house to house to see if anyone saw anything. I don't understand," she said, pacing the small living room.

"I'm sure his mother is the one who talked to police and either didn't want to get her son involved or just assumed he hadn't seen anything. I didn't talk to her, but the look she gave me was one of a mother bear protecting her cubs. She probably tries to shield Danny as much as possible from the real world," I said.

"Yes, you're right. Heather and Danny have been friends for a few years now. He's at least a decade older than her, but he's so sweet. Their friendship seemed to bring them both a lot of joy, so I never intervened. Eventually his mother even let Danny come over here a few times. I'll go talk to her, maybe she'll let me talk to Danny," Beth said.

I looked at my watch and stood. It was now past nine o'clock and I still had a lot of work to do.

"Beth, I'll be honest with you. I don't have a good feeling about Parker. I think something's happened to her. If you learn anything, call the police immediately. I already told them about the van, but keep bugging them," I said, adding, "Did you ever see a van like that in the neighborhood or any other strange vehicles around here last week?"

"No, the police asked me that, too. I can't recall any, though. This street isn't a throughway so we don't see much traffic," she said, crossing her arms and staring out the window at the empty street.

"I've got to get going if I'm going to have enough time to talk with the camp director and see the place for myself. Will you call me if you hear from Parker?" I asked.

"Absolutely, I have your card handy," she said and walked with me to the Jeep. The rain had subsided for the time being, but thick dark clouds still obscured the autumn sun. Belle was seated on the driver's side watching two chipmunks chase each other around a mammoth maple tree in the front yard.

"What a funny looking dog! What's her name?" Beth asked with a rare smile spreading across her careworn face.

"Her name's Belle. She's a basset hound and a spoiled brat," I said and opened the door. Giving Belle a shove, I got in, shut the door and rolled down the window. Beth placed her hands on the door frame and leaned back, stretching her arms.

"Robin, I appreciate you spending so much time on this story. I never knew small town reporters were so dedicated. Thank you," she said and squeezed my left forearm. "I feel I can trust you."

I mumbled something inane like, "Just doing my job," and backed out of the driveway, wishing I was anything but a reporter hunting for a scared young girl and a murderer.

Chapter Seventeen

AUDREY GASTON WAS DEFINITELY NOT an ugly woman. Her dark blonde hair was highlighted and fell in a shoulder-grazing geometric bob, a la Vidal Sassoon. Her chocolate brown pantsuit had the clean lines and quality construction of ready-to-wear high fashion and was accented by a silk scarf in a brilliant autumn foliage pattern. The ensemble fit her athletic frame to perfection, each curve highlighted in a discreet, yet appealing manner. A gold circle clasped the ends of the scarf just below the hollow of her long pale neck. She sat with her slim fingers entwined and resting in front of her on an expansive black modern desk with sections jutting off at forty-five degree angles from the central workspace. One side consisted of a computer station while an oxblood leather-clad briefcase rested on the other side.

The office occupied the third floor of a building overlooking Lake Superior in downtown Marquette. Outside, the gray water churned with whitecaps as a northwest wind howled across the massive lake, but inside it was eerily silent. I could barely hear the hum of her computer and not a hint of a heating and ventilation system. Ms. Gaston obviously didn't believe in clutter as there was not even a stray paper clip or speck of lint to be found anywhere in the sparsely-furnished room.

She had not been pleased to see me when I'd knocked on her door, but now was beaming at me with perfect white teeth after I'd asked if I could do a story on the camp itself.

"I'd love to show you the camp. I have to run up there today anyway to check on some maintenance issues. You simply must feature us in your newspaper. We haven't received much financial support from the Escanaba area, so any publicity would be wonderful," she said, grinning like a lonely, insecure woman who'd just received a marriage proposal. She seemed to have forgotten all about our prior discussion of the five missing campers. My reporter's instinct told me that reminding her of them wasn't in my best interest, either, if I intended to get much information out of her, so I played off her hunger for publicity.

"Great. I'm sure my editor will be thrilled with something out of the ordinary like this. When can we leave?" I asked.

"Right now, if you like. Although," she stopped to look out the window, "the weather isn't going to cooperate if you want exterior photos."

"No problem. You can always e-mail pictures of the camp in session. Photos with attendees at work would be more interesting anyway, don't you think?" I said.

"Of course, you're right. We have plenty of them on file. We already have signed releases from the parents allowing us to use photos of their children for publicity purposes. They sign all sorts of forms like that before the artists arrive," she said, rising from her desk and moving toward the door.

Just then I saw the photograph on the windowsill behind her chair. It was Alex Breyers, a much younger version of Alex, but the resemblance was uncanny. The black and white studio photo was encased in a simple black metal eight-by-ten frame and depicted an athletic-looking young man with a bright smile and sharp eyes standing near some sort of old bridge across a creek.

"Who is the handsome young man?" I asked.

Audrey Gaston turned and looked at me with a question in her eyes and then followed where I was pointing to the photo. She smiled warmly.

"That's my son, Eric. That was taken during his senior year of high school. He's a sophomore at Davenport College downstate. He wants to follow in his father's footsteps and go into banking," she said.

Father? I almost snorted at the lie. At least that was one mystery solved. That explained one reason why Karl despised Alex so much — he'd had an affair with Karl's sister and fathered a child. It must have really stung him if Karl really believed Alex was responsible for Mary Jo Quinn's death. "It's always about Alex, isn't it," he had sneered on Saturday. Should I let Audrey know I knew the truth or let it pass? I still had so much to learn about the camp that I decided to leave it alone for now.

"You must be very proud of him," was all I said and followed her trail of Chanel No. 5 out of the office and down to the street.

She led the way to the camp in her black Volvo wagon up County Road 550 to Big Bay, a tiny community made famous by the novel "Anatomy of a Murder" and the subsequent movie starring James Stewart and Lee Remick. We passed the iconic Thunder Bay Inn and then turned down a gravel road that wound around to the west side of Lake Independence where the Great Lakes Summer Institute took up forty acres. Several hardwood trees had shed their foliage, leaving them a darker shade of gray than the sky, which seemed to be in mourning. A massive wooden sign set in stone pillars announced the entrance to the camp. A two-piece gate of green-painted steel across the road provided the only security I could see. Audrey got out of her car, unlocked the padlock of the chain holding the gate shut and swung it open. We made fresh tracks in the dirt, washed clean by the morning rain, as we drove to a large two-story log structure with a metal placard in front stating it was the administration building.

Taking Belle with me, I met Audrey on the wide front steps leading to the metal double doors painted forest green. The air smelled earthy with the fragrance of wet decaying leaves mingling with the scent of the lake. Despite the dreary weather, the camp was stunning in its simple beauty, casting a spell of tranquility upon its visitors. Two white-tailed deer stood at the eastern edge of the property, studying us in silence while a flock of Canada geese honked overhead, languidly making their way south for the winter.

"I could spend every day of my life here and never get bored," I said, swept up in the comforting arms of Mother Nature.

"You're a writer. How come you didn't spend a summer here?" she asked, her arms crossed over her chest as though she were cold. I cocked an eyebrow at her and she laughed. "I looked your name up in the computer."

I smirked. "I didn't hear of this place until a few days ago. I never showed much talent for anything in school. I got good grades and all that, but I kept a low profile," I said. High school had been a bust for me, a seemingly endless stream of nonsensical proms, homecomings, and beer parties that captivated my classmates but left me feeling out of place. I had gladly skipped my ten-year class reunion, thumbing my nose not so much at the people as the notion that high school was something worth reminiscing about.

"That's too bad," Audrey said. "You have the soul of an artist — an old soul, full of wisdom and the colors of life. You're a sponge, soaking up the chaos of your surroundings and arranging them in a way that makes sense to the rest of us. That's a gift."

I turned to her in surprise. It was a remarkably perceptive thing to say and something I hadn't expected from a middle-aged woman driving a forty-thousand-dollar luxury car and wearing designer clothing, all the while living in the most rural part of Michigan.

"How did you end up here?" I asked.

She stepped down onto a pathway of wood chips that led toward some of the other buildings and said, "Let me give you a tour of the place and I'll tell my story along the way."

The next stop was a long narrow building with large windows facing the lake. Audrey had a master key and unlocked the door, pushing it open so Belle and I could go ahead inside.

"Do you mind if Belle comes along?" I asked.

"Not at all. I like animals," she said, shutting the door and flicking on a switch that ignited a long row of fluorescent lights stretching to the other end of the building. On the right were six doors, all open to classrooms. Small windows spaced along the left wall looked back at a series of cabins.

"All these classrooms are for the writing, music and theater kids. The last one down there," she pointed to the end, "is a soundproof room designed with acoustics in mind. The theater workshops are conducted in the next two rooms, and these first three are all writing classes. We usually have about twenty to twenty-five kids in each discipline—music, theater, writing and the visual arts. The art students work in the studio next door."

Belle was bored, lying at my feet looking unimpressed. "Let's check out the studio then," I said and yanked at Belle's chain, causing her to grumble at my disrespect.

"Certainly," Audrey said and led the way down the path to yet another two-story log structure with a wall of windows facing the lake. The cold interior smelled of paint and clay. Three long tables occupied the center while a couple of potting wheels were stashed in a corner along with several easels and blank canvases of various sizes.

"In the loft upstairs, there are two classrooms, but this room is where you feel the most creative energy. It's amazing to walk in here and see so many incredibly talented teenagers lost in their creations," she said, sweeping her arm across the now silent cavernous room.

"Are you an artist, like your brother?" I asked.

"God, no," she said with a loud guffaw. "I am a connoisseur of art, not a talent. Karl is the artist while my mother was a poet. Actually, I have a business degree. My forte is money—making it, raising it, spending it. That's how I ended up here. I was working at the Museum of Modern Art in New York City as an assistant to the vice president of endowments when my husband died unexpectedly in 1989. He was quite a bit older than me, I hated his family and they hated me, plus I had a young son to raise, so I came home and took this job."

"If you don't mind my saying, I would think you'd feel more comfortable in New York than the U.P. You, um, sort of stand out from the crowd, if you know what I mean," I said. Most U.P. natives who stayed behind or returned home were down-to-earth people put off by extravagant displays of wealth. That's one reason the newcomers who bought up all the available waterfront and built ostentatious homes often get the cold shoulder from the locals.

"I grew up in Houghton, but I was born in Ann Arbor," Audrey explained. "You see, Karl is my half-brother. My own father was killed in a car accident when I was four. I barely remember him. Both my parents were professors at the University of Michigan, my father in history, my mother in English. She was a native of Marquette, so when my dad died, she moved closer to home and took a job at Michigan Tech University in Houghton. She was one of the few females on campus at the time. She met my stepfather, Karl Maki Sr., when I was six and married him shortly thereafter and had Karl Jr. I can't say I was thrilled that my new dad was a funeral director, but eventually I grew to be quite proud of the family business. His family emigrated from Finland in 1888 and settled in what was known as Red Jacket then but now goes by Calumet after the Calumet and Hecla Mining Company that operated the big copper mines in the area. They opened a funeral home in Red Jacket shortly after their arrival and then another in Houghton around 1910. The business has been passed down through four generations now, although I don't know if it will go to a fifth. I can't see Karl's girls going into the business and Uncle John has no children. We closed the Calumet site in 1971, a few years after the last mine shut down for good, and focused our attention in Houghton. It's paid off. My stepfather, Uncle John and Karl have done quite well for themselves."

"Where does Karl get his artistic ability? His paintings are unique, very moody," I said, thinking about the monstrous work of art holed up in my dad's garage at this very minute.

"Moody? Yes, I'd say that's accurate. Actually, my stepfather has always loved to paint; he's just not any good at it. My uncle was a very talented make-up artist and even worked on Broadway in the Sixties until he was drafted to go to Vietnam. He graduated from Houghton High School in 1962, twelve years behind my stepfather, and headed straight for New York. Within five years, he was working on major productions. It was amazing, but then he was drafted in 1967 and chose to go into the Navy because he had this romantic vision of traveling the high seas. It obviously didn't work out like that. The war was just too much for him, so he never did go back to New York. As for Karl Sr., well, dementia has turned his painting from a pastime to an attempt to keep his mind from turning to complete oatmeal," she said, sorrow in her voice.

"Has your brother ever done anything with the camp?" I asked.

"Other than a little advising from time to time, no. He claims he's too busy, which I suppose is true, but I know he just doesn't like kids," she said. "Well, ready for more?"

"Lead the way," I said. The heavy fumes from the supplies were starting to give me a headache. Besides, I wasn't learning much to help me find Heather, except that I could probably write Audrey Gaston off as a suspect. I could not envision her murdering anyone. She might get a spot on her Armani suit. Karl was also sounding less and less like a possibility, unless one considered maybe he hated kids and took his rage out on other people's children. That didn't make sense, though. Of course, he did have a ponytail, which could have led Danny, the eyewitness to the brown van, to think he was a woman. Then again, how would Danny have been able to see Karl's hairstyle? Even if the van's interior light had come on, it would still have been too dark to see such detail when Heather was taken. Danny couldn't have been too close to the scene of the crime or the kidnapper would have noticed him.

We crossed back in front of the classrooms and around back of the administration building to the theater/gallery. The wind had died and thick fog was approaching off of Lake Superior, enveloping me and leaving a fine mist on my face and Belle's brown and white fur. She shook herself furiously when we stopped at the side door of the theater. Audrey turned and looked at the lake as she unlocked the door.

"The temperature's dropping fast. I hope it doesn't get icy. It's too early for that," she said. Giving the heavy steel door a shove with her shoulder, she forged ahead into the darkness. The click of her heels stopped about a dozen paces from the door and then a weak glow from a low-watt naked bulb illuminated stage-left of the theater. Belle nosed past me and sniffed the wooden floor, which creaked under my feet as I followed her inside and shut the door behind me.

Heavy black curtains were parted a few feet to reveal a large stage, empty save for a couple of straight-backed chairs and a dingy, battered kitchen table.

"They did 'Death of a Salesman' this summer. It was fabulous. The kid who played Biff has a future on Broadway, if he sticks with it," Audrey said.

"Are you here all summer, for the camp, I mean?" I asked.

"Absolutely. I love the excitement of discovering new talent. I get to know many of the students and often write recommendations for college, fellowships, scholarships, even jobs. I really believe in the mission of this place," she said, throwing her arms out in celebration. Her eyes glowed in the dim light. The stiff professional I had spoken with on the phone and in that soulless modern office was gone. In its place emerged a passionate fan of the creative mind. It was as though she fed off the energy of these students, lacking any such ability herself. Suddenly I felt a chill and wanted to leave.

I started to back toward the door but she grabbed my hand and pulled me through a doorway and down a short steep flight of stairs into the seating area.

"C'mon. I want you to see the gallery. We have hundreds of pieces on display dating back to the Institute's opening," she said with the fervor of a child on her way to the county fair for the first time.

I heard a faint thump to my right and felt my heart jump. Belle had heard it, too, and gave a low woof. Audrey still had a hold of my hand. I pulled it free and asked, "Is anyone else here?"

"Of course not. Why?" Her brows were knitted across her hazel eyes, as though I had asked a stupid question.

"I heard something."

"Don't be silly. It's just the wind," she said

"Audrey, there is no wind."

She threw open a door at the back of the theater and faced me with a smile.

"Are you nervous about something?" she asked, sounding incredulous.

Nervous? No, I thought. Creeped-out from the roots of my hair to the tips of my toenails was more like it. But why? There was nothing overtly spooky about the place, except the knowledge that five young girls had walked these grounds, only to disappear forever shortly thereafter.

"I guess it's just the quietness. It seems so empty," I finally said.

She tossed her blonde head back and laughed.

"Empty? Can't you feel the power all around you? These kids leave a piece of their souls here when they create a work of art. Look around you," she said and twirled around the middle of the gallery.

Natural light poured in from huge skylights overhead and large windows on three sides. Dozens of paintings covered the wall and stood on easels. A few elaborate papier mache birds dangled from invisible wires hung from beams crossing the vaulted ceiling. An array of sculptures and ceramics were displayed on pedestals around the spacious room.

Wrapping Belle's leash around my hand to keep her from aimlessly wandering and knocking something over, I made my way around the room. Even with my limited knowledge of art I could see these kids were way beyond the clay ash tray and tempera paint stage. I stopped in front of a two-by-three-foot oil of a moose and her calf wading in a swamp, lichen dripping from branches in the distance. I could almost feel the heat that sent the pair to refuge in the shallow water. I'd seen photos of moose on Isle Royale, but they lacked the essence of life captured in this painting. I strained to read the name inscribed in the lower right corner, and then noticed a white card mounted beneath it. "Heather Stankowski, Mother and Child in Tobin Harbor," it read and was dated July of this year.

"This was done by the girl who's missing from Rapid River," I said matter-of-factly.

"Yes, I hope they find her soon. Her hand has the perfect touch for oil—not too heavy, yet firm and definitive. Her eye for detail is breathtaking," Audrey said, joining me in front of the painting.

As we strolled around the room, I admired some pieces and scowled at others, like a metal contraption made out of old, rusted small animal traps. From the way Belle sniffed it with growing interest, I feared some of the unfortunate little victims' remains were left behind. Cringing, I jerked her away. She turned her attention to a white triangle poking out from underneath a pedestal holding a bust of a Native American maiden. She placed a thick paw on it and pulled. Audrey had her backed turned to us as she studied a colorful ceramic pitcher so I stooped and swiped the paper from Belle before she could slobber on it. Flipping it over, I saw it was a business card with the Michigan State Police emblem. The name printed below the emblem was Detective Sergeant Christine Parker.

Chapter Eighteen

"AUDREY, WERE YOU HERE YESTERDAY with a state police detective?" I asked, wincing at the accusation in my voice, but as I looked down at her business card in my hand I could feel in my bones that something bad had happened to Detective Christine Parker.

Audrey Gaston rolled her eyes and said, "Yes, please don't remind me. That woman is relentless. She wanted to see all of our files including employment records of everyone who ever worked here and she questioned me endlessly about my role here and how much contact I have with the campers and where I was Friday morning and with whom I had discussed Heather's disappearance."

Fingering the edge of the card, I said, "She's just doing her job. If we don't find Heather soon, she could die—if she's not already dead."

"What's this 'we' business? You're not a cop. I thought you said you worked for the *Daily News* in Escanaba," Audrey said, eyeing me suspiciously.

"It's the *Daily Press*, and, yes, I am a reporter, but I take my duty as a journalist seriously. I'm the one who told Detective Parker about the possible connection between Heather's kidnapper and this camp. Where did Parker go when she left here?" I asked.

"I've no idea," Audrey said, fiddling with the gold button on her blazer. "I had a meeting to attend back in Marquette so I left her here with Bill, our maintenance guy, to finish the tour of the camp. As for the files, I told her to get a search warrant because this was getting ridiculous. I just can't see anyone here harming any of our students. These are dedicated professionals we're talking about, not sickos with a thing for young girls. Frankly, I resent this whole insinuation that we're involved somehow with Heather's or anyone else's disappearance."

Ignoring her tirade, I asked, "Who is this Bill?"

She rolled her eyes again and threw her perfectly-manicured hands in the air. "Don't you start again. I can assure you, Bill is not interested in kidnapping teenage girls. He works at the Shiras power plant in Marquette, but lives with his family in Big Bay. He's done our maintenance for us since I've been here, and he does a fine job, I might add," she said.

Whether or not Bill was a fine maintenance man was of no interest to me. He was my last, best link to Detective Parker. Perhaps if I found out where she had gone from the camp, I would find Heather. Audrey refused to answer any more questions about Bill or the camp so I thanked her for the tour, told her I'd be in touch and headed back toward the town of Big Bay, leaving her fuming. Tough, I thought. Her devotion to her precious camp was over the top, and now I couldn't get the vision of Parker's two little girls, whom I'd never even met, crying over their lost mother, out of my head. I knew all too well what it was like to be a child without a mother. Who would harm a mother, I thought as I pressed down on the accelerator.

I figured finding Bill wouldn't be too hard. If Big Bay was like every other small town in America, some local business person would know where I could find a guy named Bill who worked at a power plant and did the maintenance at the Institute. Sure enough, the bartender at the Thunder Bay Inn told me Bill Mecklin lived in town and pointed at his two-story yellow house, visible from one of the front windows of the inn.

Leaving Belle in the Jeep, I walked over to the house and knocked on the door, not expecting Bill to be home but hoping someone could give me a phone number where he could be reached. To my surprise, a forty-something man with rosy cheeks and deep dimples answered the door almost immediately. I introduced myself and asked him about seeing the detective.

"Oh sure, the state cop. Real nice lady. She asked me some questions about the place and then Karl showed up and took care of showing her around the place," Bill said.

"Karl Maki? I thought he had nothing to do with the camp," I said, now thoroughly confused.

"Yeah, that's right, it was Audrey's brother, Karl. He's not an instructor or anything, but he does advise the staff once in a great while on things involving the studio, like layout and stuff," he said and then scratched his chin. "Um, what is this all about? Is something wrong?"

"I honestly don't know. Did you see the cop leave?" I asked as the rain began to fall and the wind kicked up, washing over the porch roof like waves across the bow of a freighter.

"No, when Karl came, I headed home. To be honest, I really don't care for the guy. I've done the maintenance at that place since I was twenty years old, five years before his sister came on board, but damned if that guy doesn't criticize every little thing down to the wattage of the bulbs I use in some of the light fixtures," Bill said.

I thanked him and sprinted over, around and through a half dozen puddles on my way back to the Jeep. Once inside, I dialed the number of the newspaper and left a message for Bob about the missing detective and told him I was driving to Houghton to speak with Karl Maki. I considered calling the state police post in Gladstone, but what could I say? Karl Maki may have done something nasty to your one and only detective? I had no proof that Karl had done anything, or even that something had happened to Parker. It was just a gut feeling.

In order to get to Houghton, I had to drive southeast back to Marquette and then get on the federal highway, a good twenty miles out of the way, but such is life in the Upper Peninsula. The other option was traversing a dirt logging road, which would have been shorter but taken three times as long. Despite the heavy rain, the Jeep cruised along just below seventy, once I got past Ishpeming. I figured if I got pulled over by a cop, I'd explain the situation and let them go after Maki.

In the two hours it took me to get to Houghton, I thought about what I would say to Karl when I found him. *What did you do with Detective Parker? Did you kill Heather Stankowski and all those other girls? Are you going to kill me now?* I had to finesse this somehow without getting myself in trouble by letting him know that I knew something was wrong. By the time I reached the city limits sign just south of Michigan Tech University I'd formulated a plan, albeit a lame one. Making the turn onto MacInnes Drive and following it until it merged with Sharon Avenue, I practiced my speech to Karl about how sorry I was about our conversation on Saturday and that I realized that it was Alex Breyers I needed to talk to with regard to Mary Jo Quinn's death. Then I would ask if a state police detective had been in touch with him and apologize for that as well and watch his reaction to my line of bullshit. If I saw even the faintest hint that he knew something, I would hightail it over to the Houghton City Police and beg and plead with them until they agreed to look for Parker and Heather.

Unfortunately, Karl Maki was not at the funeral home when I arrived. His wife Lily answered the door and explained that Karl was at a home in some little town called Tapiola, about fifteen miles south of Houghton, working with a family on some funeral arrangements. He wasn't expected back for a few hours. She invited me inside and offered me a cup of tea. Declining the tea, I stumbled over an explanation as to why I was there in the first place.

"I, um, wanted to apologize for upsetting him on Saturday. That was a mistake on my part," I said, swallowing hard.

Lily arched her eyebrows and said, "You drove all the way to Houghton for that? I mean, I know Karl was distraught after you left, but that's a long way to come to deliver an apology."

"Actually, I had business at the *Daily Mining Gazette* here in town, so it wasn't really out of the way," I lied. "Um, why was Karl so distraught, as you say? I certainly didn't mean to accuse him of anything."

She scrunched her face and sat on the edge of a couch in the front parlor, heaving a sigh as she sat. "I don't know, but you touched a nerve. He's been acting very strange ever since. What is this all about anyway? I mean, Mary Jo's been gone for thirty-two years. What's the point of bringing all this up now?"

"It's not just Mary Jo. There are five other girls who've disappeared under similar circumstances since then, one of them just last Friday," I said and sat down next to her. "You seem like a decent, kind-hearted woman. There's a mother in Rapid River who at this very minute is living a nightmare that won't end until her daughter is safe and sound at home. Will you help me try to make that happen?"

Lily looked startled and whispered hoarsely, "My god, I can't imagine one of my children being missing. I'd go insane."

I'd hit the mother nerve. "Lily, I have to ask where Karl was Friday morning."

"He was here all morning. We had a funeral. These past few weeks have been terrible. A strain of pneumonia hit the area nursing homes and at least four people died from it, three of them we had to handle. It's just been crazy around here," Lily said, rubbing her face and eyes. "You have no idea what this business is like. I can't tell you the number of family gatherings we've had ruined because Karl has to go retrieve a body. You can make a decent living, but it sure takes a toll on the family."

When she dropped her hands from her face, her mauve lipstick was slightly smeared. Suddenly I remembered the lipstick drawing and thought about who would have lipstick in his possession as part of his job.

"What about John?" I asked.

Lily looked at me as though I'd bit her. "Oh no, John would never harm anyone. He's the gentlest soul," she said.

"I'm sure he is, but please just tell me if he was here Friday morning," I pleaded.

Slowly, she shook her head from side to side. "No, he doesn't attend the funerals. His work is all in the back room. Besides, he lives in Calumet, at the old funeral home Karl Sr. closed after the mines shut down. It allows him to be close to the Calumet Theatre where he volunteers. In fact, he's working on a play right now," she said and grabbed my hand in an icy grip. "Please don't bother John. He's had such a tough time with simple day-to-day living. He just wants peace and quiet now."

"I don't want to hurt him, but I need to know what's happened to two people who've disappeared in the last four days, one of them a state police detective with two children. Tell me, does John ever do anything with the Great Lakes Summer Institute, run by Karl's sister, in Big Bay?" I asked. Why hadn't I asked Audrey that question, I suddenly wondered.

Lily began chewing on a cuticle and looked worried. "Yes, every year he goes down there whenever he has the time. He loves being around the kids. So?" she said. "That doesn't mean anything."

I didn't know what to say so I stared at the pale blue plush carpeting beneath my feet. Did it mean anything? Why hadn't Audrey volunteered that information when she spoke about her family's artistic efforts? John used lipstick in his job every day, ensuring the deceased looked as good as possible on their last day of visibility in this world. He was creative and had some mental issues resulting from the war, but did that make him a killer?

And what about Parker? I needed to talk to Karl about how he'd handled the tour of the camp with the detective.

"I'm sorry to have bothered you. I'll show myself out," was all I could say as I stood up and walked slowly to the door, more confused than ever. After all, what proof did I have of anything? All I had was an eerie feeling that someone was weaving me into their sinister web. What should I do next, I wondered. Should I try to find John in Calumet? What would I say? Should I try to find Karl in Tapiola and confront him? What about Alex, was he out of the picture? Just because he'd had an illegitimate child with Audrey Gaston didn't make him a killer anymore than I was bank robber just because I bounced a few checks once in a while.

"What should I do?" I asked Belle, who looked at me with big brown eyes. She whined a little, maybe sensing my distress. It dawned on me that I had no idea where the old funeral home was in Calumet. Asking around town probably wasn't a good idea because it might needlessly lead people to wonder what its occupant was up to, especially if he didn't get many visitors. If he was innocent, the increased attention would not be good for his mental state. Even if John really was the man behind all this, did I want to confront him on his own turf? Erring on what I thought was the side of caution, I pulled a map of the U.P. from the glove compartment and found the road that would eventually lead to Tapiola. By knocking on a few doors I wouldn't have any problem finding out which family had just experienced a death. After passing it once, I found Paradise Road, a two-lane country road that paralleled the highway.

As I drove I suddenly felt drained of energy, as if the weight of this whole investigation had finally flattened me like a fresh sheet of asphalt under a steam roller. I squinted through the drops splattering against the windshield at such a pace that the wipers barely made a difference. I was dimly aware of a pickup truck passing me about two miles outside of Houghton and wondered aloud why anyone would drive so fast in such dangerous conditions. Belle whimpered from her perch in the front seat and panted as the rain seemed to increase in intensity.

I was almost past the pickup when I saw it in the ditch on the right side of the road about five minutes later, its back end tilted up at an unnatural angle and its rear wheels still spinning. I hit the brakes and pulled off the road, looking around to see if anyone else was going to stop, but there were no other cars on the road, it being mid-afternoon, before the evening rush. I grabbed my cell phone, pulled my hood over my head and jumped out of the Jeep. I was soaked to the skin by the time I reached the truck, a dark blue Ford that had seen a lot of hard U.P. winters. The windows were intact, meaning the occupants hadn't been thrown from the vehicle, but there was no movement from inside the cab. Stashing the cell phone in my pocket, I stumbled through the weeds and cupped my hands to peer through the driver's side window and saw the truck was empty. Had the driver gotten out and walked to a nearby house to get help? He must have been a fast walker. I looked down the road in each direction but saw only trees and empty fields. There wasn't a house within a thousand feet of the pickup.

I thought I heard a twig snap but the hood of my jacket hindered both my hearing and vision. I turned toward the bed of the pickup, my heart now thudding in my chest. I felt a presence behind me and turned to see a familiar face. I felt a sharp pain in my arm. I looked down at the needle in disbelief before glancing up into his eyes, which were dull and empty of all emotion. Then, like seven others before me, I disappeared into darkness.

Chapter Nineteen

MY FIRST THOUGHT WHEN I woke up was of realizing I was alive, the second was of being very cold and the third was of Belle. Frantically scrabbling around me on my trembling hands and knees in a black void, I felt only cold cement underneath my fingers.

"Belle!"

The only reply was dead silence. No panting, no whimpering, no snuffling of her big wet nose telling me she was okay. Hot tears streamed down my face as I grimaced uncontrollably. My upper arm throbbed where I'd been jabbed with the hypodermic needle. *What the hell was in that thing?* I tried to swallow the lump in my throat, only to choke on the fear and dread that welled up from a dark place deep inside me. Thrusting my hands into the darkness, I found a cement block wall and slid toward its offer of relative comfort and fought against the urge to give in to the terror that was wrestling for control of my senses. I was alive but to remain in that condition would not be easy.

He's got me, I thought, angry at the naiveté that had blinded me to John Maki's madness. I had been so close and yet couldn't see the clues until they were right in front of me, the most obvious being the sorrow-filled eye painted in lipstick on my garage door. I still didn't understand how Karl fit into the whole picture, but I knew John had most likely killed five girls, possibly six, if Heather was dead, and maybe even the detective. Why he had targeted girls of a certain age with a creative nature was still a mystery, though. I knew so little about his history, just that he'd been a talented make-up artist in New York before being drafted and sent to Vietnam. As my dad had explained just the night before in the safety of his warm kitchen, far from the hell of war, John probably had a serious mental illness before heading to the jungle, but what had happened to him there could have flipped a switch that turned him homicidal. Lily had described him as a gentle soul. Perhaps he'd seen something so horrifying that his already troubled mind couldn't comprehend it, so he created an alternate reality and lived there, in a world with different rules.

I wouldn't find out anything if I didn't get out of this dungeon, though. I tried to remember the sequence of events leading to my arrival in what might as well have been a tomb. My upper left arm throbbed and my brain felt like it was shrouded in a thick fog. I'd been jabbed with a needle full of some sort of drug that knocked me into oblivion, yet designed to not kill me. My body ached from the cold, and I shivered in my still-wet cotton trousers and thin jacket. John must have loaded me into the Jeep as soon he'd stuck me because there was no way he could have gotten his pickup out of the ditch without help. That meant Belle had to be somewhere close by, unless he had tossed her out the door and left her to roam the highway. I felt my throat close up again at the thought of her wandering aimlessly along the road, possibly hit by a car. I took a deep breath, forcing my lungs to fill with air, hoping to gain some sense of composure and clear my head, but the stench of something I hadn't smelled since tenth-grade biology filled my nostrils, making me gag. Suddenly images of dissected frogs and pigs filled my head. I remembered making the mistake of going to class with a fresh wad of bubble gum in my mouth the day we began dissecting the pigs. By the end of the hour, which just happened to precede lunch, my gum tasted like that poor little pig smelled. I skipped lunch that day and probably for the rest of the week.

Was I in a laboratory or classroom, maybe at Michigan Tech University? That made no sense, but my muddled mind couldn't seem to grasp what was happening. Drawing my knees to my chest and wrapping my arms around my shins, I tucked my head down, breathed through my mouth and tried to concentrate. But images kept shifting in my brain. One second it was Detective Parker's earnest face. Was she in the same building with me? Was she dead? Then I would see Belle sitting next to me in the Jeep. Where was Belle? What he done with her? Had he just let her run loose? Had he killed her, too?

"Oh, Belle," I cried softly, finally giving in to the tears that so eagerly spilled over my eyelids and fell in my lap. She was the one link I had to Mitch. He had given her to me for Christmas nearly two years before. Just eight weeks old, she was the ugliest dog I'd ever seen, and I loved her immediately and vowed to spoil her worse than any grandparent would spoil their first grandchild. Some pet parent I was, though—Belle was probably dead and it was my fault for dragging her along while I fancied myself some great investigative reporter who was not only brave but invincible. More like stupid and reckless. If there was a hell, I would be there soon for my dereliction of duty as Belle's protector.

"Stop it!" I screamed at the noise in my head, my voice bouncing back at me, hurling the words like knives.

"Focus. You must focus," I said and eased into a standing position, stretching my arms over my head, feeling for the ceiling. All I felt was air. Somewhere outside the room but still close by, a motor kicked on. Its low hum provided welcome relief from the silence, although the room soon felt even more frigid. I tried to determine the source of the cold but it seemed to be emanating from everywhere. Taking a tentative step forward, my hands stretched out in front of me, I tried to ignore the chemical stench that seemed worse, now that I was standing. After a few more steps, the toe of my right shoe grazed something hard. I bent at the knees and let my fingers travel across the floor until they rested on a long narrow spindle of wood, grooved in some sort of pattern and shaped like the leg of a piece of furniture. Tracing the length of the wood, my hands stopped at the edge of the bottom of a flat surface. The piece had rounded edges and gave the impression of being large, like a dining room table. I grasped the thick edge and tried to shake it, but it barely moved. Creeping my way to the left, I found a wooden chair with vertical slats for a back. Was I in a restaurant? No, the wall and floor were definitely cement, hardly appropriate décor for a restaurant. And that smell, stronger than ever now, certainly didn't make me hungry.

Moving back to the right a few feet, I jumped in surprise when my arm brushed against something softer with a bit of give to it. With growing horror, my mouth dry as the Mojave Desert in July, I lifted my right hand and touched what felt like starched lace. I held my breath as I exerted pressure and felt the shape of a human arm. It must be a doll, it had to be a doll, oh please God let it be a doll, my mind screamed as my hand followed the form until the lace ended and cold dead flesh began. I screamed aloud and jumped back, my hands on my cheeks, and then I screamed again and dropped them from my face in revulsion. I had no doubt there was a dead body seated at the table.

Adding to my confusion, a vision of my mother's funeral flashed into my terror-stricken mind. I was ten years old and struck by how lifelike she had appeared in her polished walnut casket. Curious, I'd touched my finger to her neatly-folded hands. She had felt cold, stiff, like a rubber doll left outside overnight. I had pulled my hand back in disgust and run for the comfort of my father, standing with a dazed-looking Aunt Gina and my maternal grandmother.

"Mom's cold," I'd cried. My father, a strained smile on his tired yet still handsome face, took my hand and squeezed it.

"I know, Sweet Pea. That's just her body, though. Mom's spirit is free now, so it'll be okay," he'd said.

I had forgotten that touch until now and suddenly realized what that horrible smell was filling the room — formaldehyde, an embalming agent rarely used anymore because of its link to cancer. I was in the Maki Funeral Home, most likely the old one in Calumet now inhabited by John Maki. Lily would have noticed a dead body dressed in lace stashed in her home.

I'm stuck in a freezing, dark room with a dead body, I thought. *How the hell do I get out of here?*

I needed light, but then I'd have to look at the body. *Stop being such a baby,* I chided myself. *You've seen plenty of dead bodies.* Too many actually, I thought, suddenly picturing Mitch laid out in his dress uniform, brass buttons glowing in the candle light, his face turned ever so slightly toward the casket lid to hide the wound from the shotgun blast that had ended his life less than six month ago.

I felt the urge to vomit. It was all just too much to handle. All I could see before me was death in the darkness surrounding me and in the dark reaches of my mind. Panic surfaced, preventing me from stringing two coherent thoughts together. I backed up against the wall and inched to the right, my hand sweeping the blocks for signs of a door or light switch. Coming to a corner, I stopped and turned toward the wall and continued another couple of feet until my hand touched a metal conduit. Using both hands, I found a switch and flipped it up. A fluorescent light blazed to life overhead, blinding me momentarily. I blinked several times and then squinted for several seconds until I could focus.

The walls were gray cement block, unadorned by paint. A steel door, like that of a walk-in cooler, was to the left of the switch. With increasing trepidation I turned to face the table.

No matter how much counseling I receive or wine I drink, never in my life will I forget the surreal horror of that scene as my knees buckled and I choked on yet another scream, wishing I had never flipped that switch.

An oblong maple table filled the center of the otherwise stark room. In the center of the table sat a massive bouquet of white silk roses on a large, round lace doily. Six chairs were placed around that table in an orderly manner and seated in five of those chairs were Lucy Franklin, Sabrina Danelli, Caroline Baxter, Mary Jo Quinn and a stranger.

Chapter Twenty

THIS IS A NIGHTMARE OR a hallucination. This can't be happening. I'm stuck in a Vincent Price movie. Explanations for what I was seeing tumbled through my head like numbered balls in a lottery machine, my mind desperately seeking one that made sense to drop in the slot. Nothing came.

But it was real. The smell of formaldehyde, the cold of the makeshift morgue, the gaudiness of the made-up faces and the sheer ridiculousness of their nineteenth century costumes were too bizarre even for nightmares.

I recognized each girl from the photographs circulated at the time of their disappearances, but the identity of the fifth occupant, a middle-aged woman, was a mystery to me. The woman bore a slight resemblance to Audrey Gaston but looked like a statue in a wax museum, her skin leathery and yellow, unlike the relatively smooth complexions of the teenage girls.

I looked at the girl who had started it all. It had been more than thirty years since Mary Jo Quinn was last seen by the rest of the world. She would be in her mid-forties, had she survived adolescence. But she hadn't. Her fate was to remain frozen at the age of fourteen, a player on the stage of some sick, twisted fantasy created by a madman. She had obviously been embalmed soon after her death, and by an expert at that, for she appeared life-like from my vantage point about ten feet from where she sat stiffly. If not for the fact that none of them blinked, they all would have seemed very much alive, as though they were sitting down to tea and polite conversation.

Clothed in a yellow gingham gown with white lace sewn at the high collar that grazed her chin and at the cuffs, buttoned tight around her ghastly pale wrists, Mary Jo looked like a prim, proper young lady making a social call circa 1895. Her long, golden-blonde hair had been pulled up in a loose bun with a few tendrils framing her once pretty face. She stared straight across the table, past Sabrina Danelli, who stared back lifelessly.

It had been Sabrina's olive-skinned hand, resting on the table, which I had touched earlier. Repulsed, yet strangely mesmerized by the scene, like a passerby at a horrific accident, I moved closer to examine each victim, easing my way around the table to look at Sabrina's face. While Mary Jo's expression was one of seeming tranquility, as though she were daydreaming, Sabrina's visage was frozen in anger despite the best efforts of her make-up artist. Her red-stained mouth was set in a sneer, her brows permanently knitted over her deep brown eyes. Her death had not been an easy one from the looks of her face, although I saw no marks of outright violence on her or any of the other girls. *How had they died,* I wondered.

Sabrina's dress was more womanly than Mary Jo's, befitting her more developed figure, as a hint of cleavage peeked above the russet-colored silk gown. Black lace sleeves puffed at her smooth shoulders and ended in a series of black buttons at the wrists. Like Mary Jo, Sabrina's thick black hair was swept up in a bun on top of her head. That's when I noticed all of them had long hair, although Lucy Franklin's hair was left to fall across her shoulders in soft dark ash-blonde waves, and Caroline Baxter's curly brown mane was tucked under an outlandish peach hat with feathers and flowers sprouting along its wide brim. The hat was tilted at a flirtatious angle, like that of a young maiden.

The unknown lady who resembled Audrey Gaston was dressed in a white blouse with lace and ruffles spilling over the lapels of a light gray tweed jacket, her silver-streaked blonde hair disappearing under a black hat festooned with some type of gauzy material and blue silk flowers. She looked to be in her early fifties. While the girls all looked healthy at the time of their demise, with full rosy cheeks, this woman had been gravely ill, perhaps from cancer, prior to her death.

I noticed the smell of formaldehyde was strongest around Mary Jo and wondered if some other chemical had been used on the others. All of them had a leathery look about them, more so Mary Jo and less so Sabrina, the last to die.

There was one empty chair at the head of the table, perhaps reserved for Heather Stankowski. Laid out on the table were six place settings, including pristine white mats topped with rose-patterned, gilt-edged china complete with dessert plate, tea cup, saucer, silver spoons and cloth napkins. In the center sat the basket of roses and a silver tea service with milk and sugar containers. Feeling like Alice in Wonderland at the Mad Hatter's tea party, I carefully lifted the pot. Liquid sloshed inside, but the cups were empty, as though someone would pour a cup as soon as it was ready. Setting the pot back in place, I stepped back and studied each girl a bit more closely. Mary Jo's and Lucy's faces were beginning to show the effects of gravity, something even embalming couldn't prevent. They had jowls, giving their faces the appearance of wearing a Halloween mask that didn't quit fit. Each person was heavily made up with rouge, thick eyeliner and lipstick. I caught the reflection of light in one of Caroline Baxter's brown eyes and stretched across the table to get a closer look. They were glass. Of course, I thought, human eyes wouldn't hold up under embalming. I shivered. The corpses reminded me of those life-size dolls popular at Christmas. Never a big fan of dolls even as a child, I felt my flesh crawl.

I considered the empty chair and wondered how long before it would be filled. Had it been meant for Crystal Jensen? But why wait so many years before trying again? Had her escape rattled John Maki to the point of being fearful of obtaining another actress in his macabre production? I sat in the chair and joined the party, waiting for my companions to tell me their story. Shock was beginning to give way to acceptance of the strange display, but when a cough broke the cold silence I jumped out of the chair, knocking it backwards and scanned the faces around the table. No one moved. My heart pounded in my ears.

I'm going insane. Then came the second cough, followed by a series of choking sounds coming from the far corner of the room. I hit the floor and crawled around the table to the right side of the room. There in the corner lay a very ill, pale and terrified, but still very much alive, Heather Stankowski. I scrambled across the room and felt her face. It was flush with cold, rather than health. She had vomited at one point and I picked up the faint smell of ammonia from urine. No amount of shaking or prodding could awaken her, and it occurred to me she had slipped into a diabetic coma. She had been without her insulin kit for at least four days, maybe five if it was now Wednesday. I had seen movies where diabetics were given orange juice or candy to bring their blood sugar back under control, but I knew Heather was way past that point. She needed hospital care, and she needed it now.

I took off my jacket and wrapped it around her shoulders, guiding her arms into the sleeves. She had a good twenty pounds on me so it didn't fit, but it was all I could offer at this point. As I tugged it around her waist to zip it, I felt a bulge in the pocket. My cell phone! I dug it out and then had to stop myself from smashing it against the wall when I saw the "No Service" message in the display window. The phone couldn't pick up a signal from wherever we were located. I stuffed it into the pocket of my pants just in case I had the opportunity to get a signal later.

"Don't worry, Heather. I'm going to try and get us out of here," I said, more to reassure myself than her. "I think we're at a funeral home in Calumet, but I'm not sure."

Heather didn't have much time left before her body quit functioning entirely. I ran to the door and pushed down on the handle, fully expecting it to be locked from outside. To my surprise, it gave easily under my weight and the door swung open. Warily I poked my head around it and surveyed the black nothingness outside the cooler. I was beginning to feel like a mole. Would I ever see natural daylight again, I wondered. Hearing no sound other than the drone of the refrigeration unit, which had kicked on again upon the opening of the door, I made sure the door would not close and lock behind me when I went back in to Heather. How was I going to get her out of here? I didn't know how to lift her over my shoulder like a fireman. I was likely too weak for that anyway so I grabbed her by the arms and pulled her away from the wall, maneuvering her into a position where I could get my hands under her armpits. It took a couple minutes to drag her across the floor and outside the cooler. The door was on some type of spring closure so I had to hold it wide open in order to allow some light from the cooler to spill into the room.

We were definitely in a mortuary. The cinder block room that held the cooler was about forty feet long and thirty feet wide and contained two steel tables near sinks, sluices and other equipment used for embalming the dead. Between the two tables was a chair similar to those in the cooler. Not knowing anything about mortuary science, I didn't know if the chair was for the embalmer or embalmee.

Shelves full of chemicals with names like Glutaraldehyde lined three of the four walls, and stairs led up from my immediate left. Squinting into the dark, I spotted a light switch next to what looked like freight elevator doors to the right of the stairs. I grabbed a long pair of steel scissors from the shelf to my right and wedged them between the door and jamb above the middle hinge and allowed the door to spring closed until it hit the scissors. It created a six-inch shaft of light—enough to see my way to the light switch across the room. More fluorescent lights flickered to life overhead, casting the room in a stark, cold glare.

I looked down at Heather and wondered if she had seen her roommates before slipping into unconsciousness. If she had, I couldn't imagine what had gone through the poor kid's mind. My own head was spinning, both from the drug John had injected into my body and the sheer lunacy of the situation, but I had to get myself under control. It was up to me and me alone to get Heather to safety and, right now, I had no idea how to accomplish that.

I scanned the room one more time in search of some sign that Detective Christine Parker had been here. The place looked like a bizarre take on a Merle Norman Studio, with cosmetology tools and a variety of vials, tubes and jars of make-up laid out at a work station on the wall opposite the elevator, but drawing closer, I saw the hair-dryer and various curling irons were all more than twenty years old. The Sunbeam dryer was a pale yellow model similar to one my mother had used. Even the make-up looked outdated, some cracked and rancid. As I wandered around the room, I realized most of the equipment looked outdated and had a thick shroud of dust, as though it hadn't been used in many years. A path had been worn in the dust between the stairs, elevator, and cooler but otherwise appeared to be undisturbed. Then I spied another sight that gave me the creeps.

There in the corner was a pink ten-speed bicycle, the style that was popular in the mid-nineteen eighties. Carolyn Baxter's missing bicycle. He must have stashed it in the back of whatever vehicle he was driving at the time he'd picked her up so close to home, but not close enough. I wanted to cry for her, but the tears were stuck in my throat. It would do no good now anyhow. My first concern had to be getting the one girl who was still alive to a hospital and then finding the detective before there were two little girls orphaned. I walked back to Heather and caught sight of several little glass vials of liquid stored on the shelf next to the cooler. They looked ancient and had neatly typed labels that read Benadryl, Haldol and Ativan, all familiar to me thanks to having sources at the Cook County Hospital in Chicago. The three drugs were used together to form a powerful antipsychotic medication called a B52, sometimes injected into an out-of-control psychiatric patient. Were these left over from some treatment Maki had undergone upon his return from Vietnam? An injection of the three drugs together could cause a person to black out for a period of time and then awaken slowly with a myriad of side effects, including muscle contractions in the face and hands as the drug wore off and the person regained control of his bodily reactions. That would explain the shaking in my hands, that annoying tic I'd been feeling in my cheeks and the extremely agitated state of my mind.

Where was John now? I looked at my watch, an analog model that told me it was 9:08, but not if it was morning or night. There were no windows in the room to give me a hint, either.

Not wanting to risk leaving Heather behind, I pondered which way would be best to leave this dreadful room — up the stairs or on the elevator. Both had risks. The stairs would be difficult to negotiate with Heather, but the elevator would make a lot more noise. I had to risk it, though. There was no way I could get her up the stairs by myself. Pulling the scissors from the cooler door in case I needed a weapon, I stashed them in my back pocket, took a deep breath and dragged Heather to the elevator door. It was in the "down" position, meaning John had used the stairs to go back up the last time he'd been here. I pulled the freight door up and heaved Heather inside. I held my breath as I pushed the button to go up and listened to the contraption roar to life. It was so loud. If John was anywhere near the building, he'd certainly hear it. I found myself praying to every god and goddess I'd ever heard of. *Please just let me get her to the hospital.* Then the elevator stopped with a jolt.

Other than the sound of Heather's labored breathing, the building was silent as a tomb. When my hand finally found the door, I prayed John wouldn't be standing on the other side. He wasn't. The old steel door went up roughly on its track and creaked like the floors of a haunted house. I was sure neighbors within a mile of the place had heard it. Swallowing hard, I peered into the dark hallway but saw and heard no sign of human life.

I stepped outside the elevator and saw a set of double doors leading outside. Streetlights illuminated windows that took up the top half of each panel and told me it was night. I stepped into the dim light and pulled out my cell phone, but it still couldn't pick up more than two bars, indicating a poor signal. I dialed 911 anyway, but got nothing but dead air. I cursed and stuffed it back in my pocket. I could easily waste precious minutes trying to find a phone in the old house, if it even had one. I looked back at Heather. She didn't have minutes to spare.

The doors were locked from the inside but refused to give when I pushed or pulled on either handle. I felt along the edge for hinges. It was probably considered a fire exit, so the doors opened outward. I grabbed the right knob, turned it and heaved all one hundred and ten pounds against the door. All I achieved was a serious pain in my shoulder. I tried the left with the same result.

"What the hell is the matter?" I spit through gritted teeth.

Peering out the window again, I saw the problem. Apparently John Maki didn't mind if his guests wandered around the basement or the rest of the old house so long as they didn't leave. He had wedged a length of two-by-four underneath each doorknob.

I slammed my hand against the wall and cursed again.

"I'm not staying here another minute," I shouted to the ghosts that seemed to be closing in on me as I looked for a way out. I ran back to Heather and removed my jacket from her limp body. Wrapping it around my right fist, I marched through a doorway opposite the double doors toward the front of the house and found the front door, which I tried to open just for the hell of it. The handle wouldn't turn. Not caring why, I went to the nearest large low window overlooking the street and smashed my fist through the glass until the lower pane was gone and the screen pushed out, allowing me plenty of room to safely scoot onto the porch. As I watched for porch lights to come on and neighbors to poke their heads outside to see what the commotion was, I shook the glass out of the jacket and waited. Nothing stirred.

"Talk about a dead town," I whispered to myself. There was not a single light in any of the homes on the block, most looking like they'd been vacant for years.

"No wonder he was able to get away with this for all these years. There's no one around to wonder what the hell he was up to," I mumbled under my breath and headed around to the back of the building. Just before I rounded the corner, though, I turned and looked at the front of the house. A faded wooden sign above the entry said Maki Funeral Home. The shabby, ornate Victorian structure looked like the model for the house in that goofy Sixties television show "The Munsters." Perfect place for a madman, I thought, and went to get Heather.

I kicked both two-by-fours from the back doors and managed to yank one open. Not knowing how much time I had before John Maki came back, I didn't bother to put my coat back on Heather but dragged her out the door and into the alley. A rickety garage stood to the right of the house and, in the gloom, faint tire tracks could be seen disappearing under its doors. I was curious to see if the brown van Danny had described was inside, but there wasn't time. There was no sign of my Jeep, which he must have ditched somewhere.

The whole neighborhood seemed deserted. Someone had to be home. It was nearly ten o'clock on a weeknight. Dragging the girl a little farther down the cracked cement alley, I spied a light in a window across the street behind the funeral home. I pulled Heather between two houses, propped her against the front steps of one of them and then sprinted across the street and pounded on the door until a young man in a dirty t-shirt answered. I told him to call for an ambulance and the police and told him where they'd find Heather and the bodies in the basement of the funeral home. The man looked at me like he was doubtful of my sanity, or his, or both.

"Please, there's a girl across the street in a diabetic coma. She needs help now," I screamed at him. From inside, I heard a female's voice telling someone there was a crazy woman on her front porch yelling something about dead bodies and comas and that the police had to get here right away.

"Perfect, she's near the front steps of that white house. Remember, her name is Heather Stankowski and I think she's in a diabetic coma," I said and stepped off the porch and into the dark.

Had I been in my right mind, not blinded by the effects of some strange drug the sight of too many dead bodies in one place, and angered at losing my dog and the disappearance of a cop who was the mother of two little girls, I would have stuck around for the ambulance or the police. But it would have taken too much time to explain what had happened and who was responsible, and I was in no condition to explain anything. With my hair hanging in strings across my face, sweat seeping through my shirt and the smell of death clinging to my skin, I went in search of John Maki.

Chapter Twenty-one

BY THE TIME I LEFT Heather and headed toward the lights of downtown Calumet, I was completely out of my mind with fear, anger, disgust, and exhaustion, but I still knew right where to find John Maki—the historic Calumet Theatre on Sixth Street. It took me just five minutes to walk the distance guided by its clock tower, which loomed over the town, a witness to celebrations, a violent copper miners strike and even a mass funeral of mostly children who perished in a horrifying mishap in 1913. Even now, more than a hundred years after its construction, the theatre provided an Old World touch of distinction and grace to a town that had shrunk by about ninety percent in less than a century.

Lily had said John was working on a play opening soon, and sure enough, the marquee announced the local production of Shakespeare's "Macbeth" beginning a two-week run the following Friday.

"How fitting," I snarled as I stood behind a massive old tree to the south of the theatre and watched actors leave the side door, rehearsals completed for the night. After ten minutes of waiting for John to emerge, I grew impatient, threw open the door and stormed across the threshold into the vacant theatre. Dim lights illuminated the red seats and carpeting on the main floor and a balcony extending over it, while bright lights still shined on the empty stage. The proscenium arch was covered with intricately-detailed paintings of the five muses for painting, drama, music, literature and sculpture. Lining the arch and a circle in the ceiling where a chandelier had once hung were hundreds of tiny light bulbs.

The sound of footsteps came from behind one panel of a set of thick black curtains that parted across the stage, and there was John Maki, center stage.

"Maki!"

He turned and looked at me, surprise evident on his thin face.

"Remember me?" I yelled, moving closer. The fear and exhaustion were gone; only anger and disgust remained.

"Who are you?" he asked in a high-pitched voice. *It was an ugly woman,* Danny, Heather's neighbor, had said. Of course, he must have been close enough to hear him talking to Heather and mistook Maki's strange voice for that of a woman.

"You didn't get Crystal, you didn't get Heather and you didn't get me. Why did you want us?" I asked.

He looked at me like I was talking insanity. And I was. My voice didn't sound like that of a rational person, but I was long past the point of caring about what was rational.

"C'mon, John. What's your game? What's with the Victorian tea party? Tell me. I'm not going to hurt you, I just want to know why," I said and stepped onto the stage. He was now about fifteen feet away. He made no move toward me, but didn't back away either. Looking down at the white lace scarf he held in his left hand, he shook his head slowly. That far away look was in his eyes, like he didn't really know where he was or why.

"Why do you use that tone of voice? I've done nothing wrong," he said, almost in tears.

I was incredulous. *Done nothing wrong? You killed them!* But John Maki's sense of reality had probably always been tenuous, even as a child. Now it was ancient history. If I was going to find out what happened to the state police detective, I would have to try to see things through his warped vision.

"I'm sorry," I said and tried to calm the rage in my voice. Think kindly kindergarten teacher, I told myself and lowered my tone. "John, please tell me about the party."

He began to rub the scarf against his face, which, this late in the day, had stiff stubble on the surface, causing the fabric to make a scratching sound that sent a shiver up my spine.

"They're so happy. They sit and talk all day and all night. Nothing to worry about. No one to harm them," he said.

A door closed somewhere in the theatre, but I ignored the sound.

"Who wanted to harm them?" I interrupted, feeling my hands clench into fists inside my pants pockets.

Again, I got the look that said he thought I was nuts.

"Everyone. They're so special, so gentle and soft. Like my mother. They needed someone to bring them home to where they belonged. They didn't belong here, in this filthy, corrupt world where little children are given guns and mothers booby-trap their babies. No, my ladies deserve better than what this world has to offer them," he replied as though he were giving a soliloquy, sweeping his hand in a wide arc above his head when he said "world". I wasn't following him at all and could feel my frustration about ready to boil over. Booby-trapped babies? Children with guns? I threw my head back, took a deep breath and tried again.

"Is that your mother in there with them?" I asked.

"No, my mother's dead. I couldn't save her," he said fiercely and began twisting the scarf in his hands.

"But the ladies in your house aren't dead?" I said.

"Certainly not, you saw them. They're as alive as you are, you just can't hear them because your soul is closed to their conversation," he said in an exasperated tone.

The image of four young women stolen from their families and forced to die in some twisted fantasy returned. Mary Jo Quinn, the budding fashion designer. Lucy Franklin, the quiet artist. Caroline Baxter, the violinist who made beautiful music. Sabrina Danelli, the free-spirited poet. And then there was Crystal Jensen, who might have made the world laugh with joy. He had killed them all.

"You don't embalm people who are alive, John," I snarled.

His eyes narrowed into slits as he wound the long scarf around each hand.

"Get out of here!" he screamed suddenly. The hazy look was gone from his blue eyes and was replaced by hysteria.

"Not until I know what you did with Detective Christine Parker!" I yelled back.

He took a step forward and extended his hands with the ends of the scarf wrapped tightly around each one, leaving about two feet between them.

"You don't scare me, John Maki," I said and stood firm, hands still in my pockets. "What's the worst you can do, kill me? Well, c'mon!" I screamed. "After what I saw in that basement tonight, after having some asshole like you murder the only man I ever loved, do you really think you can do anything worse to me? If you kill me, you'd be doing me a favor."

He took another step forward. I felt myself lower into a squatting position, hands now free and ready to strike.

"Come and get me, Maki. But first, you're going to tell me where Parker is," I said and took a step toward him. He stopped, looked down at his hands and then at me, confusion now evident on his face.

"No, I swore I'd never kill again. Never," he said and stepped backwards.

I continued advancing, still crouched low. "Bullshit! You killed all those girls. Now where is that cop?"

"I don't know any detectives. Leave me alone," he cried.

"Liar! Where's Parker?" I screamed again. He backed up, tangling his legs in the black curtains that hung from thick ropes soaring to the rafters. Terror filled his eyes as I advanced upon his trembling form.

"You bastard! She has two little girls, do you hear me? She's a mother! Did you kill a mother?" Still he would not answer, although he swallowed hard, his Adam's apple bobbing with the effort.

"Answer me! Did you kill my mother?" I shrieked and lunged for the apple.

"Robin! Stop! Robin!"

The sound of my name being called, feet thumping down the carpeted aisle and the barking of a frantic dog were distant, barely entering my crazed mind as I watched my fingers clasp John Maki's throat. Suddenly I felt arms everywhere pushing and pulling me. Breath left my body, along with every urge to fight, move or even live. I collapsed in the center of the stage and sobbed with someone's arms still wrapped around my waist.

Chapter Twenty-two

"WHERE AM I?"

My hands shook nearly as much as my voice as I tried to breathe despite the sharp pain in my lungs from hyperventilating.

"It's all right. Everything's going to be fine." It was Aunt Gina. She was holding me, her words muffled by my hair, which hung in strings around my face. I opened my eyes and saw hundreds of red seats in front of me, thankfully all empty, save for one occupied by my dad, who stared at me in disbelief.

"The theatre. I'm at the Calumet Theatre. I came here looking for John Maki. Ohmygod! Is he—"

"Shh. The state police took him away a few minutes ago. Like I said, everything's fine," Aunt Gina whispered.

"Heather."

"I'm sure she's fine, too. The police said she's at the hospital just down the street. You saved her life, Robin. Now, just relax and take slow, deep breaths. You've had a rough time of it, but you'll be all right," she said. I drew in a lungful of air despite the pain in my chest and inhaled the scent of rosewater. My mother. I'd lost all sense of reality, completely lost it, and I had attacked John Maki for killing my mother.

"I've gone insane," I said, fear taking over, fear of what lay ahead in the realm of madness. Padded cells? Antipsychotic drugs? A life of wandering aimlessly down dark streets in search of something I couldn't define?

"Stop it. You're not insane, just very, very stressed. What you witnessed tonight, what you've been through over the last several months is more than one person can handle, even a normal, healthy young woman," Aunt Gina said. Her words did little to soothe me, but the touch of a live, warm human being was comforting. I looked at my dad and tried to smile. He got up, climbed the steps to the stage and knelt down in front of me, taking my hand.

"Robin, I'm so sorry. This is my fault. I've known for a long time that you were having trouble dealing with Mitch and even your mother, but I didn't push you to get help," he said, tears welling in his soft green eyes.

"Hank, this isn't your fault. You can't force someone to grieve a certain way. She reminds me of my mother. Always stoic, always strong, never crying, never showing the world she might have the same weaknesses as the rest of the human race. I never saw her cry when Dad died or even when Grace died," Aunt Gina said, releasing me from her arms. "Now she rules my poor brother's family like Attila the Hun. My hope is that one day, before she moves on to the next life, she realizes that emotion is not a bad thing and that letting it all hang out once in a while helps free up space in the mind and heart. This is a sign, Robin, that it's time to let go of some things, like your anger over losing your mom."

I sat silent, wishing she hadn't let go of me, but holding tight to my dad's strong hands. I wanted so much to connect with another human being, to feel alive rather than tortured and dying. I had told Maki I wasn't afraid to die, that he'd be doing me a favor. Had I really meant that? Yes, I guess I had. But was there peace in death? I didn't know. Those five women in the cooler hadn't looked peaceful. Mitch hadn't looked peaceful, stuffed into a coffin at the ripe old age of thirty-two. Thinking of him and death made me remember Detective Parker. I still didn't know what had happened to the woman.

I looked at my dad and Aunt Gina wearily. "This isn't over, you know. We still have to find Parker. Where's Karl Maki? He must know something about her since he's the last one to see her alive, at least as far as I know," I said, the quaking in my muscles finally subsiding as I focused on something besides my own bad memories.

"Karl, that's the painter, right? I'm sure he's either at the police post or on his way there by now," my dad said. "Are you all right? I'm very worried about you, Robin."

I took a few more deep breaths the way my mother had taught me as a child when my temper would get the best of me — inhale, count to five and exhale.

"I'm worried about me, too, Dad. But right now all I can think about is Parker and what will happen to her little girls if she's dead. Something happened to her at that damn camp, I just know it. I found her damn business card there on the floor in the studio. All I can think is that Karl killed her. I really believe John Maki when he says he doesn't know who she is. He couldn't fake that, I don't think," I said and crawled into a standing position.

Charlie entered the theatre from a side exit on the left side of the room.

"How is she?" he asked my dad, nodding his head in my direction.

"I'm fine," I snapped and then was sorry. He must have thought I'd gone mad as well. I started over in a calmer voice. "I'm okay, really, just wound way too tight. Have you heard anything about Parker?"

He ran his fingers through his sandy hair, something I noticed he did often when he was frustrated.

"Unfortunately, no. Robin, the state cops are going to want to talk to you. You seem to have some pieces they're missing. C'mon, I'll drive you there," he said, reaching for my dad's keys, which Hank handed over, and turned to leave.

"Wait a minute. Where's Belle? I swear I heard her barking earlier," I asked, hoping I hadn't imagined it.

"I put her in the Tahoe," my dad said. "She wouldn't shut up after Charlie pulled you off that character."

"How on earth did you find her?" I asked, thanking the gods that they had. "I don't know what I would do without her."

"Actually, she found us. Well, more like found someone who found us," my dad explained. "A lady saw her in her front yard not too far from an intersection a mile or so west of that little town called Chassell. She brought her inside and saw that ID tag on her, but it has your work phone number from the Tribune on it. She called it and got somebody who said you now worked for the *Daily Press,* so she got that number and ended up connecting with Bob Hunter. He called me. I called Charlie and then your Aunt Gina called me, saying she had a bad feeling about something. We all knew you'd gotten yourself into some nasty mess up here so we piled into the Tahoe and headed up, stopping to pick up the dog. It was your aunt, little Miss Marple here, who figured out on the drive up here that it must've been John Maki behind all this and led us to the theatre. Personally, I think she's psychic. I always told you she was spooky."

Aunt Gina smiled and fluttered her long eyelashes. "It was nothing really. Actually, it was just intuition. Something about the way you described the whole family seemed off, but especially him," she said. "Charlie told me about the eye drawn in lipstick on your garage door; I knew it had to be him."

"Do you know what he did, I mean, how he did it?" I asked. My head pounded to the rhythm of my heart, making coherent thought almost impossible.

"No, but I heard what you said to him about not embalming people who are alive. It must have been pretty awful, but we don't have to talk about it now," she said and moved toward Charlie. "You need to talk to the police first. Let's go."

The reunion with Belle was wet and sloppy, with her licking my face and me dripping tears on her soft brown head.

"I was afraid you were dead," I cried as we sat in the backseat with Aunt Gina.

Charlie drove to the state police post located on the highway south of town while my dad sat twisted around in the passenger seat, studying his only remaining child, the source of most of his silver hair.

"Perhaps it's time you took up a safer profession, Sweet Pea. This reporting business is starting to get out of hand," he said.

"Yeah. Maybe she should go into law enforcement. At least then she could carry a gun," Charlie snapped.

His retort made me think of Parker again. I pulled her card out of my jacket pocket and looked at it. The last place anyone saw her was the studio/

theater at the camp. The noise I'd heard while walking through the theater with Audrey echoed through my addled brain.

"Charlie! I know where she is," I shouted.

"Parker?" he asked as he pulled into a spot in front of the state police post.

"Yes, she's in the theater at that camp on Lake Independence," I said, pushing Belle away and jumping out of the Tahoe. I ran into the station and rapped on the window at the front desk until a sergeant appeared.

"Please, listen to me. I know where Detective Christine Parker is. Send someone to the Great Lakes Summer Institute in Big Bay. She's in the studio/theatre complex, I'm sure of it," I said, banging my palms on the counter for emphasis.

For about the twentieth time in the last week, someone looked at me like I'd lost my mind, but at least he seemed to know what I was talking about and picked up the phone on a nearby desk.

"Yeah, this is Sergeant Rhodes at Calumet. You know that detective that's missing? I got a woman here who says she might be in the studio/theater complex at some institute in Big Bay. Does that mean anything to you?" He listened for a minute, then his eyes flew open and he said," Really? Well, okay. I'll keep her here."

He hung up and looked at me with interest. Finally, he said, "I take it you're Robin Hamilton."

I smiled meekly and asked, "Gee, am I famous?"

"More like notorious," Charlie cracked from behind me. To the sergeant, he said, "Yes, this is Robin Hamilton. I'm Detective Sergeant Charlie Baker with the Escanaba Public Safety Department. I spoke with a Detective Peterson a little while ago and he said he wanted to talk to her about that deal at the Maki Funeral Home. Is he back yet?"

"Not yet, he's still out at that nightmare in Calumet. Why don't you have a seat and I'll let you know when he's ready for her," Sergeant Rhodes said, nodding in my direction, then disappearing around a corner.

Aunt Gina grinned, shrugged her shoulders and said, "He's cute, and I didn't see a wedding ring."

"Oh for heaven's sake, Gina, please," my dad groaned and threw himself into one of several uncomfortable-looking plastic chairs.

"Hey, he has a good aura, which is more than I can say for you. You're tired, cranky and bossy," she said and sat down next to him, to which my sixty-year-old dad replied by sticking out his tongue. I rolled my eyes at Charlie, who just stood near the door and smirked.

After about two hours, a muscular fortyish man of medium height opened a door to the right of the service window and motioned for me to follow him. Once inside a small, cramped office, he pointed to another uncomfortable-looking chair and closed the door behind him.

"I'm Detective Todd Peterson," he said and shook my hand before settling behind his desk, which was immaculate, unlike Charlie's, which usually looked as though a Level 5 tornado had swept across it.

"Did you see the cooler?" I asked, sitting on the edge of the chair.

He rubbed his eyes with his hands and blinked several times before clearing his throat and answering.

"Yeah, I saw it. Fifteen years, including ten around Detroit, and I've never—" His voice trailed off and he shook his head as if to clear it. He pulled a tape recorder from a drawer in his desk, plugged it in and made an introductory statement. Handing me the microphone, he said, "Why don't you start at the beginning, Ms. Hamilton?"

So I did. An hour and a half later, as he took away the microphone and handed me a white Styrofoam cup filled with hot coffee, I stopped talking and marveled at the story I'd just related. *It's just a dream, it has to be.*

"Unfortunately, it's not a dream," Detective Peterson said. I jumped, not realizing I'd spoken the thought aloud.

"Who's that other woman in there with them, the older one?" I asked and took a sip of coffee.

"One of the Calumet village officers recognized her and said that's Karl Maki's mother. She died of cancer about twenty-five years ago. John must have taken the body and, well, you know," Peterson said and shifted in his chair. "By the way, they found Parker, just where you said she'd be. She's fine.

A little dehydrated, but fine. Somebody tied her up and stuck her behind the curtains on the stage. She must have heard you when you were there with Audrey Gaston and tried to make some noise."

I heaved a sigh of relief and asked, "Who put her there? Karl?"

"No, get this. Parker said it was Audrey. Apparently she knew all along that John had probably killed that Mary Jo girl and then put two and two together when you called up there to get information about the camp and the other girls, since he volunteered there a lot. When Parker started asking too many questions on Monday, Audrey set up a trap for her at the camp and tricked Karl into taking part in it. She planned it so Karl would come down to check on some work being done and then arranged to give Parker a tour. She faked having to leave, then called Karl on his cell phone about fifteen minutes later and told him she had a flat tire and needed his help. When he left Parker alone, Audrey, who had parked back in the woods, simply walked up behind her as she was getting in her cruiser and bopped Parker over the head, tied her up and dragged her behind the curtains on the stage. Audrey then pushed the cruiser into the lake, ala Anthony Perkins in "Psycho." She didn't have it in herself to kill Parker, but she wanted to get her out of the way until she could get John out of the country. She'd already bought two tickets to Venezuela, probably figuring they wouldn't extradite him. She couldn't stand the thought of him being in prison. She claims she was going to set Parker free, once John was safe," Peterson explained as he tapped a ballpoint pen on the edge of his desk. "How she expected to get away with any of this is beyond me. If you ask me, she's not much saner than John Maki."

"Wait a minute. How do you know all this?" I said, my mind reeling. "And why didn't she do anything to me? She had me there all alone."

Peterson chuckled. "She just didn't think you were a threat. Huge miscalculation on her part. She's a fund-raiser, not an investigator. As for how I know, she's down the hall. As soon as we got the call about possible dead bodies in the old funeral home, we called Karl Maki. Audrey was there. She must have followed you up here this afternoon, because she went to the funeral home in Houghton, figured you might have gone in search of Karl and went after you. She came across a sheriff's deputy and a tow truck trying to get John's truck out of that ditch on Paradise Road. She had no idea what had happened, but she buffaloed them into bringing the pickup to the funeral home in Houghton and told them she knew where John was and that everything was fine. She even paid the tow truck driver right there on the spot. She then drove up here to look for John. I don't know what he did with your Jeep, but he must not have come back to his house because she claims she waited until about six o'clock, then went back to Houghton. Karl's in another room down the hall right now and he's totally confused by all this. He swore up and down that some guy named Alex killed Mary Jo. Isn't that the owner of that cabin you said you rented?" he asked.

Karl was confused?! I was utterly baffled . Audrey was protecting John? Why? This made no sense, and I said as much.

"Well, I can't explain why Audrey protected the old man. I don't know the family history. She keeps saying he has the soul of an artist, whatever the hell that means. The whole family is in shock right now. No one, not even Audrey, guessed that John had built up this fantasy world in his basement. No one ever went down there," he said.

I thought about how excited Audrey had been over the student-created art and the passion she showed toward the institute. It was genuine, a real love of all things beautiful, a trait she shared with John Maki, although they didn't share the same blood.

"That painting, it must just be Karl's grief coming through," I muttered.

"Huh?"

"Never mind," I said, shaking my head.

"Anyway, Karl's having a tough time accepting the fact that his beloved uncle was the murderer. He always believed it was Alex and said he hated him for taking away the love of his life and then having the nerve to sleep with his sister," Peterson said.

"What will happen to Maki? I know he won't go to prison," I said.

"No. He has a history of mental illness going back to his childhood. According to Karl, John was institutionalized on several occasions for psychotic episodes. The Navy gave him a medical discharge because of issues he was having over in Vietnam, although why the military even drafted him is beyond me. I guess they were desperate," Peterson said.

I stood up to stretch my legs as a million questions tumbled through my head.

"How did he get the girls?" I asked.

"From what Audrey said, it sounds like he built up trust with them through his involvement with the camp, giving them little gifts and sort of mentoring them. He probably had no trouble luring them into his vehicle where he drugged them with the same crap he was given during some of his hospitalizations. Some of that stuff will knock you out faster than a Mickey Finn. He brought them to the funeral home, probably under the cover of darkness, and went to work. Since he had so few neighbors, no one was around to question his activities. I haven't talked with him yet, but from what I could piece together just looking around the place, I'm guessing he embalmed the girls in a sitting position while they were still alive, just unconscious, but an autopsy will have to confirm that."

"Good God!" I said and shivered.

"I know, but I don't think they felt anything, except maybe that girl in the rust-colored dress. I don't like the expression on her face," Peterson said and grimaced.

"But how could they stay preserved so long? I mean, I don't know much about the embalming process, but I know it's not permanent," I said.

"I can't say for sure, but it was a cool, clean environment, and from the chemicals on the shelves, I'd say he touched them up from time to time to keep them looking fresh," he said.

My hands were shaking along with every other part of my body. Suddenly I wanted to cry. Peterson grabbed some tissues, jumped up from his chair and stuffed them in my hand.

"Hey, hey, listen, I know this is hard, but you saved that other girl's life," he said, tucking a finger under my chin and forcing me to look at his warm brown eyes. "I just called the hospital while I was getting coffee, and she's got a good shot at coming out of this in one piece. You got to her just in time. She's coming out of the coma. Call it a miracle, but I call it damn good investigative work, with a bit of stupid bravado thrown in, but that's okay."

I sniffled, blew my nose and took a deep breath.

"Did you find a brown van in that little garage?" I said.

Peterson nodded. "Yep. It's an older Chrysler, an 'Eighty-eight, I think. It's probably full of evidence. We'll try to check it for blood traces from that girl in Ironwood."

"What's next for Audrey?" I asked.

"Assault, kidnapping, possibly tampering with evidence," he said, ticking the charges off one by one on his short, thick fingers. "Who knows? Maybe the prosecutor will take pity on her. I feel bad for her kid."

"So do I," I whispered, suddenly wishing I'd never heard of Mary Jo Quinn.

Chapter Twenty-three

THE SUN WAS CRESTING THE horizon when we reached my apartment on Lake Shore Drive in Escanaba, around seven. My dad parked the Tahoe in front of the two-story house, and the four of us, along with Belle, eased our tense, tired bodies from the truck and stretched in the early morning light. Leaving them to chatter among themselves, I walked across the grass of Ludington Park, enjoying the brisk breeze that ruffled my hair and the feel of earth beneath my feet. Despite what seemed to be my best efforts to do myself in by chasing recklessly after a killer, I had lived to see another sunrise. What would I do with it? Mick had wondered if Mitch would have wanted me to wallow in grief and anger, as I had done for the past six months. No, he wouldn't, but my confrontation with John told me that my problems didn't start with Mitch's death. Rather, they started with how I handled, or rather didn't handle, my mother's death. I looked at my dad and smiled as he and Aunt Gina discussed the merits of owning a gas-guzzling sport utility vehicle as opposed to a fuel-efficient little car. He was twenty-nine years older than me and yet so much more carefree. She had a good twenty years on me, but, dressed in her orange tunic and colorful long flowing skirt, she looked like a young Hippie, full of joy and faith in the human race. Laughing came easier to both of them. I was jealous, yet anxious to learn their secret.

Belle and I strolled to the marina, now nearly empty since the myriad of sailboats, cabin cruisers and powerboats had been stored for the winter. Five teenage girls were dead because no one recognized just how dangerous John Maki's delusions had become. I had endangered myself by not listening to the warnings of my friends and family, that bottling up fountains of anger would only lead to an explosion.

"Robin! Are you okay?" my dad called.

I turned and waved and walked back to the Tahoe, taking my time to drink in the beauty of the towering old hardwoods that lined the park and Lake Shore Drive, now festooned in yellow, orange and red leaves.

Aunt Gina put her arm around my shoulders and said, "I hope you're going to get some rest, Kiddo."

I shrugged. "Eventually. First, I need to write the articles for the paper. Peterson and I went over what can be released today and what will have to wait until later. I want to do it while it's all fresh in my mind. I don't think I'll be able to get much rest until I've got this down on paper," I said.

She thought about that for a moment and then nodded. "Yes, I can understand that. Okay, drop off the pooch in the apartment and we'll drive you to work. Then your old man here can take me back to my car and I'll go home and get enough sleep for all of us," she said, and everyone laughed.

After depositing Belle upstairs with some fresh food and water and running a cold wash cloth over my face, I climbed into the back seat of the Tahoe with Charlie.

"So what's next? You've jumped out of a burning building and chased down a psycho. Ready for some international intrigue? How about foiling a terrorist plot or perhaps uncovering an assassination attempt on the president?" he said, tapping his fingers on his mustache.

"Please don't encourage her," my dad said, eyeing us wearily in the rearview mirror. Fortunately for me we had reached the *Daily Press* office, and I jumped out before anyone could make any further jokes.

Bob Hunter was waiting for me at the glass front door, which he unlocked, then locked behind us and followed me into the newsroom, full of questions. I held up my hands.

"Please, Bob, let me just write the stories first. Then you can read them and I'll fill you in on the details. I think I can give you three bylines today," I said and fired up my ancient MacIntosh computer. He stood in front of my desk with his arms folded across his chest and scowled.

"Don't do that, Bob. It makes you look like a buzzard. It's very unattractive," I said and started typing.

He looked at his watch. "You get two hours to write. These stories better be damn good."

An hour and fifty-five minutes later I filed the last of the package, which included a look at all five girls that I knew Maki had either killed or kidnapped. Unfortunately, unless Maki confessed to Crystal Jensen's case or solid evidence was found in his van, we would never know if the wrong man had been sent to prison to die needlessly. The other two articles focused on Maki and Heather Stankowski, who had been transferred to Marquette General Hospital and was doing fine as of eight o'clock that morning.

As I was preparing to go home and collapse into bed, the phone on my desk rang. It was Alex Breyers.

"Robin, I don't know how to thank you. You're like the terrier my parents own. That little thing will go after a mouse like a crow tying into a deer carcass, and she won't quit until she's got it. I owe a lot to you, more than you know," he said.

I didn't really have the energy to get into a lengthy conversation, but I wanted him to know I knew the truth. "I saw your son's picture on Audrey's desk."

He was silent for a moment, then chuckled. "Yes, well, I suppose I should have told you that, shouldn't I? I'm sorry. You knew I was holding something back. It's just that that relationship was so short-lived and, well, *wrong*, and I didn't want you to get the idea we had rekindled some passionate affair. It wasn't like that at all. We ran into each other in New York after not having had any contact since Mary Jo's funeral. Audrey's mother was dying and her husband, who was about seventy at the time, was cold and distant. I was lonely and one thing led to another. It was silly. Audrey's seven years older, but acts like a spoiled child. She wanted everything—to hang on to her rich husband, have her dream career and me, too. I needed more than that, though," Alex said.

"What about now? What about Eric?" I asked.

"That's what I meant when I said I owe you," he said and took a deep breath. "This isn't just about solving Mary Jo's murder. I thought about what you said about getting counseling. I made an appointment this morning and I'm bringing Karen. It won't be easy, but I want her to be a part of Eric's life. Right now, he needs as many loving people around him as he can find. It was wrong of me to hide him from Karen. He's a great kid and I know he'll like her and she'll like him."

"That's great, Alex. I hope it works out," I said, hesitating a bit before I plunged ahead with my next question. How much did he know about John's condition.

"Alex, did you ever have a clue that it might have been John?" I finally asked.

"God, no! He was such a *nice* person. I mean, he spent hours and hours with Karl and me on projects for school, helping us build forts, telling us stories about New York. He was like a second father to both us, but especially to Karl, since his own father was so distant. They shared the same name, but, I'm telling you, Robin, those two just never clicked. Karl Senior was too much like his own father, a cold son of a bitch. Their father openly despised John, while their mother doted on him. When she died sometime when John was in high school, it probably helped drive him over the edge. As for Karl, I know it really hurt him that his father looked down on his long hair and his desire to do something other than be a mortician. John was solace for him. They understood each other, well, not completely, but you get the idea," Alex said.

"Yeah, I know what you mean. You told me he came back from Vietnam with shell shock issues. Did you see any of those symptoms at all?" I asked.

"Before I answer that, there's something else I want to thank you for and that's giving me back my friendship with Karl. You see, he called me early this morning to tell me how sorry he was for holding fast to the belief that I killed Mary Jo. I drove down there and spent about three hours talking to him and Lily this morning. They talked about clues that showed up along the way that didn't mean anything to them at the time, but now make sense. For example, John never had girlfriends. He loved being around women, watching them, touching their hair, listening to their conversations, but he never dated. Karl said John was fascinated by Mary Jo and would always hang around when she came to the house, but he didn't think anything of it because he and John were so close. Then there were the strange absences over the years, probably when he was stalking his victims. They just assumed he was dealing with demons from his past. He had a few episodes where he became delusional and physically attacked Karl, Karl's dad and even Lily. He was hospitalized at Newberry mental hospital for quite some time before it closed in the early Nineties."

He paused as though considering his next words carefully. "If only someone could have linked Mary Jo to those other girls sooner, maybe it wouldn't have gone on so long. There's one thing I want you to understand when you write your stories. John never meant to be cruel. He couldn't physically kill anyone. If what the police told Karl is true, John somehow convinced each girl to get into his vehicle, then he injected them with some sort of concoction of drugs that would knock them out. Then he'd embalm them while they were still alive, but unconscious. That's why he couldn't kill Heather. She woke up too soon because those drugs were so old they had lost their potency. That threw him for a loop," Alex explained.

"Alex, we're all victims in a way, not just the girls and John. The mental health system failed him at every point in his life when he needed help. His family refused to face the fact that he had problems, the military refused to face it and then the state of Michigan refused to take responsibility for him when he couldn't function in reality any longer," I said. "There's one more thing, though. I understand why he went after females, but why girls in their early teens? What was it about that age group that set him off?"

There was another pause at the other end of the line. "We pondered that question too. I remember one strange, rainy afternoon the spring before Mary Jo died. We were talking about what it would be like to be a soldier. Karl and I were all macho, bragging that we could kick anyone's butt, or some nonsense. It was a pretty insensitive conversation to have, considering we knew that John had tough time with the memories of Vietnam. Anyway, Mary Jo, budding feminist that she was, stood up and said she could be a solider, too. Well, you would have thought she'd slapped John. He got this wild look in his eyes and grabbed her hands. God, I can still remember his exact words. He said, 'No, you're just a baby. I saw what happens when babies have guns. They die. I won't let that happen to you.'"

That made sense. On stage at the Calumet Theatre, John had said the girls were all alive, I just couldn't hear them. In his mind, he'd save them from becoming child soldiers in an unholy war, like the ones he must have faced in the jungle. What do you do when a child aims an AK-47 at you? Kill or be killed. It was just too much for him to bear.

After wishing Alex well and telling him to keep in touch and let me know how things worked out with Karen and Eric, I trudged the six blocks to my apartment and slept for fifteen hours straight. At some point my dad came and took care of Belle and brought me some fresh groceries. When I awoke, I ate a large bowl of soup with a few slices of French bread and some cheddar cheese and then went right back to bed and slept until it was time to go to work Thursday morning.

Detective Todd Peterson from the Calumet Post called that morning to tell me my Jeep had been found at the site of the abandoned Centennial Mine, parked behind a large building adjoining the No. 2 shaft house. My purse was still inside, so he sent that via overnight delivery. As for the Jeep itself, I never wanted to see it again. It would always remind me of that night in the basement of the old Maki Funeral Home, surrounded by death. I signed the title and sent it Peterson and he took care of selling it to some college kid when the police were done with it. In the meantime, I drove my dad's gas-guzzling Chevy Tahoe and listened to lectures from Aunt Gina about the benefits of small cars while my dad argued the practicality of four-wheel drive and crash test ratings. I compromised and bought a used sage-colored Subaru Outback station wagon with all-wheel drive, which Charlie promptly labeled my "Yuppie mobile."

An analysis of the lipstick on my garage door eventually matched it to a tube of Maybelline's Crushed Cranberry in John's makeup kit, one of the newer additions. As for Crystal Jensen, the truth was locked somewhere in John Maki's twisted mind. He was unable to confess to anything other than wanting to "save" his victims, never even referring to them by name. The van had seat covers, which Detective Todd Peterson in Calumet surmised had been washed often so there was no trace of blood in the van.

Each girl was given a proper burial, with more than three hundred people attending Mary Jo Quinn's Mass of Christian Burial at St. Ignatius Loyola Catholic Church in Houghton. The Baxters sent me a dozen roses and a card with their late daughter's photo printed on the outside. The Danellis, including Sylvia (minus the shotgun), came to the office after Sabrina had been cremated, her ashes scattered over Lake Michigan, not far from her home. Her mother and father both choked back tears as they thanked me for finding their daughter. I felt only sorrow that someone else hadn't found her thirteen years earlier and still alive. I never did hear from Lucy Franklin's father and wondered how he felt about finally knowing his daughter's fate. Then Charlie found out from his parents that Brian Franklin had entered a nursing home the previous February, a victim of Alzheimer's disease. It was probably for the best, considering he and his wife never wanted to believe their daughter was dead.

On a brighter note, I saw Detective Christine Parker about once a week, either at her office or the courthouse, and we quickly developed a friendship based on mutual admiration. It's never wise to become too friendly with sources, but Parker would become a powerful ally in the months ahead.

Mick came home for Thanksgiving with her new husband, Miguel, who turned out to be as wonderful as she had described. He immediately took a strong dislike to Karl Maki's rendition of a stormy Lake Superior night and pleaded with Mick to get rid of it, but, knowing the history behind it, no one in her family or mine would touch it. I finally broke down the Sunday after Thanksgiving and called Karl Maki Jr. to ask if he'd like the painting returned. He was silent for so long that I began to wonder if he'd hung up on me. Then he sniffled. In a voice strained by tears in his throat, he simply said, "Yes, thank you. We'll come get it today."

Before I let him go, I asked if there was anything special about the paint used to compose the work, and I explained the mysterious effect it had on Belle.

Sounding bewildered, he said, "No, I use standard oil paints available at any store that sells art supplies." After a short pause, he added quietly, "I painted that three years after Mary Jo disappeared. I poured all my pain into that canvas. It helped keep me sane at a time when all I wanted to do was join her."

As it was getting dark, he and Lily and the two girls, who apparently never stopped bickering, arrived at the home of Mick's parents, two blocks from my dad's place. A dozen people, including my Aunt Gina, stood in the O'Bryan garage and stared at the painting's tragic image, now aware of the meaning behind its disturbing aura.

Turning to his family, Karl straightened his shoulders and said, "This is the very first painting I sold for any significant amount of money and the first one that really meant anything to me. It was in an art gallery in Marquette in 1986. I later learned that Astrid Heikkinen bought it, the same lady who kept that scrapbook about Mary Jo. This was my memorial to Mary Jo. Its return means things have come full circle and this family's healing can truly begin."

Tears streamed down my face as I watched them pull out of the driveway. Aunt Gina sidled up to me and smiled through her own tears. "It'll soon be your turn to come full circle."

I didn't understand what she meant but was comforted nonetheless and carried her words through my first Christmas without Mitch. His parents and sister and I traded a few phone calls, some of them long and full of laughter laced with tears as we recalled why we loved him so much, but there were nights when the pain felt like it would crush me as I lay in bed and cried into Belle's soft fur.

Unfortunately, I would soon learn that Aunt Gina's words were less about comfort and more about prophecy. On New Year's Day, Nick Granati, my Chicago detective friend, showed up at my apartment with a black briefcase in one hand and a duffle bag in the other.

The rare rainstorm in January left him standing with droplets of water rolling off his dark trench coat on to the landing outside my door, he greeted me with tired, pain-filled brown eyes and a thick voice.

"I told you I'd let you know when I had something on Mitch. I know who killed him, but I need your help to get 'em."

So much for my New Year's resolution to reduce stress.

About the Author

Award winning journalist, Nancy Barr grew up in Michigan's Upper Peninsula. She graduated *cum laude* from Lake Superior State University in Sault Ste. Marie.

Her journalism career spans two decades beginning at the *Daily Press* in Escanaba, Michigan, reporting on police, court, school and local government news.

In 1998, 1999 and 2005, she received the Good News Award sponsored by area churches and has also been honored by The Associated Press and Michigan Press Association.

A lifelong connoisseur of mysteries, her favorite memories as a young child are of weekly trips to the neighborhood library with her mother to spend hours poring over Nancy Drew mysteries. Nancy's previous book, *Page One: Hit and Run* was the first of the Robin Hamilton mystery series.

More about Nancy Barr at www.nancybarronline.com.